DELICIOUSLY STEAMY ROMANCE
WITH A DASH OF SWEET AND
PLENTY OF HEAT

Table of Contents

Where to find me

Newsletter Signup

https://mailchi.mp/cd4d69a732cf/mlspannsignup

I promise not to spam you! Joining my newsletter grants you the opportunity to enter contests, get chances to become Beta Readers, and I'll update you about all of my upcoming projects.

Amazon Author page https://amazon.com/author/mlspann

Instagram https://instagram.com/mtharrte

Also, thank you so much for your support. Purchasing, reading, and reviewing my work really means a lot to me. Purchasing and reviewing go hand in hand like bread and butter. While I'm grateful for the bread, slide me a little butter by leaving a review!!! Happy reading!

SWEETLY SWIRLED

M. L. Spann

Dedicated to all the voices in my head. We've come a long way, and I'll keep writing as long as you keep talking.

SWEETLY SWIRLED

M. L. Spann

Chapter One

"Bullshit," I hissed, shoving the resume back across the table.

"Brianna!" shouted Dr. Gray. "How dare you speak to me that way." His too-round face turned bright red as his cheeks puffed out.

I dropped my head and willed my hands to stay in my lap.

You have no idea how bad I want to choke you right now.

"I'm sorry," I muttered. "But this isn't right and you know it. I've taken several of your classes, and you've known me for years. I don't understand why you can't hire me to be your assistant."

"Listen," he said, taking several deep breaths before placing his glasses on the table. "This isn't my call. I need someone that has experience. You clearly have the required educational background, but it's not enough. I'll hold on to your info just in case something comes open that's a better fit."

"Are you seriously giving me the 'we'll keep your application on file speech' right now? How hard can it be to answer the phone and file a few papers?" I asked in disbelief. Suddenly the too tight pantsuit I had on was cutting off my circulation.

"Brianna, I'm sorry."

Without mumbling another word, I snatched my resume off the table and stalked out of Dr. Gray's office.

My favorite professor won't even hire me. What a slap in the face.

I'd managed to get shot down for a job within the span of ten minutes.

But I guess that's progress, considering no one else even bothered to interview me.

I made it home and slammed my car in park. By the time I walked into my room, most of the confining business suit was off me and on the floor. I put my pajamas back on and climbed into bed, ready to shut the world out.

My plan was to go back to sleep and wake up knowing the interview from hell was just a dream. But I laid there wide awake, glaring at the ceiling instead. How did I end up back in my childhood bedroom? I couldn't believe my life had taken such a dramatic turn for the worse. My post-graduation plan included grabbing life by the balls and never letting go; not contemplating my failures while the empty eyes of 'N Sync stared at me from the posters on the wall.

Why in the hell do I still have those things?

I felt like success only came to those who took it. But when I tried to take it, life quickly yanked it away and punched me in the gut with unemployment, a nonexistent love life, and the stigma of moving back in with my mother.

My hand shot out in annoyance as I slapped the clock I forgot to disable off the table. My mid-morning alarm let me know it was time to get up from my second nap. With no job to speak of, I had absolutely nowhere to go, but it was important for me to maintain a routine. The highlight of my boring existence right now was getting my favorite morning pick me up from Drip Drop Coffee Hut. I didn't feel the need to change out of my pajamas, so the plain white T-shirt and sweatpants would just have to do. I drove through the mid-morning traffic as a fog of disappointment loomed over me.

I knew I was close to the shop because the scent of roasted coffee beans started to permeate the air. Once inside the small café, I inhaled deeply and instantly relaxed. My legs propelled me over to my favorite seat at the bar and I hoisted myself onto the barstool. I slapped the bar twice to get the barista's attention.

"Barkeep!" I yelled.

He sauntered over and wiped his towel over a nonexistent spot on the bar. "Yeah?" he drawled. "What can I get ya?"

"The usual," I sighed. "Make it a double."

The other customers were clearly confused at the playful banter exchanged between the two of us and that made it even funnier. Several coughed and a few cleared their throats, while one woman next to me took several steps to the left. Jayce and I started this little game a few months ago and it was now a part of our routine. I watched as he expertly mixed, poured, and topped my hot chocolate with whip cream.

He gently placed the cup in front of me on a small saucer. "Danish or bagel?"

"Danish," I replied, taking a careful sip of the steaming drink. Lord knows I didn't need bread, or anything sweet for that matter, but this café had the best pastries in town. Jayce returned seconds later with my food and placed it next to my cup. Flashing a toothy grin, he wiped his hands on his apron and turned to help another person at the counter.

I don't exactly swoon whenever I see him, at least not anymore. Perhaps it's because I know he's taken and, based on the Barbie doll he's with, I wasn't his type anyway. But still, I enjoyed taking in the sight of his body just the same. And man oh man what a body! Since he's Samoan his skin was genetically tan and I definitely appreciated the exotic look. He's built like a bulldozer with broad shoulders and a massive chest, but it's obvious he's a gentle giant. Jayce always had a smile plastered on his face even at o-dark-thirty in the morning. But honestly, his shoulder length raven hair was my favorite part about him. On more than one occasion, I had to force myself from day dreaming about running my fingers through it.

Taking another sip from my cup, I swiveled around in my seat to survey the rest of the café. At that time of the morning, most of the people hustled and bustled to get their orders so they could get to work. I grabbed my Danish to take a bite and stopped midway to my mouth.

A demi-god from Olympus watched me with the most seductive smirk I'd ever seen. He was definitely not a regular, I was positive I would have noticed him by now. A chill raced over my skin the instant our eyes connected, and I could feel my nipples tighten under my top.

My poor decision to go braless today was clearly evident for the entire coffee shop to see. I quickly turned back toward the bar to hide my headlights, but not before I noticed the smile widen across the mystery man's face. *Is he really smiling at me?*

I tried to discreetly look over in his direction and I caught him staring at me … again. *He must have a case of jungle fever.* Most white men were too intimidated to approach a black woman, but he didn't seem to be that kind of guy. I closed my eyes and chuckled to myself. There was no way that blue-eyed ray of sunshine was flirting with me. I found it pretty hard to believe he saw anything attractive about me right now. Today, I looked a hot ass mess with no makeup, a frizzy ponytail, and taut nipples. I wolfed down the rest of the Danish, slurped up the semi-hot drink, left my money on the counter, and quickly made my way out the door. Tomorrow I'd put some actual effort into how I looked just in case the mystery man was there again.

I intended to go straight home, clean the kitchen, apply for a few jobs, and do whatever else I needed to do. I managed to clean up, but a nap took the place of applying for jobs. A few hours later, my eyes flew open in a panic the moment I heard the rattle of the garage door being opened. I reached over, grabbed my laptop, and attempted to look hard at work. The sensor on the door chimed as Mom came into the house with an armful of grocery bags.

"Hey, Brianna, can you come help me?" she asked.

I shoved the computer to the side and slid my feet into my worn house slippers. Walking toward the kitchen, I mentally prepared myself for the daily inquisition.

"How was your day, honey?"

I paused for a moment before grabbing a bag full of stuff to put away. "It was fine. The interview went well and I managed to submit several other applications," I replied.

That was lie number one in a series of lies that were sure to follow. It wasn't that I didn't want a job, because I desperately longed to get my own place once again and support myself. In all honesty, I lost my steam for the whole job search process. I made the biggest mistake of my life when I decided to leave work for the last semester of Grad school. I figured three months was plenty of time to really focus and finish the year strong. Besides, I had plenty of money saved to cover my bills and finding a job would be easy once I finished getting my Masters.

Right? Wrong. I was SO wrong. Here I was, twenty-four years old with two degrees and no job. It seemed like I had wasted my time getting an education in the first place.

"That's great, honey. I'm sure something will come through soon," said Mom. She had been saying the same thing every day for the last six months. "Leave the pasta sauce on the counter. Gram-Gram's coming over for dinner tonight, so try to spruce yourself up a little."

Great, she's the last person I want to see right now.

Gram-Gram had a not so funny way of making a bad situation even worse. I leaned over, grabbed a cookie out of the jar next to me, wolfed it down, and reached for another.

"Honey, do you really need all of those cookies?" Mom asked gently.

I sighed and tossed the cookie back into the jar. My weight had been another topic of discussion lately as I plowed through food like a ravenous football team. Most people put on the freshman fifteen during school. Well, I had put on the college forty and it didn't seem to be going anywhere anytime soon. My love of food was the main reason why none of my jeans fit, forcing me to wear duck print sweat pants most of time. I knew Mom was just trying to help, but she actually made me feel worse. She could eat cookies and anything else she wanted and not gain a single ounce. I had to admit, she definitely looked damn good for her age, and she knew it. Her favorite thing to say was "black don't crack, it just bends a little" and she's proof of that. Being a recent divorcee encouraged her to really step her game up in terms of her appearance during her own search for love.

I decided to vacate the area before I was forced to answer anything else. Snatching my laptop and cell phone off the couch, I made a beeline toward my bedroom.

Plopping down on my bed, I scrolled through my recent contacts on my phone until I got to the one that was sure to put a smile on my face.

My best friend Kirsten was one of the reasons why I was still holding on to reality. Although sometimes wallowing in depression did seem like the better option. It's hard for us to spend any time together especially since she's a travelling makeup artist. Luckily, she was home for a few days right now.

"Hey, girl, what's up?" she asked.

"Kirsten, I'm feeling so … so … blah," I replied.

"Blah?"

I rolled onto my back and kicked my feet into the air. "Yes … blah. I guess it's just one of those days where I realize my life is going in the opposite direction of awesome."

Kirsten released her signature laugh with the accidental snort included. "It will get better eventually. What you need is somebody to help you relieve some stress. Why don't you call Avery?"

Now it was my turn to laugh. "You think sex solves everything," I chuckled.

"No I don't," she said. "But it does help take the edge off. You need somebody to bend your ankles behind your head and stroke all your stress away."

"Well it certainly won't happen with Avery. You remember what happened the last time," I muttered.

"Oh yeah," she replied after a brief pause. She then took several minutes to laugh hysterically.

I could look back and laugh about it now, but it wasn't the least bit funny at the time. Avery had been my high school sweetheart, the love of my life all through school. He moved away, we broke up, but remained good friends over the years. When he moved back home last year it only seemed right we meet for drinks. Well, those potent margaritas led to a late-night rendezvous back at my place. As soon as the door clicked shut behind us, he immediately started devouring my face like a psycho on bath salts. His sloppy kisses were everywhere as I tried and failed at dodging his wet advances. With absolutely zero foreplay involved, he snatched off our clothes and commenced to fucking me like we were still in high school, and that's no compliment.

Apparently, life and his girlfriends after me had taught him nothing about learning to finesse a woman and listen to her body. He poked me for a good five minutes and collapsed onto my chest in a sweaty heap. I tried to blink the salty droplets of sweat out of my eyes as I wiggled my way from underneath him. I quickly made up some lame excuse and escorted him to the door. In fact, that's the last time I had sex, if you could even call it that. Kirsten's right, I was long overdue for some good loving.

"Speaking of stress relievers, I saw a delicious specimen of a man at the coffee shop this morning," I said after Kirsten quieted her guffaws down to a few light chuckles.

"Oh really? Tell me more. Did you give him your number?"

"No," I replied. "Nobody exchanged numbers or anything. He looked tall, but I can't be positive though since he was sitting down. Blond hair, spiked with gel. And he has blue eyes and a very nice smile."

"Well why didn't you give him your number, crazy woman?" she asked.

"No, ma'am, I wasn't about to embarrass myself," I said. "Hopefully I'll see him again and he'll ask for the digits if he's really interested."

"You need to take the initiative, Bri. I'm pretty sure the people at the Stop-n-Shop are tired of you coming in there hoarding all of the batteries. One of these days you're going to electrocute yourself. You need a man, not a vibrator," said Kirsten.

I laughed, but she was right. Every time I shopped for new, longer lasting batteries, I did fear the cashier ringing me up knew what I planned to do with said batteries.

"Brianna!" shouted Mom. "Come down for dinner!"

"I have to go. Gram-Gram is here for dinner so you know I will be calling you back," I grumbled.

"Oh shit … yeah, good luck," Kirsten muttered.

I pressed END, changed into a pair of black yoga pants, and raced down   the   stairs.

Chapter Two

Don't get me wrong, I loved Gram-Gram to death, but she got on my last good nerve. She has an old school charm about her I enjoy at times, and at other times it makes me wish we had her locked away in a retirement home. Ever the diva, she always looks like she has somewhere to go with her full-face makeup and French rolled hair. She honestly feels like a woman's role in life includes finding a husband and having kids. So it absolutely baffled her that I managed to graduate without landing a husband. Although, I was engaged at one point and planned to head down the road to matrimony, but my fiancé abruptly decided he wasn't ready and called the whole thing off. I thought Gram-Gram was going to declare me a witch and burn me at the stake for letting a man slip through my fingers like that.

"Oh, Brianna, are you wearing a bra?" she asked with the same finesse used to ask someone if they've killed a kitten.

I glanced down and dropped my shoulders. I knew I was forgetting something. One would think that after my little faux pas earlier I would have properly covered my breasts.

"How many times do I have to tell you to wear a bra? You're going to end up with breasts sagging down to your belly button. No man wants to see that. You won't catch a husband with breasts that slide off into your armpits when you're on your back," she snapped.

"Mom!" hissed my own mother.

"What?" asked Gram-Gram. "I taught these same lessons to you. I don't know why you won't teach Brianna. It's just not lady-like at all."

"I'm sorry. Do you want me to go put on a bra?" I asked, praying the vein in my neck wasn't pulsating.

"No," she replied. "There's no point now, you're already at the table."

I shook my head and rubbed my palm down my face in an attempt to erase the scowl on it. I tried to eat my food and stay off Gram-Gram's radar, but there was zero chance of that happening.

"So, Brianna, have you found a job yet?" she asked.

"No, ma'am, the search continues," I mumbled.

Gram-Gram narrowed her eyes in my direction as she speared the pasta with her fork. Mom tried to lighten the mood by intervening on my behalf.

"The job market is a little slow right now. Brianna is a smart girl, something will come through eventually," she said.

"Evelyn, you're always coddling her. You need to show Brianna some tough love and force her to grow up. A girl her age should be married and working on baby number two by now. But oh no, she wanted to join the club of working women, which wouldn't be much of a problem if she actually worked."

My mouth flapped open in response to the imaginary slap to the face I was just issued. Mom appeared equally as shocked as she dropped her fork onto the plate, causing the loud clang to resonate throughout the room. If I were a hermit crab, now would be the perfect time for me to retreat into my shell.

"Mom, that way of thinking worked just fine when you were growing up, but this is a new era. Brianna is my daughter and if she wants to take some time to find herself, then it's fine with me. It sure beats marrying a man you don't love and having to wait twenty some odd years to find out who you really are like I did. And since I have you both here, I want to let you know I plan on going out of town for two weeks," Mom announced.

I wish I was the person in the crowd that kicked off the slow clap, because Mom definitely deserved a round of applause. It's not often that she stood up to Gram-Gram, but when she did, it's awesome. I was even happier to know she's going out of town. She deserved the vacation and I welcomed the alone time.

Gram-Gram pursed her lips into a harsh line refusing to comment any further after being put in her place.

"Where are you headed?" I asked. A broad smile blossomed across my face, thankful the attention was off of me.

"Keith is taking me to Jamaica," she gushed.

Keith was Mom's latest squeeze and she really enjoyed the attention he lavished on her. We excitedly prattled on about swimsuits and flight details while Gram-Gram sat scowling and cutting her eyes at both of us. We tried to lure her into the conversation just so she would stop looking like she had a sour taste in her mouth. She knew how to get under Mom's skin by giving her the silent treatment.

I took it as an opportunity to eat my food before escaping to the solitude of my bedroom. My hand found the light switch as I pushed the door closed with my foot. An exasperated sigh left my lips in a huff.

Gram-Gram did have a point about my whole job situation, despite her snarky way of bringing it into the light. My goal was to land a job by the time Mom got back from her vacation. If it weren't for her I would be homeless and probably getting arrested on prostitution charges. I felt obligated to hurry up and get on my feet so she could stop supporting me.

I found myself standing in front of my closet ready to take on my next task. Hopefully my mystery man would be in the coffee shop tomorrow, and I needed the perfect outfit to lure him in. Of course finding the right threads took longer than I expected. After nearly an hour and a half, I finally found jeans that wouldn't require me losing a limb from loss of circulation and a shirt that completely covered my stomach. Add a bra and a bit of mascara to the mix and I planned on being ready for whatever tomorrow had to offer.

Chapter Three

My eyes popped open before my alarm clock had a chance to go off. I darted out of bed, but I took my time getting dressed as I attempted to make sure everything was in its proper place. The chances of being approached by Mr. Blue Eyes were slim, but I was willing to put my best foot forward … just in case.

I walked into the café and headed for my usual spot.

"Well don't you look extra spiffy today," Jayce teased.

A smile tugged at my lips as I waited for my coffee. "Since when are jeans and a T-shirt spiffy?"

"It's a change from your pajamas wouldn't you agree?" he asked with an eyebrow raised.

I guess comparatively speaking I did look spiffy. My eyes scanned the shop, but there was no sign of the handsome guy from the day before. Returning my attention to my cup and pastry, I completely missed his arrival until it was too late.

His scent registered first, it was light and intoxicating. Nothing turned me on more than a man that smelled good.

"You mind if I sit here?" he whispered, his warm breath practically nipped at my earlobe.

My head made a quarter turn and our eyes met with the same intensity as the day before. *"You mind if I sit here?"* was going to be the question I would ask him at some point, only instead of the barstool, I would be referring to his face. *Oh wow … where did that come from? Let's rein it in, Bri, so you don't come off like a horn-dog.*

"No, I don't mind," I mumbled into my hot mug.

"I'm Connor," he said.

Yes! Yes! YES! This is really happening.

"Bri," I replied.

"Bri? What a beautiful name. I wanted to ask you yesterday, but you rushed out of here so fast," he said, motioning for Jayce to come over. "I'll have a large coffee, black."

"Coming right up. Bri you want anything else?" Jayce asked.

I shook my head and picked at the edge of the Danish. "Why did you want to know my name?"

He leaned forward on the counter and chuckled. If there was ever a time to swoon, it would be now. I bit my bottom lip in an attempt to help hold my lips together. The last thing I needed was drool sliding down my chin from my inability to keep my mouth closed.

"I make it a point to find out the name of any pretty girl that catches my eye," he murmured.

Yeah, the whole lip thing failed as my mouth flapped open in awe. He was laying it on thick and I liked it.

Jayce returned with the coffee and waited. He seemed interested in knowing what would happen next too. After a few awkward moments, Connor finally broke the silence.

"Uh, thanks man. I'm ready to settle the bill. Add her order to mine," he said.

"No ... no, that's not necessary," I protested.

Connor's eyes dimmed as he flashed his teeth again. "It's absolutely necessary. And tonight when I pay for our dinner, it will be necessary then too."

I couldn't stop my lips from forming the largest smile ever. My eyes could have been playing tricks, but I thought I saw Jayce roll his eyes as he went to retrieve the receipt.

"Dinner?" I questioned.

"Yes, dinner. Give me your number and I'll text you with the details," he said as he stood up to leave. "I hate to just drop in and leave so soon, but I have to get to work."

I grabbed a napkin and pen off the counter, and struggled to recall my phone number. My palms were sweaty, and my nerves took me on a roller coaster ride of emotions. With trembling hands, I handed the napkin over to Connor. He glanced down at the semi-damp napkin and flashed another grin.

"Later," he said.

At a complete loss for words, I gave a small wave instead. As soon as he's gone, I looked around just to see if anyone else had witnessed the magic that just happened.

"Are you seriously going out with that guy?" Jayce scoffed.

My smile grew smaller as a frown took over my face. "Yeah, what's wrong with that?" I asked defensively.

"He seems really fake to me, and I don't think he's being honest with you," he replied, his voice taking on a very matter of fact tone. This was the first time I'd seen him with something other than a smile on his face. *What the hell is his problem?*

I rolled my eyes and leaned back in my seat. "How could you possibly know any of that from the few seconds of conversation we exchanged?" I asked.

Jayce put both hands on the countertop and leaned forward. The stance caused his shirt to strain against his muscles just a tad.

"I'm a man, that's how," he replied. "But hey, if I'm wrong I will let you get your usual for free for the next month."

"Wow," I muttered. "Thanks for the vote of confidence. Sorry it's so hard to fathom that a guy could like me."

"Wait, that's not what I meant!" he called out, but I was already halfway out the door.

Chapter Four

I couldn't believe the nerve of Jayce trying to rain on my parade. It was perfectly plausible for Connor to actually be interested in me. Jayce couldn't even offer a legitimate reason behind why he thought those things about Connor. I couldn't help but wonder if he said that because of my looks or something. I pulled my car into the driveway at home and put the car in park. I would show him. It was okay for a guy like Connor to like someone like me. Right? It didn't take much to unlock the delicate box that held my insecurities at bay, and the door was definitely wide open now. My mind scrambled to find ways to mask all of my imperfections thanks to Jayce planting a seed of doubt in my mind.

I plowed into the house and took the stairs two at a time. Operation Transformation was about to take place. I didn't have a clue where we were going or what was planned, but I was going to do everything in my power to look good doing it. The chime of my cell phone drew my gaze away from my closet.

"Kirsten!" I squealed. "You called at the perfect time. Drop whatever you're doing and get over here."

"Oh my," she said. "Sounds like somebody is excited."

"Mmmhmm, I'm more than excited. I have a date with the hot guy from yesterday."

Kirsten released a loud yelp into the phone. "Damn, you didn't tell me it was a Code Blue! I'll be there in a few."

She hung the phone up in my face before I had a chance to say goodbye. Minutes later I heard the door downstairs open and close. I knew it was Kirsten based on her heavy stomping coming up the stairs. She burst through my door and shoved her makeup kit to the side. Grabbing my shoulders, she propelled me to the bed while she found a spot on the floor.

"Start at the very beginning and don't leave out a single detail," she ordered.

I beamed from ear to ear as I made myself more comfortable on the bed. Since I finally had good news to deliver, I took my time dragging out the story. Kirsten eagerly sat there hanging on to my every word. It was fun watching her face go through a series of exaggerated expressions. Once I finished my tale, Kirsten jumped to her feet with a sinister smile dancing on her lips.

"All right, chick, it's time to go to work. Have you decided on what to wear?" she asked.

I rolled off the bed and joined her next to the closet. "No, not really. Something cute and comfortable I guess."

Kirsten, ever the fashionista, scowled at me as if I'd said plaid and flannel.

"What?" I asked with a shrug. "My options are limited. None of the cute stuff I own fits anymore."

She rolled her eyes and thumbed through the clothes. "If they don't fit ... you make them fit. Don't you have a body shaper or something?"

"Yes," I replied slowly. "But I want to be able to breathe through dinner or whatever we do. Those stupid shapers cut off my circulation."

"If you play your cards right you won't be wearing it for long," said Kirsten with a wink.

I smiled and sat back down on the edge of the bed waiting on her to find something suitable. Everything she pulled from the closet didn't look or feel right. Most of my dresses were short from back in the day when I had killer legs and no cellulite. I held on to the too-tight clothes in hopes that I would one day fit in them again.

Finally, after a lot of back and forth, we found something that would work under the right circumstances. The dress was black and hit right above my knees. It was also formfitting, so a body shaper would be needed in order for me to have a smooth silhouette. I placed the dress on the bed and made my way to the closet where Kirsten was crouched down examining my shoes.

"Since we don't know the specifics of the date I think you need something comfortable for your feet," she murmured.

Oh now my comfort matters.

Our heads whipped around simultaneously as my phone chimed. There was a mad dash to the bed, and we wrestled over the hand-held device.

Kirsten won and managed to hold me at bay with one hand as she scrolled through my messages with the other. "Wow," she whispered.

I stopped flailing around and froze. "Wow? Wow what? Is the message from Connor?" I asked anxiously.

"Yes," she said with a smirk. "He said he made reservations at *Maison de L'amour* for eight o'clock. And he wants to know if you want him to pick you up."

"No!" I yelled, snatching the phone out her hands. "You know I need to be able to leave just in case things don't turn out right."

Kirsten narrowed her eyes into tiny slits as she folded her arms across her chest. "Why do you always set yourself up for failure? You want to drive your own car because you have already planned on this date failing."

True.

"That's not it," I protested.

Instead of being a sympathetic understanding friend, all I got was a skeptical arched eyebrow in my direction.

"It's not," I said firmly. "I need some semblance of control. He chose the restaurant. I don't think it's unreasonable for me to drive my own car."

"Mmmhmm, okay, Bri. Whatever you say," she replied, her voice dripping in disbelief. "Go on and get showered so we can finish pulling the rest of your look together. Make sure you shave everything. You have to be prepared … just in case."

I smiled a little at the implications of "just in case" as I grabbed my towel and razor. Kirsten barely gave me a chance to step out of the shower before she started her primping session. Based on all of the pulling going on, I was positive most of my hair had been ripped out. This had better be worth all the trouble, no … torture, I was going through. After a few more brush strokes of blush, Kirsten stepped back and leaned her head to the side to admire her work.

"I think you're ready," she said.

I walked over to the mirror and almost didn't recognize myself. She made my skin look flawless. Surprisingly, I still had hair attached to my scalp and it was cascading down in large curls.

"Wow, Kirsten, you really outdid yourself this time," I murmured. "I have cheekbones now."

"I told you I'm a magician. Makeup is nothing more than a magic trick. I know how to create the right illusion to work in your favor," she explained. "You know I can talk all night about the ins and outs of the beauty world, but it's seven o'clock. We need to get you into your dress and on the road headed to the restaurant."

I grabbed the body shaper and shimmied halfway into it before I needed help. We pulled, tugged, and tucked all of me into the tight straitjacket-like garment. I couldn't deny the obvious transformation of my body as the dress was zipped into place. Kirsten coupled it with some bangle bracelets, stud earrings, and leopard print heels.

With my keys in tow, we headed out the front door. My heart raced and I was eager to find out what was coming next.

Chapter Five

I blinked my eyes and tried to get my breathing under control as I raced toward the restaurant. A sheen of sweat started to develop on my upper lip and brow, and I gently dabbed at both areas with the back of my hand. Either my nerves were taking control or I was dangerously close to passing out because of the body shaper.

I pulled up to the restaurant and decided to park on my own rather than valet. I didn't have twenty bucks to waste just to park a car. Unfortunately for me and my feet, the closest space available was a block away. I checked my makeup and took a deep breath before I opened the restaurant door. My eyes roamed over the other diners, searching for Connor, but he was nowhere to be found.

"Ma'am, do you need some help?" asked the hostess.

"No," I said. "I'm waiting on someone."

A couple came up behind me, so I inched over to the side to get out of their way.

The lights were low, creating the perfect romantic mood for the evening. I craned my neck around, attempting to get a better look at the decor. Each table had linen tablecloths and candles. I shifted my weight from one foot to the other in the not so comfortable shoes Kirsten insisted I wear. Evidently she had no clue what the word comfortable meant.

"You're breathtaking," a voice murmured into my ear.

Connor took a couple of steps back as I turned around. "Thank you," I replied. "You look quite handsome yourself."

Actually, he looked better than handsome in his black pinstripe suit. I was even more impressed by the dark purple tie and matching handkerchief combo. There was no denying the man definitely had style. But then again, he could have been standing there in a loincloth and I would probably comment on how good he looked in his outfit.

"Shall we?" he asked, offering me his arm.

I nervously latched on and moved with him toward the hostess guarding the reservation book.

"Reservation for two under the name Connor O'Neil," he said.

"Yes, sir," she replied. "Do you have a seating preference?"

Instead of offering a response, Connor turned to me and arched an eyebrow. "Preference?" he asked.

"Um," I said. *Damn, I wasn't expecting to be put on the spot like this. "A booth will be fine."*

Connor dropped his eyes and smiled. *Did I say something funny?*

"This restaurant doesn't offer booths, we have tables. In terms of preference, I meant center dining room, or perhaps by the window," the hostess explained with a bit of a bite in her tone. If it wasn't inappropriate to call me a dumbass I'm positive she would have.

I was so embarrassed now and the date hadn't even started. At the rate I was going, my frazzled nerves would have me sweating through this dress before the night was over.

"The window will be fine," said Connor.

If I could shrink down and disappear right now, I would.

The snarky hostess led us to an intimate private table, away from all of the other patrons. I grabbed my chair so I could sit down, but Connor gently batted my hands away as he pulled out the chair for me. This date was shaping up to be one for the record books, minus my earlier incident. I'd never had a man be such a gentleman before. Most of the guys I dated didn't open doors, let alone pull out chairs.

"Your server will be with you in just a moment," said the hostess, before shooting a nasty glare in my direction.

"I'm glad you showed up, Bri. For a moment I thought you were giving me the cold shoulder when you said you wanted to drive yourself," he said.

My hands nervously gripped the clutch in my lap as I gathered the courage to look him in the eyes. "Of course I showed up," I said. "I'm still in shock you even asked."

"The night's still young, so I may shock you even more. You never know what I might have up my sleeve," he murmured. My mind illustrated in vivid detail all of the possible outcomes for this night and they all involved being naked. Something about him awakened a part of me that had been hidden for quite some time.

"So, Bri, what can you tell me about yourself?"

Shit, I knew that question was coming. Let's see, I'm unemployed, overweight, and living back home with my mom.

"Well, I'm twenty-four, no kids, I have my own car, and I just finished getting my Master's degree," I said. "How about you?" I desperately wanted the spotlight off of me. My plan was to avoid the embarrassing parts of my life at all costs.

Connor scanned one side of the menu and then the other before responding. "I'm twenty-nine, independent, and I'm the leading pharmaceutical rep in this area," he replied proudly.

"Wow, impressive," I said.

Our server appeared from the shadows with pen and pad in hand. "Hello, my name is Sylvia, and I'll be waiting on you tonight. Have you made your selections for the evening?"

"Yes. I'll have the steak, medium rare and a side of lightly steamed vegetables. I want them to still have a bit of crunch to them," he said. "I'll have a rum and coke from the bar and a glass of water."

Sylvia nodded and turned to me with her pen poised over the pad. I quickly scanned the menu and tried to find something that wouldn't scream "fatty." Everything that caught my eye was either swimming in gravy or covered in some type of creamy sauce.

"I'll just have the watercress salad with low-fat vinaigrette … and a glass of water," I said.

"What?" asked Connor. "That's all you intend to eat?"

I nodded and handed my menu to Sylvia. "No wait," he said. "Do you like seafood?"

"Yes," I replied slowly.

"Great. She'll have the seafood pasta. Bring her a rum and coke and a glass of water as well," he said, handing his menu to the server.

My eyes widened at the brazen move he just made.

He likes control.

Sylvia paused for a moment and waited to see if I agreed with the order. Connor immediately cut the moment short. "That'll be all," he said firmly, casting a dark glare at her. She took the hint and scurried off to fill our orders.

"What do you do for a living?" he asked.

Think of something clever, think of something clever. I repeated the mantra to myself over and over as I tried to come up with an excuse.

"Right now, I'm just exploring my options," I said.

"Oh," he replied slowly, evidently catching the true meaning of my statement. "I see."

I nervously glanced down at the table and waited on him to make up an excuse to leave. Couldn't say I would blame him, given the circumstances. The deafening silence was awkward and extremely uncomfortable. I looked up, ready with an excuse of my own.

To my surprise, Connor had his eyes trained on me with an odd intense hunger that made me squirm.

"Are you single?" he asked.

I nodded and nervously wiped my sweaty palms on my dress.

"I know this is going to sound a little forward, but do you want to go back to my place after dinner?" he asked.

Holy shit. Is this really happening? I pinched myself just to be sure. And sure enough, it hurt like hell.

"Yes!" I blurted out faster and louder than necessary. My outburst garnered a few glances in our direction, but I didn't give a rat's ass about those nosy people. I exhaled slowly and tried to smooth over my response. "I mean … if you want me to, then yes I'll go."

Our food and drinks arrived at the same time and neither of us wasted any time digging in. I wanted to hurry up and shovel the food into my mouth as fast as possible.

"Would you be interested in participating in a small focus group tomorrow? It's for my job," said Connor.

I quickly worked to clear my mouth and nearly choked on the partially chewed food.

"What's it for?" I gulped, grabbing my glass of water to help wash down the lump in my throat.

"It's for women and you'll be asked a series of questions based on your individual needs. It would help me out a lot and you'll get paid for your participation," he replied quickly.

Paid? Now he's speaking my language.

"Sure, just let me know when and where. I'm stuffed, do you mind if we get our food to go?" I asked.

A seductive smile spread across Connor's face as he glanced down at my plate and then back to me. *He knows I'm rushing just so we can get back to his place.* "Ready to go so soon?" he teased.

"You said you were full of surprises, and I'm curious to see what will happen next," I replied as I leaned over the table, allowing him to peek at my cleavage.

He glanced down at my breasts and slowly met my eyes with a knowing look of amusement.

"Just know some of my surprises are a little rough," he whispered.

"Oh I can handle anything you throw at me," I purred.

He signaled for Sylvia to come over and requested the check and to-go boxes.

My head was telling me to slow down, but my hormones were running this show. Tonight the chips could fall where they may, and I would deal with the consequences tomorrow.

Chapter Six

I dangerously weaved in and out of traffic, struggling to keep up with the red mustang racing ahead of me.

My palms were sweaty again, and my heart pounded like a bass drum. I wasn't surprised when we crossed over to the nicer part of town. Expensive condos towered above us and I was curious to see which one belonged to Connor. After a few more sharp turns and ignored traffic lights, we slowly pulled into an underground parking garage. The mustang zipped into a parking space and I parked my dingy gray sedan next to it. Before I had the chance to open the door Connor appeared and did it for me.

"You are the perfect gentleman," I said.

"Yes … for now," he growled, grabbing my hand to help me out of the car.

He led me over to the elevator and pushed the button. The doors opened instantly and he gestured for me to step inside. He pressed a few numbers on the keypad and the elevator started going up. It wasn't long before it slowly came to a halt on the fifteenth floor. The doors opened, and I stepped out into the hallway. We had two options to choose from, left or right. Connor pulled me toward the left and opened the door.

I assumed his lights had motion sensors in them because they immediately came on and illuminated the room.

"Make yourself comfortable," he said.

The house was expertly decorated and looked like something one would see in a magazine. Everything looked delicate and expensive and I didn't have the courage to touch anything. I found myself admiring a painting on the wall when Connor slipped his arms around my waist and nuzzled my neck.

"You smell so good," he murmured.

My breathing quickly became more and more labored as I struggled to get air. The hardness of his erection poking me wasn't helping my asthmatic situation either. With one arm still circling my waist, his other one snaked its way up to my breasts. He cupped one and gave it a hard squeeze causing a small yelp to pass my lips. That must have been the response he was looking for as he placed his lips on my neck and moaned. He dropped his arms and despite the minor pain he'd inflicted I wanted his hands back on my body. The sudden forward thrust of his hips into my ass took me by surprise and I stumbled over my own feet.

"Walk," he growled.

I quickly regained my balance and inched forward a few steps. "Walk where?" I asked tentatively, not sure about what was coming next.

He's a little aggressive.

I don't mind a little pain with my pleasure, but if he pulled out a whip and a dog collar or some type of weird shit like that, I was going to leave.

"To the end of the hall, now go," he ordered giving me another push.

Okay, Bri, you can do this. Just breathe and keep an open mind.

The moment I entered the room, the lights popped on just like the ones in the living room. I barely had a second to look around before Connor turned me on my heels and cupped my face. His lips were soft but the kiss wasn't. His technique was rough as he aggressively pressed his mouth to mine. He dropped his hands and shrugged out of the suit jacket without breaking our connection. I closed my eyes and relaxed, giving myself the opportunity to explore his mouth with my tongue. My arousal was building and I could feel the familiar wetness forming between my thighs. I pressed my body into his even though there wasn't an inch of space between us to begin with. Connor abruptly moved back and loosened his tie.

"Lose the dress," he commanded.

I wanted to snatch the dress off, but I didn't want him to see all of the garments holding me together. "You mind if I use your bathroom? That alcohol is getting to me," I sputtered.

He nodded to the door to my left. "Come back naked," he ordered.

Naked?

I knew being naked was part of the package, but being naked with the lights on was asking a bit much.

"Can we ditch the lights?" I asked nervously.

Connor sauntered over to the bed and sat down. He tugged his shirt out of his pants and started unbuttoning it. I waited on an answer, but he didn't give me one.

"Still going to the bathroom?" he asked.

I sighed and ducked into the sanctuary of the bathroom. My eyes scanned for something to cover my body with. Maybe a towel or robe? I spotted a plushy black towel with a monogrammed "C" on it and grabbed it off the rack. Placing it on the granite counter, I quickly freed myself from my clothes and shoes. I wondered if Connor was doing the same. As soon as I managed to roll the shaper down, I felt my air passages open and I ushered in deep breathes of air. I wrapped the towel around me to hide my imperfections and stepped out into the bedroom.

Connor watched me with his intense blue gaze as I tried to seductively walk toward him. I was happy to see he was shirtless. It was clear he was no stranger to working out as each muscle was perfectly defined without a layer of fat to hide under. My heart dropped a little when I noticed he still had his pants on, but at least they were unbuttoned. I got within arm's length of him and he yanked the towel away from me. Every roll, every stretch mark, and every dimple of cellulite was out in the open for him to see. Horrified, I tried to bolt back into the safety of the bathroom. He grabbed my hand and brought me to a standstill.

I trembled as his eyes roamed over my body. Talk about a buzz-kill.

"Your skin looks like chocolate," he murmured. "But do you taste like it as well?"

Not only did his question take me by surprise but what he did next surprised me too. Instead of ordering me to cover my lumpy body and leave, he pulled me in close and latched on to my breast with his mouth. The warmth and gentle rolling of his tongue over my nipple made my knees weak. He wasn't lying when he said he was full of surprises. My whole body tingled and I needed to feel him inside me. He switched sides and gave the other breast some much needed attention too. I was all moans and groans as I gave in to the pleasure.

"Like I told you, I'm into a bit of rough sex and some other stuff," he murmured.

"How rough is rough?" I asked quietly.

I'm open to explore … just don't pee on me or something.

He chuckled and caressed my ass with his hand before giving it a hard smack. I yelped loudly.

"Rough enough that I like to add a little pain to the pleasure I give," he whispered. "Can you handle it?"

His hand slid up my thigh and he gently slipped one finger inside of me. My knees wanted to immediately buckle, but I willed myself to remain upright. My head dropped back as I opened my legs wider and titled my hips toward his hand. Unfortunately, the slow stroking of his fingers didn't last long.

He released me and gently guided me to the bed as he stood up. He took his time rolling down his pants and finally his boxers. The length of him bobbed up and down, seemingly relieved at being released from the tight confines of his clothes. His dick was thick, long, and hard, and absolutely aching to do its job. Going on instincts alone, I flattened myself out against the satin sheets and waited. Connor took position between my thighs and pulled me to the very edge of the bed. There was a brief rattle of a condom being opened and then silence.

The initial thrust of his hips forced me to release a breath of air I wasn't aware I'd been holding. A sharp pain ricocheted through my body, but it was quickly replaced by pleasure. He was thicker than I had anticipated and I wasn't ready to accept the girth of him. I could feel him glide over every crevice inside my body and the nerves in each spot were electrified. He developed a slow, deep rhythm as the thrust of his hips melded our bodies together.

"You like that?" he growled. "Hmm? You like that, bitch?"

Um ... excuse me? Bitch? Where the hell did that come from?

"Yeah, you like it," he groaned, "because you're a dirty, filthy whore."

Okayyyy ... the insults are a bit much. I'm all for dirty talk but this is pushing the envelope.

We were a tangle of arms and legs as he expertly flipped me over onto my stomach. He took position and thrust back inside me with enough force to make me wonder if he was trying to come out the other end. His hand grabbed a fistful of hair and snatched my head back, eliciting a loud gasp from me. The rough sex was a turn on, minus the degrading insults. His hips fervently pumped in and out of me, and I reached back to gently put my hand on his thigh to stop him from thrusting so hard. He grabbed my hand and jacked my arm up behind me. The other hand found my clit and massaged it until it throbbed, begging for a release.

His hand, coupled with his deep hard strokes, was about to pitch me over the edge. The first orgasm slammed into me with enough force that I momentarily became dizzy, and thought I saw spots before my eyes. Connor slapped my ass repeatedly, clearly not ready to be done with me yet. Each stroke made me moan and bite my lip. This one encounter was enough to keep my sexual appetite at bay for the next two years. Just when I thought I couldn't take it anymore, Connor pulled out, removed the condom and covered my ass in his warm wetness before collapsing onto the bed next to me.

"I'll be ready for the next round in a few minutes," he said panting.

Next round? Is he a man or a machine? I can't handle another round of anything.

"Actually, you have completely tired me out. I think we better call it a night," I suggested.

"Okay," he chuckled.

I gave a small sigh of relief and attempted to stand. My legs were weak and threatened to drop me down to the floor. I forced my feet forward to the bathroom and leaned against the door once it closed behind me. Connor was definitely a force to be reckoned with. I could question a lot of things about him, but his stamina sure wouldn't be one of them. There was no point in forcing my aching body back into the body shaper. Besides, he'd seen all there was to see anyway. I took my time washing up, being especially gentle with my delicate sore parts. I slipped my dress on and scooped up my shoes before exiting the bathroom.

"Leaving so soon?" he asked playfully.

I glimpsed the new erection he was sporting, and felt the dull throb between my legs quicken. He was going to have to take care of that one by himself.

"Yes," I replied. "It's late and I need to get all the rest I can get so I will be able to make it to the focus group in the morning."

With a sly grin of satisfaction, Connor grabbed the towel he'd taken from me earlier and wrapped it around his waist. "You're right. You need to get some sleep. I'll text you all of the details you'll need for tomorrow," he said.

He walked me to the door and gave me a quick kiss goodbye before closing the door behind me.

I'm going to sleep like a baby tonight, I thought with a smile.

Chapter Seven

I groaned my contempt for the buzzing alarm clock rousing me from my sleep too soon. Morning came faster than I wanted it to given my level of exhaustion. I needed at least six more hours of sleep in order to fully recuperate from last night's activities. Today I would have to skip my morning pit stop at the coffee shop. Based on the time and my overzealous swatting of the snooze button, I was running a little late. I jumped in the shower and carefully washed my body. My legs were a little sore, but I didn't care. I smiled at the pleasant reminder instead.

Today was going to be a ponytail and no makeup kind of day. I cursed myself for not getting up the first time the alarm went off. Cloaked in my oversized robe, I stood in front of the closet trying to narrow down my options. My phone vibrated, alerting me of new messages.

I hope it's Connor.

My mouth transformed into a thousand-watt smile as I glanced at the screen. I did have a message from Connor and five from Kirsten. Connor's message had the information he mentioned last night.

Connor: 112 Waylan Ave Suite 208. Be there at 9. Dress comfortably.

Just like last night, he seemed to be able to anticipate everything. I was thankful he mentioned the bit about dressing comfortably, because I certainly didn't want to embarrass him by showing up dressed wrong. My outfit, a T-shirt and yoga pants, was completed by a pair of running shoes I'd never used before. The address was across town in the business district and since I didn't want to get trapped in the morning rush hour, I hurried on out the door.

I had every intention on being on time, but the bumper to bumper traffic had other plans. Since traffic wasn't moving, I grabbed my phone and looked at the messages from Kirsten. Each text she sent was funnier than the last.

Kirsten: Are you there yet? How's dinner?

Kirsten: Hello! Give me an update! Don't make me come down there.

Kirsten: No response?! I hope you're ignoring me because you're naked.

Kirsten: I should stake out your house so I can see you do the walk of shame.

Kirsten: OMG really, no answer! I hope he hasn't done something to you. Call me.

A horn blared from behind, and scared the hell out of me. Traffic had started moving, but I hadn't. I dropped the phone in my lap and inched up a little to close the gap I'd created. Not wanting to be bothered with typing a long drawn out text, I grabbed the phone and called Kirsten.

"Oh my goodness, what the hell happened to you last night!" she shrieked.

"What didn't happen to me last night is the better question," I replied smugly.

She squealed into the phone loud enough to burst my eardrum. "You fucked him didn't you? How was it? What happened? I need every sordid detail," she said.

I spent the next ten minutes rehashing last night's events. Verbally reliving the moment caused the familiar ache between my thighs to return.

"And," I drawled, "he invited me to a thing at his job."

"Wow, I'm so jealous right now," she murmured. "What's it for?"

"I'm not really sure about the details. He said it was like a focus group thing. Listen, I'm pulling up at the building right now. I'll call you as soon as I'm done," I said.

"All right, call me as soon as you finish," she ordered.

Circling the building for the fourth time, I desperately searched for a place to park. With no spaces available, I was forced to use the parking garage on the side of the building.

I hope I can get my parking validated.

I swerved into the first space I came to and got out of the car. Following the signs and arrows, I found the elevator and made my way upstairs. The doors opened on the second floor and I was greeted by a blast of cold air. I glanced up and down the hall, searching for the right suite. The glass door down on the end led to the place I was looking for. I pulled open the heavy door and waited for the receptionist.

She sashayed in with orange stringy hair flowing behind her. As if the hair alone wasn't enough, she was wearing bright blue eye shadow. "Hello," she said, her eyes gliding over my body from head to toe. "You must be here for the case-study?"

"Case-study? No, I'm here for the focus group. Mr. O'Neil invited me, Connor O'Neil," I replied.

She offered a not-so-pleasant smile and stood up to hand me a clipboard. "Of course he did. Sign in and then follow me. They're about to get started."

I frowned at the woman's lack of polite customer service.

You're rude and look like a clown.

After I scrawled my signature on the paper, I followed her through a side door. Everything was white and looked very sterile. She abruptly stopped in front of an opening to a space that looked like a classroom.

"Find an available desk and fill out the paperwork on top," she instructed.

I stepped into the mid-sized room and gave a tight smile to other ladies there. They offered similar smiles and shy waves. I found an open seat near the door and slid into the blue chair. Several sheets of paper were neatly stacked with a black ink pen holding them down. I grabbed the pen and got started. Most of the information they wanted was general; age, race, occupation, weight.

Weight? Why in the hell do they need that?

Before I had time to ponder the meaning of the odd question, a pair of men walked in wearing white lab coats.

"Good morning, ladies. We want to thank each and every one of you for participating in this case-study," said the man with the glasses.

Case-study? Maybe Connor got it wrong and this wasn't a focus group after all.

"As you know, we are ready to start testing our new weight loss drug that will specifically target obese minority females," announced the other man.

What. The. Fuck.

My hand shot up into the air like an eager first grader, ready to answer the teacher's question.

"Um ... yes, ma'am? You have questions already?"

"Yes," I snapped. "What's going on? I was told this was a focus group."

Both gentlemen glanced at each other and back at me. "Mr. Glasses" shuffled around a stack of papers for a moment.

That's right, check your list. Obviously, I'm in the wrong room.

"No, ma'am, the representative that invited you here should have explained all of this to you," he replied nervously.

"Whoa, wait a minute. You mean to tell me I was told to come here to test a drug for fat black people?" I growled.

The other man in the room held up his hands in front of me as if he were warding off an impending attack. "Nobody said black people specifically. We said *minorities*. Our scientists believe they have found a common link that will allow us to target the different biological needs in our participants."

I felt my rage building as I surveyed the room again. No one else seemed as outraged as me. Clearly they knew what was going on, and I was the only one in the dark. Horrified and humiliated, I grabbed my bag and yanked open the door to leave.

"Ma'am, if you leave now you won't get your ten-dollar check at the end," one of them yelled.

Ten dollars? That's the damn check he told me about? Ten measly dollars!

It was a good thing I had on my running shoes, because I was in a full-blown sprint as I went by the tacky receptionist and out the door. My hands trembled as I pushed the button for the elevator. I didn't think shit could possibly get worse, but I was wrong. The elevator arrived and the doors slid open to reveal Connor standing there leaning against the rail.

"Hey, Bri, where are you going?" he asked.

"You are a fucking liar!" I bellowed, pointing an accusatory finger in his face. "You said this was a focus group!"

Connor reached out and pulled me into the elevator. "I didn't lie," he said through clenched teeth. "I just didn't give you all the pertinent details. You need to get your ass back in there before I lose my commission."

The elevator doors sprang back open, and a gentleman with a briefcase stepped in and pressed the button for the parking garage. Connor nodded a greeting and flashed him a smile. "You invited me here to take an experimental drug," I barked. I didn't give a rat's ass about the man trapped in the elevator with us. "Why didn't you tell me the fucking truth? Why invite me to dinner and allow all of the other stuff to happen? You could've just said, 'Hey, come to a case study for fat people.' You didn't have to screw me first."

We made it to the bottom and the man eagerly exited the elevator. I stepped between the doors so they wouldn't close and waited on an explanation.

"You want the truth?" he snarled. Darkness washed over his face and startled me just a bit.

"Fine, here it is. I saw you and thought you would be perfect for the program. I invited you to dinner because you have a cute face and I wanted to know what it would be like to fuck a black chick. And to be perfectly honest, it was a disappointing experience. I expected you to be feisty, dominant, and a lot more aggressive. Isn't that what black women are known for? What you should be doing is thanking me for giving you an opportunity to get the physique you obviously want. You and I both know you aren't comfortable with your body based on how shy you acted last night. So, are you happy now? Was finding out the truth to your satisfaction?"

My mouth dropped open as I looked down at my chest to check for blood. The invisible knife was plunged deep into my heart. I wanted to punch Connor in the face and show him just how aggressive I could be. He scowled at me with a blatant look of aggravation. I took two steps back and allowed the doors to close as he mumbled something about losing out on his commission again.

My heart pounded in my ears and despite the sticky humid air, I was shivering. It took me several attempts to steady my hands long enough to get the car unlocked and the key in the ignition. My foot hit the gas and revved the engine. Luckily, the car was still in park or I would have completely smashed into the cars parked behind me. I grabbed the steering wheel with both hands and tried to calm my nerves. After a few minutes of slow deep breaths, I managed to get out of the parking space. I paid the parking attendant and zoomed off before getting my change.

I hadn't felt this low in years, and I struggled to focus on the road. My vision was blurred by tears and my hands started trembling again. How could somebody have such a disregard for someone else's feelings? I found myself passing the same sign for the third time before I realized I was driving in circles. If I weren't driving right now, I would curl up into a ball and cry. Actually, I wanted to find the tallest building in the city and jump off of it. I'd opened my fortress of solitude and broadcasted every flaw and weakness I had, this was the end result. I needed to find a quiet place to help settle my nerves before I did something drastic. My little sedan lurched forward with a set destination in mind: Drip Drop Coffee Hut.

Chapter Eight

I sought the comfort of food and the reassuring scent of coffee beans. My mind screamed at me to go home, especially since relying on food for comfort was how I got into this situation. I swept my hands over my face and tried to erase the tears. Tears or no tears, my puffy red eyes proved I'd been crying. Since it was just after the morning rush and right before lunch, the café was nearly empty. A few people were sprinkled here and there; a couple whispering over a plate of scones, a twitchy weirdo with a laptop, and a relaxed elderly man with a newspaper.

No one stood behind the register, and I assumed Jayce was in the back somewhere. I sat down at the far end of the bar and dropped my head. The double doors swung open, but I didn't bother looking up to see who was coming through them.

"Hey, Bri, what's shaking?" asked Jayce playfully.

Hold it together, Bri. Just hold it together, I chanted over and over.

My eyes finally lifted to meet his and the floodgates opened. I immediately became a sobbing shaking mess. I felt a hand gently patting my arm.

"Take a deep breath. Ssshhh, calm down. Tell me what happened," he whispered.

My head snapped to attention as I remembered the recent conversation we had. "You were right," I sobbed. "I should have listened to you. He humiliated me."

Someone near the register cleared their throat to get Jayce's attention. He glanced over his shoulder and shot them a dirty look. The man quickly became extremely interested in the magazine rack.

"C'mon," he murmured. "Let's go in my office and talk. I'll get Leani to handle the front."

I eased off of the stool and followed him through the swinging doors. He ushered me into an office where a pretty girl with long dark hair sat frowning over a stack of papers. "Leani, do you mind taking over the register for me?"

She took one look at me and quickly exited the office. "Have a seat," he said, motioning to the chair. He opted to lean against the desk with his arms folded. "You said 'he' humiliated you. Are you referring to the asshole from yesterday?"

I couldn't produce the right words necessary to explain the situation so I nodded. I sat down in the chair and dropped my head into the palms of my hands.

"Do you want something to drink?" he asked.

"Hot chocolate won't help this situation," I mumbled.

Jayce moved to the side of the desk and shuffled a few things around. "No, I meant a real drink. I can make you a cranberry vodka if you want."

Alcohol? Hell yes.

"Yes, please," I replied. Alcohol wouldn't undo the situation, but it would bring my emotions down to a tolerable non-suicidal level.

I grabbed the glass and downed the contents, welcoming the burn in my chest. There was more vodka than cranberry, but I didn't mind, not one little bit. The liquid courage gave me the strength to tell Jayce the truth. We didn't know each other outside the café, but I felt like I could talk to him. I gave him the quick version of the events and waited for him to respond. He grabbed my glass, refilled it, and made a drink for himself.

"I'm going to break his face," he muttered.

I chuckled at his alpha male response. "No need to break any faces. I just appreciate you taking the time to listen. Everything has been so hard for me lately. I have no job, and two useless degrees hanging on my wall at home. Speaking of home, I live with my mom since I have no money to support myself with. Right now, I'm not living, I'm just existing. I'm the knockoff version of who I thought I would be."

He emptied his glass and stooped down to meet my eyes. "You're one of my favorite customers and I hate to see you upset like this. Since you don't want me punch this asshole in the face, let me help you another way. Leani is my sister, and she'll be leaving in the next couple of weeks for school. There's a job waiting for you if you want it. As an added bonus you can eat and drink whatever you want."

"I can't ask you to do that," I stammered in disbelief.

"You didn't ask," he said, placing his hand on my knee. "I offered, and I hope you'll say yes. You've seen what a madhouse this place can be, so I could honestly use the help."

I wasn't sure what the proper protocol was in a situation like this, so I did the first thing that popped into my head. My arms wrapped around Jayce in appreciation.

"Thank you," I whispered. His arms returned the gesture, and the hug made me feel just like I thought it would: safe.

Chapter Nine

I was thankful Jayce offered me a job, but I'd created more problems in a single week than I ever could have imagined. Aside from a salt and sugar mishap, I managed to set the kitchen on fire … twice. Well, technically today would make three times, as Jayce burst through the doors with an extinguisher in hand.

"It's okay!" I exclaimed. "I put it out this time."

He looked around just to be sure and placed the extinguisher on the counter. "Bri," he said slowly.

I'd been expecting this conversation since day one, the whole "This isn't working out, so good luck with your next endeavor," speech.

"Don't worry, I already know what you're going to say," I muttered. "Listen, thank you for the opportunity, I'll just get my purse and go."

"Wait … what?" he stammered, stepping in front of the door. "Slow down, Bri, I'm not firing you. We just need to figure out what you're good at. No offense, I like you, and the customers like you despite the salty coffee you served the other day, but you are a major liability."

If my skin was lighter, I'd be red like a tomato, but I'm sure the flushed undertones were still a dead giveaway. A hot flash surged through my body as I listened.

"Here's the thing. You said you have two degrees, right? Well, what are they in?" he asked. Jayce leaned against the counter and folded his arms. That seemed to be his standard pose, and I don't know why, but I liked it. The sheer size of him was comforting to me somehow. I knew the hug we shared was a spur of the moment thing, but I found myself wishing he would put his arms around me again.

"Earth to Bri," he said, waving his hand in front of my face.

"Oh, sorry," I sputtered. "My mind went blank for second. I have a bachelor's degree in finance and my master's degree is in business administration."

"Really? Wow, I probably should have asked you that question in the beginning. This is going to work out perfectly," he replied.

He walked into the small office and grabbed a few pieces of paper. "Take a look at these and tell me if they mean anything to you."

I put my purse down and accepted the sheets of paper. My eyes gave them a quick scan before handing them back. "Yeah, one is a ledger, and the other one is supposed to be a balance sheet, but it's wrong."

His eyes lit up like a Christmas tree and his lips rolled back into a smile. "I'm so glad you know what this mumbo jumbo means. Vivianne was taking care of it all, but now I need somebody else to do it."

Vivianne. What he should call her is Bitch.

Vivianne, his Barbie doll girlfriend, had taken some days off so she could have her breasts enlarged. What's a Barbie without boobs? She should have saved that money and bought etiquette classes instead. I was hoping she didn't come back at all. In my opinion, she was actually the one responsible for my mishaps in the café. My nerves get rattled when I'm under pressure and she'd deliberately hover over me like an annoying insect.

"Great, I'll be happy to take over," I said.

"Awesome. Listen, I have a huge favor I need to ask you. Actually, think of it as part of your new job requirements. How about dinner?"

I narrowed my eyes and tilted my head to the side. "Dinner? You know I'm leery of any man asking me out to dinner these days."

Jayce tossed his head back with a laugh. "No, no it's nothing like that. By dinner, I meant pizza and beer at my place."

I smiled in return and nodded. "Sure, I'm game. What time?"

"We can actually leave now," he said, glancing down at his watch.

Together we finished the last minute cleaning and I headed out the door to my car. I waited patiently for him to lock the doors and lead the way to his house. It didn't take long for us to get to get there because it was literally right around the corner from the café in a small neighborhood similar to where I lived. We pulled into the driveway and Jayce went to unlock the door.

You could tell the house had a woman's touch to it based on the fruity air fresheners and decorations.

"Do you mind taking your shoes off? Vivianne has a thing about the carpet getting dirty," he said.

Yes I mind, mainly because I don't want to do anything SHE wants me to do, and my socks don't match.

"All right," I muttered. "But don't laugh at my socks."

The instant I kicked off my shoes, Jayce zoomed in on my feet and commenced to laughing.

"You should have known I would laugh. Not only do those socks not match, but one is neon pink and one is neon green. It looks like you have lights on your feet!" he said between chuckles.

I glanced down and laughed too. He was right; the neon colors did make it look like my feet were shining. "Shut up," I said, playfully punching him in the arm.

"Ow," he yelped. "No hitting, you know I'm delicate merchandise. C'mon into the living room, but watch your step. The light switch is on the other side of the room."

He didn't speak fast enough, because I slammed my foot into what felt like a giant brick. I howled in pain and collapsed to the floor just as he flipped the light switch.

"Oh shit, I'm so sorry about that," he said, crouching down in front of me.

I took several deep breaths in an attempt to keep the tears at bay. My eyes shot to the floor to see what just assaulted my foot. A giant hand-weight was the culprit.

"You brought me to your house to break my foot?" I asked, trying to lighten the mood.

"Oh stop it, your foot isn't broken," he said as he gingerly examined it.

"I bet it is. I don't think I can even stand up," I whined. My toes throbbed, and I planned to milk this situation for all its worth. The smile on Jayce's face showed he knew it too.

"C'mon, you big baby, let's get you on the couch so I can take a closer look at your foot," he said positioning his arms around me.

Is he about to pick me up? Oh hell no.

"No, no, no," I protested. "I can't have you throwing your back out trying to pick me up."

Jayce of course ignored me and cradled me with ease as he carried me over to the couch. "You're not as heavy as you think you are," he said.

"Thanks," I muttered.

He put me down and positioned himself on the other end with my feet in his lap. Within the blink of an eye, my pink sock was missing and Jayce was lightly squeezing my foot.

"You don't have to do that," I said, trying to swat his hands away. "I'm sure it's fine."

"Stop it," he said. "Nothing appears to be broken."

"Thank you, doctor," I teased.

He smiled and gently continued massaging my foot. "I used to play football, I've seen a lot of injuries, so don't worry, I'm a pro at this."

We sat there in an awkward silence as the mini-rub down continued. I enjoyed his hands touching me more than I probably should have.

I hope my feet don't stink.

"I'll be right back," he announced. "I'm going to order the food and grab some beers from the fridge."

I nodded and slid my legs off his lap so he could get up. Fifteen minutes later, he came back with two Bud Lights in tow. He handed one to me as he sat back down on the other end of the couch motioning for my foot. I didn't bother with protesting this time. I put my legs back where they were and allowed him to continue rubbing the pain away.

"Listen, here's the thing," he said. "I have a small problem and I need your help."

"Okay, what is it?" I asked after taking a big gulp of my beer.

If he says he needs help taking his clothes off, then I'm all in.

"Vivianne and I are going through a rough patch. Rough patch is an understatement. The truth is we broke up."

Yes, yes, yes!

" … and I need you to help me get her back."

What? Nooo!

"Get her back? What caused the breakup in the first place?"

Not that I care.

"These last few months have been a little rocky and we just weren't seeing eye to eye. She wants more than I'm willing to sacrifice," he explained.

I frowned and took another swig of beer. "Wait, if you aren't willing to sacrifice, then why do you want her back?" I asked.

"Because the things she wants are superficial. I need to make her remember why we fell in love in the first place. I want you to help me figure out ways to do that. At first I thought we were just having a spat and she'd get over it, but I realized it was serious when she moved all of her stuff out."

"Damn," I muttered under my breath.

"So that's the favor I wanted to ask. Are you willing to help me?"

"I have just one question before I give you an answer. Do you love her?"

"Yes," he replied firmly. "I do."

His response wasn't one I wanted to hear, but I wouldn't stand in the way of love. "All right, I'll help you," I sighed.

Chapter Ten

"I thought you hated Vivianne," said Kirsten.

I watched her expertly glue on a pair of fake eyelashes and add several coats of mascara. Kirsten was always putting makeup and accessories on herself or whoever was close to her. She said it was because she needed to practice her craft at all times. Personally, I thought she just liked playing in makeup, but I guess it was worth it since she's made a career out of it.

"What's the point of the mascara on top of the fake lashes?" I asked.

Mentally, I was taking notes, but I already knew any attempt I made would probably result in my eyes being glued shut.

"It helps add dimension. I'm going for a super glam look right now. Quit trying to avoid my question. Why would you volunteer to help Jayce get back together with that evil witch?"

I sighed and grabbed one of the makeup brushes to sweep over my eye. "It's complicated. He helped me when I was at my lowest point.

That douchebag Connor, made me feel like trash, and Jayce was there to pick up the pieces. I feel like I owe him," I explained.

"I've told you over and over, don't apply the same eye shadow all over your entire eyelid. It makes you look like a clown. You need to add a highlight and a crease color too," she said. "And then you need to blend. Blending helps bring it all together.

I rolled my eyes and put the brush back with the others. If I had to spend over an hour like Kirsten putting makeup on, I would probably shoot myself. The way I saw it, you only need a little eyeliner, mascara, and some lip gloss.

"Have you heard from Connor at all?" she asked.

"Nope, and if he's smart he won't contact me," I growled.

She finally seemed satisfied with her face and came over to join me on the bed. "I wish you would let me call my cousin. Ricky would set Connor straight and make him apologize too," she said.

Yeah, and Ricky would break the man's legs, and I wouldn't have to pay him extra to do it. Wait ... maybe that's not such a bad idea.

"No, Kirsten," I said firmly. "I'm a big girl. We can't run to Ricky every time something goes wrong."

"Fine," she huffed. "But the option is out there … I'm just saying." She rolled off the bed and jumped to her feet. "I think we should get dressed and put on our dancing shoes since I'm all glammed up."

My lips pulled back into a scowl as I groaned. "I can think of a million things I would rather do other than go out. For example, I have a few books I've been dying to read lately."

Kirsten grabbed my leg and started pulling me off of the bed. "Books? Seriously, Bri, where's your sense of adventure?" she asked.

Probably between the pages of one of those books.

"Please," she whined. "I'm always on the road, and we never get the chance to go out and do anything. If you say yes, I promise not to keep you out past midnight."

A defeated sigh crossed my lips and Kirsten smiled at her mini-victory. This was one argument I knew I couldn't win.

I ended up changing clothes four times before Kirsten gave me her official stamp of approval. She also wouldn't let me leave without a full face of makeup. I glanced over to my friend and zeroed in on the short skirt and halter top tight enough to look like she had painted it onto her non-jiggly body. I was the fat friend. I knew it, she knew it, and everybody in Club Flame knew it. For once, I wanted to wear a sleeveless shirt and not have batwings whenever I lifted my arms.

Kirsten immediately headed to the dance floor and I found an open seat at the bar. My job, no matter where we went, was to watch our purses and drinks. I wanted to dance, but I found myself over-thinking the rules of dance floor etiquette. What if I walked up to someone to dance and they shot me down? I wished Kirsten would consider doing some of the things I wanted to do, like sipping on glasses of wine while laughing through a horror movie because I think they are absolutely hilarious. The killer was always in the closet and everybody knows if you fall, you're screwed.

"Hey, what's up?" shouted a familiar voice. I immediately snapped out of my scrambled brain and came face to face with Jayce.

I was surprised to see him, but it was a happy kind of surprise. "I'm here with my friend," I yelled over the blaring music.

"Why … " he asked frowning.

I missed out on the rest of the question. I shook my head and leaned in for him to repeat it. The music suddenly got louder and I still had no clue what he had said.

His lips are moving again, but I couldn't hear him. All I heard was a guy in the DJ booth yelling for all of the ladies to drop it low. I shook my head again, shrugged my shoulders, and pointed to my ear. My hands reached for my purse as I fished around for my cell phone. If I couldn't hear him, then I could at least see whatever he's saying through a text message.

Before I was able to retrieve my phone, he was pulling me to my feet and out onto the dance floor. I snatched up our purses as a look of horror flashed across my face. I attempted to dig my heels in to stop myself from going any further. Jayce stopped in the middle of the floor and turned around. He started dancing, but I stood there frozen in place.

I can't move ... I can't move.

He stopped moving and cocked his head to the side. Instead of allowing me to return to the safety of my seat at the bar, he planted his hands on my hips and guided me to the beat of the music.

Awkward. This is awkward. Move, Bri! Move something, anything, so you don't look like an idiot.

I took a deep breath and slowly allowed my body to do what I knew it could do. A playful smile lingered on Jayce's lips as I finally found the right rhythm. Before long, I was a hot sweaty mess and my shirt was sticking to my body. Kirsten danced her way closer to us and gave me two thumbs up as she nodded her approval of him. I would have kept dancing if he hadn't pulled me over to a reserved table in the corner. Since we were further away from the DJ it was much easier to hear now.

"Look at you," he teased. "To be such an unwilling dance partner, you went out there and danced circles around everybody."

"Yeah," I shouted. "I'm usually too freaked out to dance with strangers. I actually love dancing; I do it all the time at home."

He leaned over, wrapped his arm around my shoulder, and gave me a light squeeze. "You're good at it; you should do it more often. Listen," he said, dropping his arm away from me. "I'm going to see Vivianne tomorrow. Do you have any tips or ideas I can use to get back in her good graces?"

Ughhh. You just killed my vibe.

"Where is she?" I asked, reaching for the menu. If I was going to be forced to discuss the Wicked Witch of the East, I'd need a few drinks in my system first.

"She's at her mom's house recovering from surgery. I'm a little nervous to see what she looks like because Vivianne believes in going big or going home. The chances of her having two giant watermelons on her chest are significantly high."

I tried very hard not to laugh, but I couldn't hold it in. My mind instantly painted a picture of Vivianne's tiny stick figure body with two huge orbs for breasts.

"I'm sorry," I said, trying to choke down the rest of my chuckles. "Take her some flowers, maybe a card, and a few balloons," I suggested.

That's what I would want.

He shook his head and waved the waitress over. "Jack Daniel's please. How about you, Bri?" he asked.

"Amaretto sour," I said, handing the drink menu to the girl. "Why did you shake your head no? What's wrong with my suggestion?"

"Vivianne likes gifts. I think she'll like shoes or a purse instead of flowers and balloons," he explained.

Wow, materialistic much?

"You definitely need to pick whatever you think she'll like. But, I thought the whole point of asking for my help was so I could help find ways that don't feed into her greedy side. We are supposed to be reminding her that your relationship is built on more," I said.

Jayce paused and seemed lost inside his thoughts for a moment. He was almost in a trance when the waitress returned with our drinks. I sipped mine slowly and waited for him to come back to reality.

"You know what? You're absolutely right. Flowers and balloons it is," he announced. He grabbed his cup and finished his drink in one gulp.

"Hey, I'm going to go ahead and call it a night. We have a truck coming in the morning with new supplies and I need to be there to unload it," he said.

I glanced at my watch and was shocked to see it was nearly two o'clock in the morning. "Wow, I didn't realize how late it is. I need to find my friend so we can head home too," I replied.

"Yeah," he smirked. "You need to get some rest. I heard your boss can be a real asshole if you show up late."

"Tell me about it, he's the biggest asshole ever. He actually let me keep my job even after I put salt in the sugar containers. Can you believe the nerve of that guy?" I said with a lop-sided grin.

Jayce's smile spread even wider, creating deep dimples in his cheeks.

Aww dimples. Now he's ten times cuter than before.

"Don't worry about the check," he said, reaching for his wallet.

I thanked him for the drink and watched him make his way through the throngs of people still dancing. Kirsten must have been waiting on him to leave because she suddenly appeared out of nowhere.

"That guy was hot! Please tell me you got his number," she said. Her hair was damp with sweat, but her makeup was still flawless. I wondered what she put on to make it stay like that … glue?

"Of course not," I replied. "I already have his number. That's Jayce, my boss."

Kirsten's eyes widened like a deer caught in headlights. "No way! Mr. Coffee Shop is sexy! Instead of helping him get back with his ex you need to find a way to take her spot."

I laughed at her suggestion. Leave it to Kirsten to always have some type of plot going on in her brain.

"Are you ready to go?" I asked. "You know I have to go to work in the morning."

"Honey, I don't blame you for wanting to go to work especially if I had *him* to look forward to," she said.

She was right. I wanted to be there bright and early, just to see Jayce.

Chapter Eleven

Jayce burst through the office doors with an arm full of stuff as I sat trying to make the balance sheet actually balance.

"Oh wow, what's all this?" I asked, catching a bouquet that was about to hit the floor.

He made it to the desk and dropped everything in a pile. "I plan on taking this stuff to Vivianne and I wanted to get your approval first."

The man had splurged and picked up every flower known to mankind. "Are you sure you want to take all of this over there?"

"Do you think I should?" he asked, narrowing his eyes at the faux garden spread across the desk.

I zeroed in on my favorites and scooped them up. "I love lilies and calla lilies. They are so elegant and tropical at the same time."

Instead of paying attention to me, Jayce was holding up a bouquet of roses. "I think she'll like these a lot better," he mumbled.

The twisted look on his face spoke volumes. He really wanted to make a good impression on Vivianne and I still didn't understand why.

"Roses are so cliché, trust me. Take her something she won't expect," I said.

His eyes bounced back and forth a few times between the different flowers and his brow buckled into a look of concentration.

"Yeah," he said slowly. "You're right."

He grabbed a vase from the pile on the desk and shoved the flowers into it. "How's this?"

I rolled my eyes and shook my head. Something told me I should have explained the right way to arrange the flowers. "It looks a mess. Scoot out of the way and I'll fix them," I ordered.

The vibration from my phone drew my attention away from my Martha Stewart moment. "You mind if I take this? It's my mom," I said.

"No, go right ahead. I have some stuff to do in the front anyway," he replied. He walked … no sauntered out of the office.

Is that what sauntering looks like? I never thought I would actually see someone saunter.

His stride had a lazy pace to it … a sexy, lazy pace. I noticed more and more things about him with each passing day. Today, it was the way he walked, yesterday it was his ass, and the day before that I found myself staring at the noticeable bulge in the front of his pants.

"Hey, Mom, how's your vacation?" I asked, trying to refocus my attention.

"Hello, sweetie, my vacation is excellent. It would be nice to sit on the beach drinking mimosas every day if I could. How are things at home?" she asked.

"Things are great. In fact they're so good, I managed to snag a job," I said, just as I accidently broke one of the lilies by trying to shove it into the already full vase. I didn't want to throw it away and let it go to waste, so I stuck it in my hair, right above my ear.

"That's wonderful, honey! I'm so proud of you; I knew you could do it. You'll have to tell me all about it when I get home. Listen … are you going to be busy later?"

Here it comes. She's going to ask for a favor. Mom only asks if I'm busy when she wants something from me.

"No," I said slowly, waiting on her to get to the point.

"Well, here's the thing, I need a favor," she said.

Bingo. I knew it.

"Gram-Gram called and you know how she goes on and on about being lonely and bored. I felt bad, so I told her you would take her to dinner tonight," she explained in a rush.

"Mommm," I whined.

"Honey, I know … I know. But she's your grandmother and it won't kill you to see her and spend a little time with her," said Mom.

I gave an exasperated sigh and closed my eyes. This dinner was going to be an absolute nightmare, but my options were limited. If I go, I'd get to listen to Gram-Gram complain for a couple of hours, and if I don't go, Mom and Gram-Gram would BOTH complain.

"Fine," I grumbled.

"Thanks, honey, I'll call back later to check in. Love you, bye," she said.

"Love you too, bye," I replied. I shoved the phone back into my pocket and tried to stay focused as I stood back to admire my work.

My mind was on autopilot as I walked to the dining area to help with the evening cleanup before closing time. I had to prepare myself for tonight, because I could only take Gram-Gram in small doses, and dinner with her was a very big dose to handle.

"How's it look?" asked Jayce.

"How's what look?"

He squinted his eyes and searched my face for a few moments before it dawned on me. "Oh! You're talking about the flowers, right? They're sitting on the desk if you want to check them out," I replied.

"Are you feeling okay?" he asked.

"Yes … no … well … " I stammered. "I have dinner tonight with my grandmother and she's a bit of a handful."

Jayce nodded and took the sugar container from me. "Grandmother's usually are handfuls. Maybe you should just wipe the tables down."

"Why?" I asked, pulling my face into a frown.

"Because you're about to refill the sugar containers with salt again," he pointed out.

I looked down and realized the mistake I was about to make. "Sorry," I muttered.

Jayce laughed and threw his arm over my shoulder. "I'm sure it will be okay. Don't worry about doing the refills; I'll take care of those in a little while."

He gave me a tight squeeze before disappearing through the double doors. I was nearly done cleaning up when I heard the main door chime. Connor walked in and our eyes met as he made his way to the register.

"Hey, Brenda," he said casually in my direction. "You're working here now?"

I tossed the towel onto the table and folded my arms. "My name is Bri, you asshole," I snapped.

The grin on his face expanded tenfold. "That's no way to talk to a customer," he replied. "Especially a customer you caused to lose a very large commission."

Oh, I amuse you? We'll see how amused you are when I pour a cup of steaming hot coffee down your pants.

"You're not a customer," barked Jayce, coming back through the double doors. "Now get out of my café."

"I'm a paying customer and I don't have to go anywhere," said Connor. He leaned against the counter in an act of defiance. He clearly didn't plan to leave quietly.

Jayce smiled, but it was not his usual smile, it was more of a sinister scary smirk. He looked like he planned on rearranging Connor's face, and the scary part was, it looked like something he would enjoy. A sense of panic coursed through my veins as he took several steps toward Connor. My hands involuntarily trembled as the pair came toe to toe.

"Don't test me, and don't let this apron fool you into thinking you won't get hurt," Jayce muttered.

"Oh really, tough guy? You don't know me," Connor snarled.

I prepared myself for a fight … just in case.

Do I jump in and help Jayce or will that make it worse? Will it embarrass him? This is technically my problem. I wish Connor would just leave. Maybe I still have time to grab that hot cup of coffee.

"Really?" asked Jayce. "Because I think I know you quite well. Mr. Connor Benjamin O'Neil, residing at 2824 Bevlin Way, on the 15th floor, with a house code of 11292. Your vehicle and condo are in your grandmother's name, Beverly O'Neil. How's that cat of hers doing? Butterscotch is her name, right?"

My mouth flapped open at the high level of creepiness oozing from Jayce. Connor's mouth dropped open too as he fluttered his eyes. His skin quickly paled, making him appear washed out and ghostlike.

"If you even think about going near my grandmother," he stammered.

"I don't have an issue with your grandma, my issue is with you. Listen to me real well … stay away from Bri. If you see her on the street, make sure you go the other way. Stay away from this café too. You can get your coffee from somewhere else. If you choose to ignore my advice … just know … I'll find you."

Connor's eyes briefly cut over to me as he took a few steps back. He slowly turned on his heels and made his way out the door with one last look over his shoulder.

My eyes flickered over to Jayce, who was calmly watching the door.

"Are you okay?" he asked, glancing over at me.

My voice was trapped in my throat but I managed to squeak something out that resembled "yes."

"If he comes back or messes with you again let me know," he said gently.

"Okay," I mumbled.

He grabbed his towel and looked around the sitting area. "Well, I think we're done here. I'll lock up and walk you to your car."

I followed him to the office to get my things. "Thanks for standing up for me. You didn't have to do it, but I appreciate the fact that you did. How did you know all that stuff about Connor anyway?"

"First of all," he said, scooping up the vase of flowers, "I did have to do it. Your feelings are important to me, and I won't allow someone to treat you like crap and get away with it. You're a good person and you didn't deserve to be treated the way he treated you. And to answer your other question, I know people that can find out anything I need to know. After your little fiasco, I did a little digging just to see what I could find," he replied with a wink. "That guy is a poser living off his grandmother. I know you don't want me to, but I can't guarantee that I won't hurt him if he bothers you again."

Wow. That's the sweetest, creepiest thing anybody has ever said to me. I kind of wish Connor would show up just so I can see them fight. I'd be there to wipe away the sweat from Jayce's hot body ....

"Bri, are you okay? You keep spacing out on me."

I walked with him to the parking lot and opened my car door. "Uh yeah, sorry about that. Good luck with Vivianne tonight," I said.

"Thanks, try to have a good time with your grandma. I'm sure it won't be as bad as you think," he said.

His kind words fell on deaf ears, because one thing I knew for certain, there was no such thing as a good time with Gram-Gram.

Chapter Twelve

I had just enough time to get home and shower before running back out the door. Gram-Gram was already standing outside in front of her house with her arms crossed by the time I rounded the corner. My tires brought me to a screeching halt right in front of her.

She opened the door and the familiar scent of her Chanel perfume made my stomach do a series of flips.

"You're late, Brianna, you're always late. I pray you don't drive like that on the way to the restaurant," she muttered.

"Hello, Gram-Gram," I replied under my breath. "My day was great, thanks for asking."

She cut her eyes over at me before yanking her seatbelt across her chest. "Don't you dare get sassy with me, young lady."

"Sorry," I grumbled.

"Turn the radio to something I want to listen to," she ordered.

I took a deep breath and counted to ten before reaching over to change the station.

What difference does the station make? You're just going to sing over whatever song is playing ... and it won't even be the same song.

Gram-Gram started singing her own tune right on cue.

Seriously? You could at least sing the song that's playing. I'm going to develop some type of nerve condition from being around her too long.

"Brianna, watch the road! Don't you see the light is yellow? That means stop," she shouted.

"It just turned yellow, and it doesn't mean stop, it means slow down," I replied, trying to calmly explain the rules of the road.

Gram-Gram leaned her head over and folded her arms again. "I've been driving longer than you have been alive. I think I know what a yellow light means. Speaking of lights, why were you late picking me up? You know I hate being late."

Speaking of lights? What in the hell did lights have to do with me being late?

"I have a new job and I needed to shower before I picked you up," I explained.

That response seemed to satisfy her long enough for us to get to the restaurant and get seated. My hand involuntarily clutched my fork as Gram-Gram had the waitress go through nearly everything on the menu before ordering her usual baked chicken and steamed vegetables.

What's the freaking point of asking about the specials if you have zero intentions of actually selecting one!

As soon as we handed the menus back to the waitress, I caught a glimpse of a devious look in Gram-Gram's eyes, which spelled trouble for me.

"Brianna, I have a little surprise for you," she said.

My heart pounded in my chest and I heard a not-so calming rush of blood in my ears. "Really?" I croaked.

"Yes," she said. "I have a friend whose grandson is single, so we worked a little magic and now you have a date."

"I have a what?" I asked nervously, praying I heard her wrong the first time.

Gram-Gram grinned from ear to ear as if she'd just announced I'd won the lottery. I'm not sure if it was because of the look of horror plastered on my face or if she really thought she was doing me a favor by setting me up with somebody.

"He's an absolutely lovely young man. I believe Gladys said he worked on computers or something as a technical engine," she said.

"Engineer?" I asked.

"Yes," she snapped waving her hand, dismissing my correction. "Engine … engineer … it's all the same."

No it's not.

"Hmmm let's see," she said. "He has dark hair, very stylish, and he's over six feet tall. I'm just asking you to give the man a chance. Nobody is going to make you marry him … although it would be nice."

I closed my eyes, pinched my leg, and counted to ten again.

"Brianna, wake up!" she yelled. "I have one more surprise for you."

Dear God, no! No more surprises.

I held my breath and waited for her to break the news to me.

"I have an appointment set up next week for you," she said beaming.

"An appointment?" I asked carefully.

"Yes," she said. "Well, actually it's for the consultation you'll need to have before you're able to get your eggs frozen."

It felt like a bomb had gone off in the building. I felt flames of rage licking over my skin as I trembled from head to toe.

"YOU DID WHAT?" I bellowed.

Everyone's heads swiveled over in our direction. One couple leaned over and offered hushed whispers to one another as they shot nasty glares at me. The man to my left cleared his throat and looked on in disgust.

"That's no way to talk to this elderly woman," he snapped. "You should be ashamed of yourself."

I'm not sure what clicked in my brain, but I freaked the hell out.

"Me? I should be ashamed? How about you turn around, eat that dry ass steak, and mind your own damn business!"

The entire restaurant was eerily silent now. "It's quiet enough to hear a mouse piss on cotton" as my deceased grandfather would say.

"Brianna," hissed Gram-Gram. "You apologize to this gentleman immediately. In fact, you apologize to this entire restaurant for being so rude."

"Gram-Gram, I'm going to the car. If you want to eat your food, then that's fine. I will be outside waiting," I said through clenched teeth. I was afraid to sit in the restaurant any longer, because if I did the table may end up flipped over. My mouth was clamped together so hard the muscles in my jaw ached.

Once inside my car, I closed my eyes and leaned my head against the steering wheel, my emotions stewed in a pot of fury.

My life is a fucking open book available for everybody to read and criticize. I'm the one that deserved a damn apology, not her.

The door opened and closed as Gram-Gram got in. I heard the soft rustling of plastic bags being situated as she shuffled around some more.

"Your food is boxed up to go, and I suppose you can eat it at home. Your rude behavior inside was unnecessary," she huffed. "You embarrassed me in front of that entire restaurant and then you had the gall to use foul language in front of me. Just wait until I speak to your mother about this."

"The only thing that's unnecessary is your unwelcome meddling," I said, trying to remain calm.

I ignored her as she inhaled sharply, probably ready to protest. "I'm not trying to be rude or disrespectful, Gram-Gram. But this is my body and you can't dictate what I do with it. It's not right. I'm a human being, not some farm animal. I'm not going anywhere to have anybody do anything to my eggs."

"I'm only trying to help," she replied. "I don't want you to get too old and can't have kids. I'm getting on in age and I want to see my great-grandbabies. Is that too much to ask?"

"You're not that old and I have quite a few baby making years ahead of me. There's still time," I said.

"I just don't want you to end up all alone like me," she whispered, dabbing at the tears in her eyes.

Shit.

"Gram-Gram, you're not alone. I'm sorry for anything I've done to make you feel that way. My time will come soon enough, but until then let's just enjoy each other's company," I said. "And leave my eggs out of it."

"Okay," she said, perking up a bit. "We can leave it alone for now. Let's go to my house and eat our dinner. I doubt the restaurant wants us to come back inside."

"Sure, Gram-Gram, whatever you want," I said with a sigh of relief. I was just glad she stopped crying.

Those people probably think there's a special seat in hell for me because of the way I behaved anyway. I was so relieved we had finally had this talk, and I felt less on edge about everything. Maybe she'll back off a little and let me breathe.

"Will you still go on the date I set up for you?" she asked with an exaggerated sniffle. Leave it to Gram-Gram to capitalize on my weak moment.

"Yes, ma'am, I will," I replied politely.

She turned her head toward the window and formed the biggest smile I had ever seen.

Chapter Thirteen

After my semi-decent dinner with Gram-Gram, I headed home ready to relax. Tonight was going to be a pajama kind of night especially since I had the day off tomorrow. I quickly changed clothes and went into the kitchen to fix a little refreshment tray for the *Golden Girls* marathon coming on in half an hour. The bottle of wine chilling in the fridge was perfect for the occasion, so I grabbed it and searched for a clean wine glass. A few minutes of fruitless searching ended with me realizing I needed to wash dishes at some point in the near future. I opened the cabinet one last time and settled on a mason jar.

A mason jar filled with wine, how classy.

I grabbed a bowl for the cheese balls and took my snacks to the living room. All I needed to complete the picture was a cat purring by my side, but there was no hope in getting one of those. Mom's allergic and thought cats were sneaky and just a touch creepy.

I got my blanket and settled in for the marathon. In the middle of the second episode, I heard a knock at the door. I kicked the blanket off and muted the TV just to be sure I'd heard correctly. Another knock pounded on the door as confirmation.

Who in the hell is that?

I tip-toed across the carpet and grabbed the baseball bat I kept next to the door. My mind ran through the list of people that would show up at this time of the night, but none of them would knock on the door. Whoever was knocking better be prepared for what I had clutched in my hands.

"Who is it?" I yelled.

"It's Jayce! I know it's late, but I wanted to talk to you," he replied.

I pulled open the door still holding on to the bat.

"Am I interrupting baseball practice or something?" he teased.

"No," I mumbled. "You scared the crap out of me. C'mon in and have a seat."

Jayce walked in and eyed the living room as he made himself comfortable on one end of the couch. I sat down and his eyes zeroed in on my mini picnic on the table.

"It looks like I'm interrupting your personal time. I can leave if you want me to and just catch up with you later," he offered.

I snuggled back under my blanket and grabbed my wine. "Don't be silly. I don't mind the company, it's not like I'm doing anything. Would you like some wine? I don't have any clean wine glasses available, so don't laugh at the mason jars."

"You're drinking wine out of that jar?" he asked before erupting into a fit of laughter.

"I told you not to laugh!" I yelled playfully throwing a pillow in his direction.

"By now you should already know telling me not to laugh at something is pointless. Once you tell me that, I feel required to laugh at whatever you're about to say or do," he said still chuckling.

I rolled my eyes and sipped my wine. "Oh shut up. How did everything go with Vivianne?"

The smile on his face dimmed just a tad at the mention of the wicked witch. "Well she wasn't too happy with the flowers. She complained about them not being roses. I tried to explain to her that roses are overdone, but she didn't care. She wouldn't even accept them at all. Aside from that, her breasts are huge, just like I thought they would be. She claims she's still swollen and they won't be that big after she heals, but I'm not so sure about that."

I gathered my nerves and asked something I'd been dying to ask for a long time. "Why are you fighting so hard to keep her?"

Jayce shrugged his shoulders and clasped his hands behind his head. "I love her, plain and simple. She didn't used to be so bitchy, but I still have faith she can go back to being the old Vivianne, my Vivi."

Good luck with that happening. I think the stick up her ass is permanent.

"What caused her to change so much?" I asked. My eyes were glued to the TV, but I was not paying attention.

He took a deep breath and dropped his hands back into his lap. "I hate to say it, but I think the reality TV shows have gone to her head. She sees the wives and girlfriends of these athletes and she feels like it should be her. All she's focused on right now is the glitz and glam of that lifestyle."

I scrunched my nose and turned toward him to see his face. "What? Why do you think she feels that way?"

"I had the chance to play professional football and I turned it down. I've played for what felt like my whole life and I just didn't want to go any further. Don't get me wrong, I loved playing, but the passion wasn't there anymore. My uncle offered me a chance to run his coffee shop during my downtime and I fell in love with it. I had the opportunity to interact with people and that's what changed my mind about playing ball. The shop started doing so well, my uncle asked me if I wanted to buy it from him, so I did, and I've been there ever since."

"Wow," I mumbled into my glass. "It's great you followed your heart."

"I'm glad you think so, but Vivianne doesn't see it that way. She thinks the coffee shop is just a hobby of mine," he said.

What a bitch. And that's the girl you're trying to win back?

"I hope she can see what a great guy she has before it's too late," I said, hoping my compliment was subtle enough to glide under the radar of suspicion. "Do you love her enough to let her go if things don't turn out the way you planned?

"Yeah," he muttered. "I'll let her go if we can't get on the same page. I don't want to be miserable and I don't want her to be either.

Let's change the subject to something less depressing. How did things go with your grandmother?"

"I thought you wanted to talk about something less depressing," I said sarcastically.

I filled him in on the highs and lows of the conversation with Gram-Gram and the whole date situation.

"That's awesome, maybe this guy will turn out to be better than the last one," he said.

I shrugged and took a gulp of wine. "I'm sure once he sees me the date will be over anyway," I said.

"What makes you think that?" he asked.

The wine was definitely making me feel more open. I probably couldn't stop myself from expressing my true feelings even if I wanted to. "Take a good look at me. The guys I'm attracted to aren't attracted to me ... at all. I've tried every diet and exercise program known to mankind and my thighs are still rubbing together. And knowing my Gram-Gram, she probably fudged on the details of my appearance."

"Wow, that's not very attractive," he replied.

I narrowed my eyes and considered kicking him in the leg. "Fuck you. Everybody can't be perfect like Vivianne, the human Barbie … with her fake boobs and extensions. Some of us have cellulite and stretch marks, asshole," I growled.

Jayce chuckled and repositioned himself so he was facing me completely. "Easy there, tiger, give me a chance to explain. I didn't mean you weren't attractive, I meant putting yourself down isn't attractive. You're beautiful, Bri, and the sooner you accept that and own it, the sooner everybody else can see just how beautiful you really are."

I snorted in disagreement and folded my arms across my chest. "Don't start that whole 'you're beautiful on the inside' crap. I want it too show on the outside too," I muttered.

"It does show, but your insecurities show too. Confidence is sexy, try it out some time. But hey, if you really want some help, I'll be happy to work out with you and give you some of my health tips," he said.

"Really?" I asked.

"Of course. But trust me, your self-confidence is the key to everything. Even if you get the body you think you want, if you aren't confident then it won't matter anyway. We'll finish the night with a bang and eat whatever we want, and tomorrow we can start fresh," he suggested.

"Good," I said with a laugh. "I really wanted to finish my wine and cheese balls."

Chapter Fourteen

I was thankful to have the day off because last night was a late one. Jayce accidently stayed until nearly five o'clock in the morning. He finally gave in and had a few drinks with me, and it wasn't long before we somehow ended up asleep. I needed to stop spending so much time with him. The small stuff he did in friendship made my heart long for more. For example, he carried me to bed last night after I passed out.

Of course, I woke up on the way up the stairs and asked him what he was doing. I thought it was so sweet that he wanted to make sure I was in bed and comfortable before he saw himself out. I was also concerned about him throwing his back out from carrying me. Vivianne didn't deserve him, hell I didn't even deserve him, but at least I appreciated the effort he put into just being my friend.

I rolled over and glanced at the red numbers glowing on the alarm clock. There was no way in hell I was getting out of bed before noon. Needless to say, my rest and relaxation lasted another ten minutes before my bladder had other plans for my day. Once I was out of bed there was no going back. I trudged down the stairs and headed straight for the kitchen. A piece of paper that wasn't there before was now stuck on the fridge. I nervously inched forward to inspect the note.

Eat one cup of oatmeal and two egg whites. Call me at lunch time.

Jayce.

Awww. What a sweet creepy thing to do.

I didn't think he was serious about helping me out with my weight loss issue. I decided to take his advice and opened the pantry to retrieve the oatmeal. If he was going to take the time to give me tips the least I could do was follow them. He didn't mention anything about the seasoning and sweeteners I should use so I grabbed my phone to give him a quick call.

"Hey, Bri, are you out of bed yet?" he asked.

"Yeah," I mumbled. "I'm up. Listen, thanks for last night."

"No problem, buddy," he said.

Ouch. Buddy? Something about that word makes me cringe.

"I saw your note on the fridge. I'm not sure what to put in the oatmeal. I know sugar is probably not an option," I said.

"No," he laughed. "Definitely no sugar. You can add a touch of cinnamon and some honey if you have it. Don't go overboard with it though. You don't need anything on the eggs, try to eat those plain. Drink some water with a twist of lemon to help wake up your digestive system first."

Eww.

"All right, great. Well I won't hold you up. I just wanted to make sure I didn't do anything wrong," I replied.

"It's cool, you're not interrupting anything. In fact, what are you doing later on?" he asked.

I thought for a moment and drew a few blanks. "I don't have anything planned," I said.

"Great, do you mind going to the mall with me? I need your help picking out a few things."

"Sure, I'd love to go," I said, even though more time alone with him was not what I needed.

"I'll be there around lunchtime that way we can grab a bite to eat too," he said. I could tell he was smiling just by the way he sounded and it made me crack a grin too.

"Well, I'll be here waiting. Later," I said.

"Later," he replied before hanging up.

I wolfed down the bland breakfast and headed upstairs to find something decent to wear.

Maybe I should get a new outfit for my date tonight?

I weighed my options as I thumbed through my clothes. A new casual outfit couldn't hurt. My hands gravitated toward a simple black maxi dress for my mall outfit and I paired it with some sandals. I preferred wearing dresses when I shopped because they made trying on clothes a lot easier.

My mind drifted back over to my weight loss situation. Jayce didn't mention any type of exercising. Maybe he planned on giving me some information about it later. In the meantime, I wasted time surfing the internet for quick calorie burning workouts. I paid very little attention to the time and before I knew it, I heard three quick beeps outside. I peeked out the curtains and saw Jayce motioning for me. He didn't say he planned to pick me up.

I reached for my house keys and purse and hurried out the door. "Wow, I get a chauffeur for the day?" I said jokingly.

Jayce laughed as he pulled out of the driveway. "I guess you can call me that. How was breakfast?"

Nasty. Bland. Icky.

"It was interesting. I guess it takes some getting used to. Usually I have something covered in frosting for breakfast," I said.

"You'll get used to it, and it will pay off in the end. We can get something to eat for lunch when we get to the mall," he explained. "Thank you for coming with me today. I'm trying to surprise Vivianne with a gift. I think things may go a little smoother if I get her something I know she likes and pair it with something a little outside the box like a poem."

"Okay," I said with a shrug. "Sounds like a great idea."

Are we going broom shopping? That's the only gift a witch like her needs.

"I'm glad you asked me to tag along, now I can get a man's perspective on my outfit for my date tonight."

"This should be fun. I guarantee whatever outfit I help pick will have the man begging for a second date," he said flashing a toothy grin at me.

His smile was intoxicatingly dreamy. Those full pink lips were practically asking for me to come closer … or at least I'd like to think so. I loved the way his smile reached his eyes, because they appeared to sparkle even with the tiniest of grins.

We entered the mall and went straight for the food court. Just the smell of food caused my mouth to water. I'd do anything for a cinnamon pretzel right about now.

"Go on and have a seat. I'll be right back with our food," said Jayce.

I found a nice table off to the side by the window and sat down. If he didn't hurry up and come back I was going to put ketchup on some of these napkins and chow down.

Jayce returned with two plates of rabbit food and I desperately searched for the meat in vain.

Please tell me there's ranch dressing.

"Any dressing?" I asked.

"Yep, two tablespoons of low fat vinaigrette. I know it doesn't seem like much, but just trust me," he said, stabbing a forkful of lettuce.

My hunger forced me to eat the entire salad plus two cups of water. I felt a migraine coming on from the lack of sugar. We put our trays away and I followed Jayce to one of the many boutiques in the mall. While he busied himself with a table of purses, I went over to a rack of very cute stylish shoes. My eyes settled on a pair of black pumps with spikes on the heel. Those would definitely turn heads if I wore them out somewhere. I grabbed one of the shoes to check the size and price, and my heart nearly stopped. *Who the hell do these people think are willing to pay four hundred dollars for a pair of shoes?* I practically threw it back down, almost afraid of holding it too long.

"Hey, Bri, do you like the black one or this yellow one?" asked Jayce, holding up two different purses.

"It's mustard," said the store clerk.

"What?" we asked in unison.

The lady glared at us like we both had two heads. "The handbag isn't yellow, the proper name for the color is mustard."

Jayce and I exchanged looks with one another before turning back toward the lady.

"Um, thank you," I muttered.

"Yeah, thanks," said Jayce with a smile. "So which one? Black or yellow?" He cut his eyes at the woman almost daring her to correct him again. I couldn't help but laugh as she turned a dark shade of red.

I moved closer to him to get a better look at both bags. If these bags were anywhere near the price of those shoes then I definitely wouldn't like either one. I searched for the tag and found it hanging on the zipper on the back.

"Do you realize this thing is over one thousand dollars?" I croaked.

He turned the bag over and looked at the price and then looked back at me with a grim expression. "Vivianne didn't mention how much it cost when she asked for the bag," he muttered.

"Of course she didn't. No sane person would even suggest something so outrageous," I replied. "I just put back a pair of shoes that were over four hundred dollars. I'm sure we can find her something just as cute in one of the outlet stores."

"Yeah," said Jayce. "But this is the one she wants."

Honey, if you like it then I love it. There's no way I intend to buy anything in this place.

"Okay, well get the yellow one then," I suggested. There was no point in putting up a fight, his mind was made up anyway.

Jayce scrunched his nose and held one bag in the air and then the other. He sighed and put them both back on the table, thought for a moment, and picked up the yellow bag.

"Well, I guess I'll get this one," he said.

I gave a tight smile and followed him to the register. He looked back at me and looked positively green as the lady gave him the final total and waited on him to pay. He passed her his credit card and sighed as he pinched the bridge of his nose.

"Here," she said, shoving the box at him.

He took it and offered her a charming smile. "Thank you. My girlfriend is really going to enjoy this purse. She really likes yellow."

The way he was teasing the woman was absolutely hilarious. The woman's top lip peeled back over her teeth like an agitated pit bull. We walked out of the overly-priced boutique and headed for the more reasonably priced stores.

"Do you know where you're going for your date?" he asked.

"Nope. Gram-Gram didn't offer too many details. I don't plan to dress up anyway. My plan is to just find something casual," I replied.

"Casual," he repeated, thumbing through a rack of clothes. "Do you have a favorite color?"

"Mmmhmm. Black."

"Black? That's a rather morbid color. Black makes me think of death and funerals," he said frowning.

"Black is slimming," I replied.

"Okay great, that means no black. You don't have anything that needs slimming. Just be yourself and be confident remember? How about something purple?" he asked.

What sage advice, sensei.

"Fine, purple it is then," I said. A few minutes later Jayce tapped me on the shoulder with an arm full of clothes.

"Here, get started with these," he said.

I could barely hold the pile of stuff he shoved at me. I stumbled my way to the dressing room and took a look at what he selected.

Size ten? Size twelve? Who the hell does he think he's dressing?

"Um, Jayce, I need bigger sizes!" I shouted.

It took a few moments for him to make his way to the dressing room. "Okay, what do I need to swap out?"

"Everything," I mumbled in embarrassment. "The pants need to be a fourteen."

"Pass me the ones that don't fit and I'll get the sizes you need. Are the tops okay?"

"Yeah, I think so," I replied.

I tossed the pants over the top of the door and waited for Jayce to come back. He returned with a few pair and threw them back over to me.

"Make sure to come out and model the outfits for me."

I made a face at the door and waited for him to walk away. Based on the clothes he picked out, I could tell the man had taste. It took me a few wardrobe changes before I had the courage to actually leave the dressing room. As soon as I rounded the corner, Jayce pulled his face into a frown.

"I don't like the shirt, it's a little big," he said. It was a little awkward standing there watching him scrutinize my appearance, but I found myself open to trusting his opinion more and more.

"Try the fitted top and the gray pants," he suggested.

Like an obedient child, I returned to the small room and changed clothes. The top he suggested was clingy and cut very low. My breasts were pushed up and out making a special appearance for whoever glanced in my direction. I tried to tuck them down so that they weren't so out there.

"Are you okay in there?" he asked.

I answered his question by stepping out into the open. The pants cling to my body like a glove, although they were not as uncomfortable as I thought they would be.

"That's it, that's the perfect outfit," he said, scanning me from head to toe.

"You don't think it's a little snug?" I asked nervously.

Jayce's eyes lingered on my breasts for a few seconds before gravitating to my face with a seductive smile. "Trust me, there's no way this guy doesn't ask you for a second date. You look great and you have an excellent personality too."

"Aww, thanks for the compliments," I said. My cheeks flushed and I quickly wiped my damp palms on the pants.

"Go on and get changed," he said. "Once you get undressed hand me the clothes."

I quickly shimmied out of everything and pulled my own clothes back on. By the time I made it out of the dressing room, Jayce was already standing at the register.

"Here you go," he said handing the bags to me. "Consider this your 'thank you gift' for helping me out with everything."

My mouth flapped open to protest as I fished around in my purse for some cash.

"I won't accept any money from you, Bri, I'm serious. If you don't mind, I only have one more stop to make," he said.

"Thank you," I mumbled. "For everything you've done. It really means a lot to me."

"No problem, I like seeing a smile on your face," he said. "Now I need you to help me pick a new cologne. I love having a woman's input separate from the sale's person before I buy a new one."

We walked over to the fragrance section and I inhaled enough scents to make me dizzy. The person at the counter handed us a small container of coffee beans to "clear our palettes" but it really didn't help.

I was ready to throw in the towel and suggest whatever we sniffed next. Luckily the next scent was one that touched me in all the right places. If a man walked by me wearing whatever this was, he would find me naked in his bushes ready for whatever he had in mind.

"What's the name of this one? This one has my vote," I said, fanning the little strip of scented paper in front of my nose.

"It's by Tom Ford, we just got this fragrance in this week. Everyone in Paris and New York are absolutely raving about this scent," said the woman behind the counter.

"Thank you, give me just a moment to think it over," said Jayce. He grabbed the bottle and turned it over in his hands for a few seconds. "Listen, there's a guy to your left whose been checking you out since we came in here. I think you should casually move a little closer to him."

"What?" I hissed, turning around in a complete circle. Sure enough there was a very handsome gentleman with hazel eyes staring in our direction.

Well, well, what do we have here?

Our eyes met and he offered a friendly smile. His gaze flickered to Jayce then back at me before beckoning me to come over.

"He wants me to come to him. What do I do?" I whispered through clenched teeth.

"You get your cute little ass on over there," he replied nudging me in the man's direction.

I walked over and smiled nervously. "Yes?" I asked.

"My name is Damian," he said.

"Hello, Damian, my name is Brianna, but you can call me Bri," I said with my smile widening. Just like Jayce, Damian's smile was infectious.

"You have such a beautiful smile," he said. "I don't want to be rude or step on any toes, that's why I called you over to speak to you privately."

"Oh you're not stepping on anybody's toes, that guy over there isn't my boyfriend. I'm single and open to meeting new people," I explained eagerly … maybe a little too eagerly.

"That's nice," he said, glancing over my shoulder. "But actually, I'm asking about your friend. Is he single?"

What the fuck? Huh?

"Him?" I asked, jerking my thumb in Jayce's direction.

"Yes … him. You're very pretty, but I'm gay. You're friend caught my eye and some guys act a little weird when you approach them and I didn't want to cause a scene."

My eyes widened in shock. I walked over here to flirt with a gay man. That's the icing on the cake for today.

"He's not gay," I grumbled.

"Oh," he replied, with a hint of disappointment in his voice. "That's too bad. Well, Bri, enjoy the rest of your day with that handsome specimen of a man."

He turned on his heels and walked out of the store. My feet were frozen in place like I was standing in cement. I didn't even hear Jayce come up behind me.

"What's up, what happened?" he asked.

"Um, he wasn't interested in me," I said.

"Huh? What do you mean?"

"Well … he wanted to know your relationship status," I said with a chuckle.

Jayce's eyes bucked as he searched the crowd for the guy. "What?" he stammered. "That guy was gay? He didn't look gay ... are you sure?"

I tossed my head back and laughed until my sides hurt. "How does a gay person look? Not all gay men walk around throwing glitter at everybody."

"But ... but ... " he stuttered.

"Don't worry, I set him straight," I said, trying to reassure him. "Er ... um ... I mean I set him as straight as could be expected."

"Oh, um ... okay. I'm sorry, I thought he was checking you out, not me. I'm glad you told him I don't swing that way. I have a cousin that would have been right up his alley though. Well anyway, can you give me a quick whiff and tell me if you still like the cologne. You know it tends to smell a little different once you put it on."

I expected him to extend his wrist, but he leaned down and turned his head instead. I inched a little too close and my lips grazed the side of his neck. A rush of heat immediately coursed through my veins. Not only did he look and smell good, but I just touched him ... with my mouth.

"Sorry," I mumbled. "It still smells nice. I think you should get it."

"All right, thanks," he said. He stood up and I caught the faint telltale signs of him blushing. "Well this is the last thing on my list of things to do. Did you have somewhere else you wanted to go?"

"Nope," I mumbled as I tried to store the close encounter away in my memory bank.

"Cool. I had fun hanging with you today. We need to do it again sometime. And before I forget, I wanted to let you know I plan to start putting together your fitness chart later today after I see Vivianne," he explained. "When you get home, grab a piece of fruit or eat some vegetables to hold you over until dinner. Tomorrow I'll have everything a little more organized."

"Sounds good," I replied.

The ride home was quiet. We seemed to be lost in our own thoughts, I was thinking about his neck and he was probably thinking about Vivianne. I thanked him again for the clothes before heading inside. My plan started out with me helping him get Vivianne back, but my heart … or it could be my overactive imagination had plans for getting him for myself.

I exhaled and toppled onto the bed. Hopefully my date tonight would be so awesome, it would make me forget all about Jayce.

Yeah right, that's wishful thinking.

Chapter Fifteen

I lounged around the rest of the afternoon waiting on the tech guy to call or text. Gram-Gram said she gave him my number, so what was the hold up? If he didn't call soon, I was heading to dinner on my own. There was no sense in starving to death waiting on him. I paced the floor and wiped off the coffee table for the sixth time before my phone rang.

"Hello?" greeted a whiny voice. "Is this Bri?"

Please don't let this be him ... please don't let this be him.

"Yes it is. Who's calling?"

He sneezed a couple of times and cleared his throat. "I'm Shawn. We have a date tonight. Your grandmother gave me your address, so I'll be there to pick you up in half an hour. Okay ... bye."

Is this a joke?

I looked at the phone just to verify the call had ended. Sure enough, the screen was black. Shawn was shaping up to be a weirdo already.

Try to give him the benefit of the doubt, Bri. Don't be so judgmental.

I tried to convince myself to take it easy on the guy but damn. Half an hour to get ready? I needed at least that long to shower and brush my teeth. There was no way I'd get all of that done, get dressed, comb my hair, and attempt to apply makeup in half an hour. I ran around my room like a mad person in a race against the clock. Since I was so pressed for time, styling my hair wasn't an option, so I settled on a simple bun at the nape of my neck. I didn't have time for makeup either, but I tried to spruce up my appearance with lip gloss and cute earrings. At least my outfit was cute, maybe that would make up for the slacking in the other areas.

A firm knock on the door officially informed me my time was up. I wiped away the beads of sweat off my nose and inhaled sharply before I pulled the door open.

What fresh new hell is this? This can't be Shawn.

"Are you Bri?"

I was at a loss for words as I released the breath I was holding with an audible whoosh. My head nodded on its own, and I struggled to keep my mouth from dropping open.

"I'm Shawn. Are you ready to go?" he asked.

I tried to mask the shock on my face, but I was confident I'd failed. Shawn was half the man Gram-Gram said he would be ... literally. I'm five feet even, give or take an inch. So the fact that my date was able to look me straight in the eye let me know he was nowhere near six feet tall. This man was hobbit sized! He looked like an outdated high school nerd. Shawn's T-shirt had the Mario Brother's on it. I was a fan of a T-shirt for the right occasion, but this was supposed to be a date! He looked like the creepy neighborhood adult that only hung out with teenagers because they "understood him."

What the hell has Gram-Gram done to me?

I closed the front door and locked it behind me.

I'm going to make this a great night even if it kills me. And then later ... without any witnesses around ... I'm going to kill Gram-Gram.

Shawn was in the car and waiting before I even had the chance to make it out down the walkway. I got into the car and immediately wanted to gag.

What's that smell? Did something die in here?

I tried to discreetly cover my nose and mouth so the funk wouldn't get into my body. "Where are we going tonight?" I asked in an attempt to make polite conversation.

"My favorite place in the whole world, so prepare yourself to be amazed. It has great entertainment and tasty food," he said, perking up.

"Sounds great," I muttered.

I endured the rest of the smelly ride in silence. We pulled up at a building that looked abandoned. Shawn got out of the car and immediately headed for the dingy front doors. My eyes scanned the surroundings, trying to identify all the escape routes. I had my mace ready to go just in case shit hit the fan.

I hope this little weirdo isn't a serial killer or something.

I got out of the car and practically ran into the building. At least it had a little bit of light shining from inside, unlike the pitch black void of the night we were in. The door creaked shut behind me and I immediately wanted to go back outside.

He brought me to a fucking arcade?

"Come on, let's get a table," he said.

I followed him in a daze as I tried to convince my flight skills to kick in. My exercise plan was going to start early because I planned to run the hell out of here.

"They have the best pizza in town," he said. I wasn't the least bit surprised to hear him actually sound excited to be here. As we sat waiting on the food to arrive, I tried to make small talk.

"My Gram-Gram told me you're a technical engineer," I said, clasping my hands together nervously.

Shawn pushed his glasses up on his face and snorted. "I just tell my grandmother that so she doesn't get confused. I'm actually a professional gamer. She won't understand if I tell her I play video games for a living," he explained.

She's not the only one not understanding. A gamer? A video game playing hobbit ... if he starts whispering about his precious ring ... I'm leaving.

Somewhere between the invention of the first gaming machine and his not so secret love of Pac-Man, I zoned out and started fantasizing about Jayce. Even though I barely grazed his skin for a split second, the feel of him was engraved into my mind. The memory of his warm smooth flesh caused an electric current to pulse between my thighs. I tried to recall the few instances he had his arms wrapped around me. The night he carried me to the bedroom would have been perfect if he had joined me. Shawn waved his hand in front of my face and I found myself getting instantly upset at having my daydream interrupted.

"The food's here," he said, reaching for the greasy triangle.

I'm sure Jayce would have a fit if he found out I'm eating this.

I grabbed a slice and vowed to only eat one, but the cheese, bread, and marinara sauce did a happy dance in my mouth. Frodo was right about the pizza, but I certainly wouldn't be coming to the sketchy part of town to get it.

Shawn devoured three slices and quickly abandoned me at the table. After I finished eating my own slice, I had to talk myself out of eating another. I washed it all down with a glass of questionable water that left a tangy taste in my mouth, and searched for my date from hell. He was nothing like the geeks I saw on TV, those guys at least had some type of appeal to them. I felt like I was babysitting, and I didn't like it one bit.

I found Shawn in deep concentration at one of the old fashioned gaming machines. "Hey, are you having fun?" I asked sarcastically.

The only response he offered was a grunt.

Okayyyyyyyy.

"Do you mind if I play?" I asked. I had no idea why I was trying so hard at that point.

"Not right now," he grumbled. "I'm on level thirty-two and I'm about to power up."

Excuse me? To hell with this, it's time to go.

I reached for my cell phone and did a quick search for a cab. "All right, Shawn, have a nice evening," I said over my shoulder. I was one hundred percent sure he didn't hear a word I'd said, but I officially stopped giving a damn.

Chapter Sixteen

I thought of several angry text messages to send Gram-Gram, but erased each one before hitting send. I wasn't angry at her per se, I was angry I wasted my time and effort to go on a date that cared more about video games than life itself. If Shawn knew what was good for him, he'd lose my number and forget tonight ever happened. What a waste of a cute outfit.

The pizza was another mistake I wished I could undo because my stomach was suffering from all of the grease. I practically ran to the bathroom. After a few minutes of nothing happening I decided to get undressed and lay down for a while. I curled up on the bed and hoped the pain would go away, but the cramps in my stomach had me writhing.

Damn, do I have food poisoning?

My phone was ringing, but I couldn't find it. The chiming stopped for a moment and then started again.

That has to be Kirsten. Nobody else calls back-to-back like that.

I finally found my phone under a pile of clothes on the floor. As soon as I answered it, Kirsten immediately started talking.

"Damn, Bri, we need to work out a new system for communication. Where are you? What are you doing?"

"Hey, I'm home in bed … dying," I groaned.

"What? What's wrong?" she asked.

I wiped off a thin layer of sweat from my forehead and pulled my blanket up around my neck.

"I think I have food poisoning from that whack ass date," I mumbled.

"Aww, I'm sorry you don't feel good. Too bad I'm out of town until Friday. I would've come over," she said. "Do you feel like talking about the date or should I call you back later?"

I rolled over and curled up into a tight ball, bringing my knees up to my chest. "No, we can talk now. Hopefully talking will keep me from thinking about throwing up. Hold on just a sec," I said.

My line beeped again and I glanced at the phone to see Jayce's name flashing across the screen, so I clicked over to answer.

"Hello?" I moaned.

"Oh hey, I'm just calling to see how things are going with your date. You sound like crap, is everything okay?" he asked. The concern in his voice was very sweet.

"I think I have food poisoning," I explained, kicking the blankets down to the end of the bed. "I'm home now, having chills, and my body can't decide whether it wants to be hot or cold."

"Shit, do I need to come over?" he asked.

"No," I mumbled. "Hang on. I'm going to click you into my conversation with my best friend, Kirsten. That way I only have to tell this horrible story once."

I merged the calls and made sure everybody was still on the line. "Kirsten, I have Jayce on the line too," I said. "Jayce, are you still there?"

"Yep," he replied. "Hello, Kirsten."

"Why hello," she said, practically purring into the phone. "Bri has told me so much about you."

"Good things I hope," he said with a laugh. "Did she tell you about my devilishly good looks?"

Kirsten's voice dropped a few octaves, "As a matter of fact … she did."

"So anyway," I interrupted, trying to steer the conversation away from the current slippery slope of embarrassment. "My date was a pint-sized little weirdo. Gram-Gram said he was six feet tall, actually he couldn't have been taller than five two."

I paused and allowed them to get done laughing. My hands groped around for my blanket so I could pull it up to my chest again.

"Yeah, yeah … hardy har-har," I said sarcastically.

I tried to quickly tell them the rest of the details, because I suddenly felt the need to revisit the bathroom. The phone dropped to the floor and I dove head first into the porcelain bowl. I heard my name being shouted through the phone, but I couldn't respond.

The violent heaving continued and brought tears to my eyes. I clutched my sides and leaned my head on my arm. My stomach gave me a short break before the heaving started again. I heard what sounded like the front door opening, but I was too weak to move. My heart thumped as the footsteps on the stairs got louder.

Is this how it all ends? There's a burglar in the house and I'm about to be murdered with my head in a toilet.

I tilted my head so I could look into the eyes of my murderer.

"Jayce," I murmured.

"Yeah, Kirsten told me where to find your spare key. I couldn't leave you here alone throwing up everywhere," he said, placing a cool wet towel on my forehead.

"My robe," I croaked. Under normal circumstances, I would be horrified for anyone to see me in my bra and panties. I was still slightly horrified, but the only thing I could think about was the stomach cramps. Jayce draped the terry cloth robe over my shoulders and stood next to me while I put it on.

"Are you finished?" he asked gently.

I nodded and closed my eyes. Shawn better hope I never saw him again because I was going to knock him the hell out for taking me to that shady looking place.

"All right, let's get you back into bed," he announced. He helped me to my feet and scooped me up into his arms.

I guess vomiting uncontrollably has its perks, I'm back in his arms again.

The coolness of the sheets felt so comforting and relaxing. I exhaled loudly and rolled over to the edge of the bed. A garbage can appeared next to my face.

"Thanks," I groaned.

Moments later the mattress shifted with Jayce's weight as he got into the bed with me.

"I'm just going to stick around until you fall asleep," he said.

I mumbled something incoherent and everything went dark. At some point in the night between the cramps and cold sweats, I found myself wrapped in his arms. My head was against his chest and I spent a few minutes listening to the steady rhythm of his heart. I watched him inhale and exhale slowly in a deep sleep. His lips were slightly parted, silently begging me to kiss them.

Too bad I have vomit breath and haven't brushed my teeth.

The rubber band holding his hair back was gone, allowing his dark tresses to partially cover his face. The robe he helped me put on was now halfway open, and most of my uncovered body was pressed against his.

This is nice, minus the vomit. I could get used to this.

I shifted around, trying to get more comfortable. Jayce stirred and pulled me in closer to him.

Ummm …

I froze and held my breath, afraid my moving would wake him.

His lips pecked my forehead in a light kiss. "You okay?" he asked groggily.

The kiss took me by surprise and my eyes widened. Maybe he's too sleepy to realize it's me next to him and not Vivianne.

"Um … it's me … Bri," I mumbled.

He tightened his hold on me and gave a throaty chuckle. "I know. Are you okay? Do you need to throw up again?" he asked.

So he knows it's me? Am I in some type of special version of the Twilight Zone where stuff happens the way I want it to?

"No, I'm good," I replied.

"Okay," he said.

I waited on him to say more or push me over a little, but he went back to sleep instead.

Does this moment mean anything? And if it does ... somebody ... somewhere needs to tell me what the hell it means. I was too tired to think about it too much, so I drifted off to sleep.

Chapter Seventeen

I woke up groggy with a dry mouth. Jayce was gone but I was left with traces of his cologne on the sheets. The events of last night forced their way to the forefront of my mind.

Do I call him or wait until he mentions our G-rated sleepover first?

I searched for my phone so I could call Kirsten and ask for her opinion. A message from Jayce was on the screen.

Jayce: Sorry for just up and leaving. Issue at the shop. I'll drop by to check on you later. Stay home and rest.

His thoughtfulness was getting to me. The line between us had already been crossed and he probably didn't even know it. There was no way I could continue giving him advice about Vivianne. I wanted him for myself. Last night definitely helped me make my decision about him. If he was this great as a friend, I could only imagine what he was like as a boyfriend. I didn't want to sabotage his relationship, but I couldn't allow him to end up with her.

Before I had the chance to call Kirsten, she called me first.

"Hey, Bri, are you feeling better?" she asked.

"Yeah, I feel so much better. You'll never believe who came over to take care of me," I replied.

"I already know," she chuckled. "Jayce text me when he left this morning. I would tease you about having a late night, but I'm pretty sure you didn't have sex with him, not with all of the throwing up you were doing."

"No, but I wanted to. I can't keep helping him with Vivianne. He took such good care of me last night, Kirsten. Girl, he saw me in my underwear and I didn't feel as bad as I thought I would. I'm not sure if I should say something about how I feel or wait to see if he says something first," I said.

"Hmmm," she replied.

I looked at the phone and frowned. Kirsten didn't sound like her usual self. Typically she was talking a mile a minute and now she was not saying anything. Clearly she knew something already. "Kirsten, what's going on?" I asked.

"Well," she said slowly. "Don't freak out okay."

Thanks for the disclaimer. Now I know I'm going to freak out.

"Okay?"

"Jayce and I have been texting … and he seems to really care about you. He didn't come right out and say it, but I can tell. I think you should wait until he brings up how he feels … just in case. Bri, I have a good feeling about him. I can't put my finger on it just yet. And guess what? We're invited to a barbecue at his house this weekend," she gushed.

Wow.

"What did he say to make you believe he cares about me?" I asked nervously.

"When you dropped the phone and started yakking all over the place the only thing he wanted to know is whether or not you had a spare key outside. What guy does something like that if he doesn't care? And then he asked for my number just in case you called me back before he got there. Jayce took the lead, no questions asked," she explained.

"Aww," I murmured. "He's truly a selfless person and Vivianne doesn't appreciate him."

Kirsten chuckled. "Well let's take her out of the picture. You know Ricky's number is on speed dial," she teased.

I laughed too, although her suggestion did sound tempting. We chatted for a few more minutes before Kirsten had to abandon me to do a bridal makeup trial. My stomach growled, but I didn't have an appetite. In fact, the very idea of eating something made my stomach start cramping again.

I needed to get out of bed and move around some, so I pulled my robe closed and eased down the stairs. My eyes zeroed in on the couch and I forced my feet forward. Today was going to be long day. I reached for the remote and flipped through the stations before settling on a show about paternity test results. Shows like this made me realize my own life could be a lot worse.

I bet he's not the father ... or him ... or him. That guy on the end has the same nose as the baby ... but so does the guy next to him.

As the host went down the list of men the guest had slept with, my eyes closed.

I could hear myself snoring, but I was too tired to move. All of the throwing up had left me so drained and weak. As soon as I felt myself going into a deeper sleep, I sensed a presence looming over me. A coolness came over my skin and made me shiver. I was awake and alert, but my eyes remained glued shut. I didn't hear the front door open or close, but I knew someone was standing over me. The scent registered in my nose and I immediately started snoring again hoping Gram-Gram would go away.

"Brianna!" she shouted, shaking my shoulder. "Get up, girl, it's the middle of the day and you're lounging around like a lizard."

I sighed and cracked open one eye. She stood over me with her arms folded across her chest. "Shawn called Gladys this morning and told her you were kidnapped. He said he looked up and you had disappeared into thin air. Brianna Marie Davis, I can't believe you walked out on him like that," she hissed.

Both of my eyes popped open as I sat straight up on the couch. "Kidnapped?" I asked, sleepily.

Gram-Gram sat down in a huff and cut her eyes at me. If looks could kill, we would both be dead, because I was returning the hard glare right back at her.

"Clearly Shawn wasn't all that concerned about my wellbeing because he hasn't called or text to make sure I'm okay. But that's beside the point, because everything you told me about him was absolutely wrong."

"There's nothing wrong with that young man. You keep expecting Prince Charming to swoop in on a white horse and that's not going to happen," she grumbled.

"I may not be a princess, but I know I didn't deserve the toad you set me up with last night," I muttered. "Gram-Gram, he plays video games for a living and he took me to an arcade in the seedy part of town," I explained. "And I got food poisoning too."

I don't care what you say ... nothing can justify last night's disaster.

Instead of chastising me even more, she reached over and put her ice cold hands on my forehead. "You need some seltzer water and crackers," she said, getting up from the couch.

Now I know I'm sick ... this isn't the Gram-Gram I know at all.

She came back with the water and crackers and passed them over to me. "Here, take this stuff and turn the TV over to channel two. My stories are about to come on," she said.

Gram-Gram sat down in the recliner next to the couch and put her feet up.

"Can we watch something else? I don't really like watching those soap operas. There's too many storylines going on for me to keep up with," I complained.

The expression on her face was one for the record books. Her eyebrows went up in surprise and her lips puckered. "You're sick, and you don't need to watch TV anyway. Close your eyes and go to sleep," she ordered. I rolled my eyes and changed the station for her.

I hope this keeps her occupied and quiet.

I reached up and grabbed the throw off the back of the couch and got comfortable. Gram-Gram tried to fill me in and explain the show, but it was pointless. I attempted to keep up with who was sleeping with who, but it seemed like everyone was sleeping together. Somebody was supposed to be dead, but they were not, and they took another person's baby. This was enough drama to give someone a migraine. I thought I was in the clear when the first show went off, but unfortunately for me, a different one came on right after. A knock on the door interrupted everything and Gram-Gram jumped to her feet to answer it.

"Pause that," she ordered.

"We don't have that function with our TV package," I explained, craning my neck around to see who was at the door.

"Hello, ma'am, my name is Jayce, and I'm here to check on Bri."

His eyes connected with mine over Gram-Gram's head as she whipped around like she'd seen a ghost. She stepped back to let him in and gave him a complete once over from head to toe.

"Bri," she said, closing the door behind him, "you didn't tell me you had a new gentleman caller."

"He's not a gentleman caller, he's my boss," I replied with a tight smile.

"Your boss?" she questioned. Her eyes glared at us over the rim of her glasses. "Mmmhmm."

"Yes, ma'am, I'm her boss and her friend. I own Drip Drop Coffee Hut down the street," he explained, taking a seat next to me.

"You're working at a coffee place?" she asked, arching her eyebrows.

Before I had the chance to explain, Jayce jumped in and answered for me. "She's the account manager there and I would be lost without her," he said with a smile. He reached over and playfully grabbed my foot.

"And you say you're just her boss? Mmmhmm, it doesn't look like it to me," she mumbled under her breath.

"Gram-Gram!" I hissed. This was awkward enough and she was about to make it worse.

"Are you hungry, young man?" she asked, ignoring me.

"Um no, ma'am, I'm fine," he replied.

She nodded and headed to the kitchen anyway. "I'll just fix you a little something."

Jayce took it all in stride and simply smiled again. "Thank you," he said politely.

I mouthed an apology to him and sat up. "Did you take care of the issue at the shop?"

"Yeah," he sighed. "I'm training my cousin to help out and then Vivianne called me, wanting to talk."

My heart raced and I my stomach knotted up. I wasn't sure if it was because he mentioned Vivianne, or if I was still feeling the last remnants of the food poisoning.

"How did everything go?" I asked.

"Well, Keon, that's my cousin, jammed one of the machines and had hot water spewing everywhere. It took us some time to get it fixed and the floor mopped," he explained.

I don't care about that. What did Barbie want?

"I'm glad you got it fixed. I haven't met Keon yet have I?" I asked, trying to appear interested.

"No, he just came into town and needed a job to help him get on his feet," he said. "That reminds me … did Kirsten tell you about the get-together at my house this weekend? I want to introduce Keon to everybody and make him feel welcomed."

"Yeah she told me this morning," I replied. "What happened with Vivianne?"

Oh my goodness Jayce, get on with it.

"Well, Vivianne called to tell me about a surprise trip she has planned for us. We leave tomorrow, and I wanted to give you the head's up. My cousin will need your help running the shop until I get back in town," he said. His face wasn't showing any type of emotion at all. I thought he'd be happy about spending time with her.

"Oh, sounds like fun! Bring me back a T-shirt," I replied jokingly.

"Yeah," he said.

"What's wrong?" I asked. The response was so dry I nearly asked if he wanted a glass of water.

Go on and say you love me and don't want to go. I know it's wishful thinking ... but still.

"Nothing," he muttered. "I just don't know where this is going. Don't get me wrong, I love Vivianne and will do anything for her, but I shouldn't have to work this hard just to get back the love we used to share. It would be different if I'd cheated on her and broke her trust or something. We used to have so much fun together, but now everything is so strained."

Kick her ass to the curb. I'm fun ... I'm tons of fun.

"It sounds like you're holding on to the hollow shell of who she used to be. People grow and change all the time," I said.

"Growing and changing are fine, but completely changing the foundation of who you are is something totally different," he grumbled. "But I have to give her credit, this is the first time she's taken the initiative to plan anything on her own."

"Well hopefully it works out," I lied. "Listen, I haven't showered yet, and I really need to. I'm not putting you out or anything, just giving you an excuse to use so you can leave before my grandmother comes back to harass you."

Jayce smiled and leaned back with his hands behind his head. "I'll wait until you finish," he replied.

Just then, Gram-Gram returned with a tray full of food. "Here you go, young man," she said sweetly, putting the tray down in front of him.

"Go on," he said, turning to me. "I'll be here when you get back."

I slowly walked up the stairs completely terrified to leave Gram-Gram alone with Jayce. There was no telling what would come out of her mouth. It was too easy to get information out of her, because she readily and eagerly volunteered to give away your secrets. By the time I come back I was positive Jayce would know every agonizing detail about my life, including the time I went commando underneath my skirt and the wind made it fly up, revealing my bare naked ass to everyone and I do mean everyone.

To my surprise, they were laughing and talking when I come back down the stairs. Gram-Gram looked excited to have someone to talk to about something she enjoyed.

"Bri!" she exclaimed. "You need to bring this young man around more often. I've never laughed so hard in my life."

Jayce glanced up at me with a satisfied look on his face. I'm surprised he didn't run out of the house screaming after being left alone with her.

"I like your hair," he said.

I reached up and self-consciously touched the giant puff on my head. "Yeah," I said. "It's naturally curly. I usually have it straight, but when I get it wet, it curls up."

"It looks really nice," he murmured.

Gram-Gram grinned from ear to ear as if he was talking to her.

"Well, ladies, I do need to leave. Thanks, Mrs. Carter, for the lunch and interesting conversation," he said, cutting his eyes at me.

Shit. Should I be embarrassed or no?

"Let me walk you out," I said, moving toward the front door.

Jayce leaned down and hugged Gram-Gram. She smiled and gently patted him on the back. I liked how comfortable he was around her.

"Make sure you come back to see me," she said.

"Yes, ma'am," he replied as he walked over to the door.

I stepped outside and watched as he closed the door behind him. "You should get some rest," he said.

"I'm planning on it. I feel a lot better now, so I plan to be a work tomorrow."

"Okay," he said. He pulled me over to him and gave me a big bear hug before whispering in my ear. "Just make sure you don't wear a skirt, I hear it's supposed to be windy tomorrow," he teased.

He laughed and got into his car as I stood there with my mouth wide open and my eyes bucked. Gram-Gram had the biggest mouth ever.

Chapter Eighteen

Even though Gram-Gram embarrassed the hell out of me, I was glad she came over yesterday. She cleaned up a little while I took another nap, and I definitely appreciated that. I got dressed in a hurry and headed down to the coffee shop. Keon … or at least I assumed it was Keon, was leaning against the counter looking down at his phone.

"Bri?" he asked, glancing up from the screen.

"Yes," I replied, sticking my hand out toward him.

He looked at my palm like it had acid on it, and quickly pushed it aside before wrapping his arms around me.

"You're family," he said playfully. "I've heard so much about you, and I'm happy to be able to put a name with a face."

I smiled and stepped back. "I get nervous when people say they've heard things about me," I said.

"Don't worry, it was good stuff," he replied. "I just know I need to keep you away from the salt and sugar."

We laughed and started the usual prepping before the morning rush came in. Keon was definitely handsome and I could see the family resemblance. His dark hair was cropped short and he had a smile that brightened his entire face just like Jayce. I discreetly took a peek at his ass when he bent over to get some coffee filters and it was nice too.

Damn their family has good genes.

The morning rush hit, and it hit hard, but I was proud of our accomplishments. We burned one pot of coffee and managed to only mess up a handful of orders. I'm still not sure how we managed to burn the coffee, but it definitely tasted scorched.

"You do this every day?" Keon asked.

"I'm usually in the back working with the different accounts. We learned the hard way my place is not out front taking orders, but I'm proud of today. The shop is still standing so I think we'll be okay," I said. "Did Jayce mention how long he'll be out of town?"

Keon smiled and leaned against the counter. His smile was more of a lazy grin, like he had a trick up his sleeve, unlike the playful one Jayce had.

"No, but hopefully he won't be gone too long," he said. "There's really no telling how everything will work out when Vivianne is involved in it."

"Oh yeah," I said nonchalantly.

"Yeah," he said with the smirk on his face growing even wider. "I think he needs to cut her loose and move on to someone new."

I agree ... .

"Well, people change. Vivianne could be on the road to being her old self again," I said.

Keon snorted and shifted his weight from one foot to the other. "You can't sugarcoat shit," he growled, folding his arms across his chest. His sleeve rolled up a bit to reveal a Marine tattoo.

"Military man?" I asked, pointing at his arm.

"Yeah," he muttered. "That is a beehive you don't want to poke right now. I got out a little while ago and life has been tough ever since. I'm happy I was able to link back up with Jayce. One thing I can say about my cousin is, he's there when you need him."

"I know what you mean," I said. "I was at my lowest point and he helped pull me back onto my feet."

He nodded and smiled again, but it was not as bright this time. "Well we're here now and I'm sure everything will work out just fine.

Jayce is a great guy and takes care of the people in his life. I just hope he gets rid of the leech that's trying to suck him dry."

Do I agree or disagree? Um …

"I just want him to be happy," I said. *That's a safe answer … right?*

"Yeah … me too. I'm going to go ahead and restock the stuff that's low," he said, grabbing a towel off the counter.

"Cool, if you need me I'll be in the back doing a little work."

A few hours later, we're ready for the evening rush and Keon and I had developed our own little system. Everything was much better this time around than it was this morning. Keon's military precision started to peek through a little. He kept moving stuff until it was arranged just right on the tables. I was finally able to get him to leave nearly an hour after the usual time. I waited while he turned off the lights and locked the door. There wasn't another car in the parking lot so I wasn't sure how he got to work. Before I knew it, he was pulling me in for another big hug.

Okay, apparently he's serious about the whole hugging situation.

"Today was a good day, and tomorrow will be better," he said.

"Yeah," I mumbled into his chest. "That sounds like something you would read from a fortune cookie."

He let me go and stood back with a big grin. "I'll see you in the morning," he said turning to leave.

"Are you walking home?" I asked.

"It's not far," he replied.

"Come on, I'll drop you off," I said, walking to my car.

After a few adjustments to the seat in order to accommodate his large size, we were ready to ride out.

"Thanks, Bri," he said once we got to Jayce's house.

"No problem. I'll be here bright and early to pick you up tomorrow!" I yelled out of the window.

He nodded and disappeared inside the house. I liked Keon, he reminded me of Jayce, but he was a bit more mysterious. Kirsten would probably hit it off with him, she liked mysterious men. I made it home and searched for something to eat. Jayce left without going over the rest of my health plan, so I tried to find a relatively healthy snack that wouldn't upset my stomach.

I ate, showered, and climbed into bed in the same spot Jayce was laying in before. The faint scent of his cologne still clung to the sheets, and I fell asleep with him on my mind.

The next few days went by in a blur, but Keon and I managed to hold down the fort. I had to admit, I was starting to get nervous because neither one of us had heard from Jayce at all.

"Have you tried to call him?" I asked.

"Yep, but he didn't answer," he muttered. "I thought about calling Vivianne, but I absolutely can't stand the sound of her voice."

I tried to keep the smile from spreading across my face, but I couldn't help it. "Why don't you like her?"

He snorted a laughed and arched his eyebrow. "I've never liked her. I can see right through her bullshit. Jayce is just now starting to see her for who and what she is. No matter how pretty the house is on the outside, if the foundation is fucked up, then the house is too," he grumbled. "I'm just glad he hasn't gotten into a situation he can't reverse, because he'll really be stuck then."

I decided to step out on a limb and see where the conversation could lead. "What kind of woman do you think he needs?"

Keon narrowed his eyes and smiled. "I think he needs a woman that understands his dreams instead of trying to tear them apart. Family is a very big part of our culture, we're all very close, and it's hard to be around Vivianne. No one in our family likes her, and that's a problem. Of course I'm the only one that will say it out loud," he explained. "Are you coming to the barbecue tomorrow?"

"Um … yeah," I stammered, thrown off by the change in topics. "You're still having it?"

"Hell, yeah," he chuckled. "Make sure you bring some friends. We're gonna have food and drinks while we party all night long!"

I smiled at his excitement, but my mind was stuck on Jayce.

Chapter Nineteen

I woke up with a familiar leg thrown over me. "Kirsten," I mumbled. "What the hell?"

She groaned and rolled over. "I got in late last night and didn't feel like driving all the way to my house."

"Well scoot over," I muttered. She shuffled over a little and started snoring again. Kirsten always showed up at weird times and just made herself comfortable. It didn't bother me though because I enjoyed her company. She's the sister I never asked for, but I loved her just the same.

A couple of hours later, I woke up again with our arms and legs intertwined. Most of the time, Kirsten's cute and put together, but she looked so funny asleep. Her eyelids were half closed and her mouth was wide open. She was such a horrible sleeper with all of her tossing and turning. I tried to push her over a little, but she didn't move an inch.

"Kirsten," I whined. "Moveeee."

"Huh?" she snorted.

I pushed her over again and managed to wiggle free this time. By the time I brushed my teeth and showered, Kirsten was sitting on the edge of the bed yawning.

"Are you cooking breakfast?" she asked.

"We have oatmeal," I replied. "Do you want that?"

She frowned and stretched as she headed toward the bathroom. "I want waffles," she muttered.

I rolled my eyes and went downstairs. Waffles sounded great, but I knew Jayce wouldn't approve. Kirsten would just have to eat some eggs and oatmeal like me. Today was my day off, but I was thinking about going to the coffee shop just to check on things. It hit me last night: I'm the only person working in the shop that's not related to Jayce. Was that weird? I grabbed my phone to text Keon to see if he'd heard from him yet and to find out whether or not we needed to bring anything for the party tonight.

I had two messages on my phone, one from Mom letting me know she was coming home tomorrow and one from Jayce. My heart raced and my palms were sweaty from anticipation. I'd been waiting to see his name flash across the screen for a long time and now I was nervous to open the message. I clicked the flashing envelope, held my breath, and waited.

Jayce: See you tonight.

See you tonight? That's it? Damn, no explanation or anything?

I was happy he was back, but I wanted the details. Actually, I wanted to be nosey and find out what happened with Vivianne.

"I don't smell waffles," said Kirsten, coming up behind me.

She'd showered and had put on one of my T-shirts. "I know you don't smell waffles, because we don't have waffles. We have oatmeal and eggs," I explained.

"Yuck," she muttered. "Oatmeal reminds me of eating a bowl of glue. It's so sticky and it clumps together."

"When have you eaten glue?" I questioned.

She leaned against the fridge and crossed her ankles. "I'm a curious person, Bri," she said.

I shook my head and reached for a small pot to boil the water in. "You're an adult eating glue."

Kirsten laughed and walked into the living room. "I'm so glad I came home this weekend. I can't wait for the party to get started tonight.

Do you think there will be any single guys? Maybe I'll snag a man," she said.

That reminded me, I never did text Keon, but now that Jayce was home I felt like I should text him instead. I decided to play it safe and text them both. Kirsten was on the floor propped up on her elbows flipping through a magazine when I came into the living room with my food.

"Where's mine?" she asked.

"What? You said oatmeal tastes like glue," I huffed.

"Well that doesn't mean I'm not hungry," she said.

I puckered my lips and narrowed my eyes, and I was pretty sure I looked just like Gram-Gram right then. "Go get some out of the kitchen," I replied. "This is mine."

She frowned and stuck her tongue out at me as she walked back into the kitchen to get her own food. "What else is on the agenda for the day?" she asked.

"I don't know," I said with a shrug. "I don't have anything planned other than washing clothes and cleaning up around the house."

"Lame," she mumbled.

My phone buzzed and I picked it up to read my messages.

Jayce: Nothing.

Jayce's message was short and straight to the point. I was starting wonder if he was okay, because he was usually a little more upbeat in his messages. I scrolled down to read the next message and smiled.

Keon: Bring hot girls…really hot girls.

Keon's response seemed like something he would say. I pictured a goofy grin on his face while he typed it. Even though I hadn't known him long, I felt like we were old friends.

"There's a guy I want to introduce you to at the party," I said.

Kirsten's eyes widened and she cocked her head to the side, batting her lashes. "Really? Give me all the details. Is he hot? Does he have kids? What about his teeth, does he have nice teeth?" she asked all at once.

"Calm down," I said, nearly choking on a mouthful of the thick oatmeal. "His name is Keon, he's one of Jayce's cousins. He has short dark hair, and a very nice smile. I'm not sure if he has kids or not. I know he just got out of the military not too long ago."

"You know I love a man in a uniform," she murmured.

"Yeah, well he's wearing a different uniform now, but I think you'll like him," I said.

"Hmmm, now you know I definitely have to make sure I'm looking my best tonight," she said.

Damn, I shouldn't have mentioned him until after we had left the house. Now she's going to take all day and part of the night to get ready.

"He's a simple guy, I don't think he cares about stuff like that," I said.

Kirsten frowned and folded her arms across her chest. "Guys always care about that stuff. No man is going to be proud telling people you're his girlfriend if you are looking a hot mess," she said.

We finished our breakfast and in classic Kirsten style, she took all day to get ready. I looked like the ugly step-sister standing next to her. She served nothing less than straight Hollywood Red carpet from head to toe. Her long tresses were piled on top of her head in a messy bun. The skin-tight black dress she wore had a mesh covered opening in the front, giving an excellent view of her cleavage.

"Why are you putting that dark powder on your face?" I asked.

She carefully swept the brush down the sides of her nose and into the hollows of her cheeks. "I'm contouring. This helps make the face look slimmer if you do it right."

Slimmer? I wonder if it works on thighs too …

"Hurry up," I whined. "I need you to do my makeup too."

We were going to a house party but Kirsten acted like we were going to a movie premiere. My taste was a bit tamer than hers, so I decided to wear the outfit Jayce picked out for me the other day.

"I'm almost done," she muttered, widening her eyes for yet another coat of mascara. Minutes later she was finally done and ordered me to take several pictures of her, just so she could see how the makeup looked in photos.

"Seriously, Kirsten, are we almost done now?" I asked. "At the rate we're going my makeup will never get done and we'll be late for the party too."

"Just four more, okay?"

I rolled my eyes and tossed the phone onto the bed. "C'mon, Kirsten, I don't want to be late."

A smile spread across her face. "You've never been this impatient about getting your makeup done. You usually complain the entire time. Is this because your boyfriend is back?"

"He's not my boyfriend," I grinned. "I just want to look nice."

She crossed her arms and puckered her lips, making kissy faces at me. "Bri's gotta boyfriend," she teased.

"You're such a big kid," I joked. "But if you don't hurry up, I'll do my own makeup and tell everybody you did it."

She snatched her brushes off of the bathroom counter. "Let's get started. I refuse to allow you to embarrass me like that."

As usual, she was able to work her magic and I looked amazing, nearly completely unrecognizable. She did some of the contouring stuff on my face this time, and she was right, it made me look noticeably smaller. We grabbed our purses and headed out the door. I reminded Kirsten several times on the way to the car about her dangerously high dress as it inched up even higher.

Her entire ass is going to be broadcasted to the World before the night is over.

"I think you like your dress being like that," I said.

She tilted her head to the side and fluttered her lashes. "I'm just having a little fun, *Mom*. One of these day's I'm going to get you into an outfit like this."

"There's not a snowball's chance in hell of that happening," I snorted.

Chapter Twenty

My hands trembled as soon as we rounded the corner to Jayce's house. Seeing all of the cars parked outside gave me pause. I was so much better being one on one with people as opposed to large groups.

"Girl, look at all the cars. It looks like we're about to have a real good time," said Kirsten excitedly.

My stomach did a series of small flips as I parked and took several deep breaths to settle my nerves.

"All right, let's go," I said with a sense of forced courage.

Kirsten pushed the door open before I had the chance to fully stop the car. Together we knocked on the door and waited. The sound of loud music and muffled voices could be heard through the door. After a few more minutes of knocking, somebody finally answered.

"Hello, you must be Bri," said the young woman.

"Yes," I mumbled. "And this is my friend Kirsten."

"Awesome," she said moving to the side. "I'm Mya, one of Jayce's cousins. C'mon in. Everybody that comes through the door has to take a shot!"

Kirsten bulldozed her way past me and sashayed to the small tray full of miniature drinks. She grabbed one and immediately downed the clear liquid.

I took the shot and cringed as the alcohol burned my chest on its way down. Vodka alone typically wouldn't be my first choice. I preferred sweet drinks, but I was willing to go along with the program.

"Let me introduce you to everybody," said Mya. She led us all through the house and introduced us to groups of smiling faces and open arms. I'd never been hugged so much in my life, but I liked the friendly atmosphere. We walked into the kitchen and I was relieved to finally see Jayce. His back faced us so he hadn't noticed us yet. He looked damn good in his white wife beater and skirt.

Wait what? What the hell is up with the skirt?

I scanned the kitchen and realized all of the men were wearing them. Before I had the chance to get Jayce's attention, a pair of arms wrapped around me from the back and lifted me off the ground.

"Bri! You made it," shouted Keon.

He gently put me back on the floor and physically turned me around for another hug. "Hey, Keon. Yeah, I made it. I wouldn't miss this for the world. By the way, this is my friend Kirsten," I said.

Their eyes locked and they gave each other a longer than necessary once over. "I'm Keon," he said with a nod. "Are you going somewhere when you leave here?"

"No," I replied slowly. "Why?"

"Because you're dressed like you're going out," he said with a grin. "I've never seen you wear so much makeup before.

"Yeah," I muttered. "I noticed we're a little over dressed when Mya introduced us to everybody." Everyone else in the room had T-shirts and shorts on. I felt out of place and Kirsten definitely stood out with her barely-there dress.

"I think you look great," Jayce whispered into my ear. I whirled around and tilted my head to meet his eyes.

"Thanks, my personal stylist picked it out for me," I said with a wink.

Jayce gave me a tight hug and I used the moment as my opportunity to recapture his scent. The Tom Ford cologne coated his skin like a new layer, but I could smell his natural earthy scent too. It took a moment for me to gather my thoughts when he released me.

"I like your … " I said, gesturing to the skirt like thing wrapped around his waist.

"It's called a lava-lava. I only wear mine when I cook unless it's a special occasion and I'm required to wear it," he explained.

"Yeah," said Keon. "It's a Poly thing."

"Poly?" questioned Kirsten.

He cut his eyes at her and folded his arms. "Poly as in Polynesian. We're Samoan," he said in a clipped tone. It sounded like he was annoyed with her already, which was odd because it was an innocent question. To be fair, I didn't know what Poly meant either. I just didn't intend to ask the meaning.

Judging by the way they kept glaring at each other, maybe I was wrong about them possibly wanting to get to know one another. Kirsten looked like she wanted to punch Keon in the face, and the feeling appeared mutual.

"Do you need any help in here?" I asked, trying to diffuse the tension in the air.

"Nope. We just need to set the food on the table and we'll be ready to dig in," said Jayce. "Go on and grab some drinks while you wait."

He led us over to a table covered in alcohol and red cups. We mixed a couple of drinks and found some empty seats. Kirsten immediately struck up a conversation with the people next to her as I sat and observed. Everybody was really friendly and welcoming despite my standoffish demeanor. If I got a few more drinks into my system, I'd be the embarrassing life of the party.

"It's chow time everybody!" yelled Keon.

Everyone stampeded into the kitchen, and quickly pushed us to the head of the line because we were guests. I soon realized Kirsten and I were the only people here not related to someone in the room.

"The food is pretty standard," said Jayce, grabbing the plate out of my hands. "There are a few things here that may be a little different for you. This is called *Oka*, it's raw fish mixed with some other things. I'll just give you a little so you can try it."

My plate had a colorful array of things piled on it. It was incredibly sweet of Jayce to fix my plate and slightly awkward.

Vivianne didn't seem to be anywhere in sight, and that too was a pleasant relief. I followed him outside to the patio and sat down in one of the chairs. The backyard was empty and I liked the privacy it offered.

"This is nice," I whispered.

"Yeah, I wanted to talk to you privately," he said.

My stomach practically dropped down to my knees. I hope you didn't secretly marry Vivianne or something.

"Okay," I stammered. "What's up?"

"Well my trip didn't turn out the way I thought it would. Everything started out great, but things didn't end that way," he said.

I tried some of the food on the plate and choked down the moan in my throat. The food was amazing and I seriously considered licking the plate after I finished.

"I'm all ears," I replied.

"She set everything up like it was all her idea. She failed to mention she contacted a coach from my football days. Coach Jackson really wanted me on his team in the past and basically told me I could come play for him whenever I got ready. Vivianne convinced him that I was on board with everything. He paid for the room, the plane tickets, and all of our food, thinking I planned to come to the open tryouts."

"Wow," I muttered. What a clever, sneaky bitch.

"I didn't want him to feel used or anything so I did go through with the tryout. He approved of my performance and so did the other coaches and trainers for the team. They offered me the opportunity to come to training camp in a couple of months. I didn't want to seem like an asshole so I told them I'll think about it," he said.

"Are you really considering it?" I asked. My hand wiped away the sweat on my forehead and I was pretty sure it was because of the spicy chicken and not my nerves this time.

"Hell no, and that's the same thing I told Vivianne. She basically told me the trip was her way of giving me a small push toward making our lives better. I told her I was done with her. My heart can't take the manipulation anymore."

Would I be wrong to cheer? How about a cartwheel?

"I'm glad you followed your heart," I said.

Jayce narrowed his eyes and arched his brow. "Tell me how you really feel, Bri," he said.

I took a deep breath and placed my empty plate on the small table between us. "Well, I really am glad you followed your heart. Vivianne isn't exactly the nicest person in the world and I thought you deserved better than her anyway," I said in a rush.

He nodded and put his plate on the table before folding his arms across his chest. "You actually helped make the decision easier for me," he explained. "You were right when you said I was holding on to a hollow shell. Vivianne isn't my Vivi anymore and it's because she chooses to not be that person anymore."

I opened my mouth to respond, but Mya poked her head out the door. "Hey, Jayce, we're about to leave," she said.

"I'll walk you out," he said, standing to his feet. "Come on in the house, Bri. I don't want to leave you out here alone."

"It was nice meeting you," said Mya. "I hope to see you again sometime."

"Likewise," I said with a nod.

As the living room emptied, I searched for Kirsten in the dwindling crowd. I found her sitting on the couch scowling with her arms folded across her chest.

I plopped down next to her and nudged her with my elbow. "What's up? What's wrong?" I whispered.

She slowly turned her head, and for a split second I thought her head would keep right on spinning. Her nose flared and there was a tinge of redness to her cheeks. I could almost feel heat radiating off of her.

"Keon, or whatever his name is, happens to be a major asshole. I couldn't believe you thought I would like a douche like that," she snarled.

"What happened?" I asked, leaning in closer.

"He keeps making little digs at me. He basically told me I must look like a gremlin underneath my makeup since I'm wearing so much of it," she said.

My eyebrows jumped up in surprise. "I can't believe he said that! Keon does have a no bullshit type of approach to him. Do you want to leave?"

Please say no. Please say no. I really want to talk to Jayce some more.

"Of course not," she hissed. "I'm waiting on him to come back."

"Huh?" I asked, my mouth went slack in confusion. "If he's such an asshole, why are you waiting on him?"

She crossed her legs and flared her nose again before offering an explanation. "Because I'm not leaving until I prove my point. There's nothing wrong with my face and I can take all of my makeup off and still be ten times hotter than anybody he's ever been with," she grumbled.

Just then, Keon returned with a soapy towel and held it out to Kirsten. All I could do was shake my head at the two of them.

"Well go on," he urged. "Take that mask off."

Jayce walked back into the house and closed the door behind him. His eyes bounced back and forth at the scene unfolding. "What's going on?" he asked slowly.

"There's some type of bet going on between the two of them. Keon thinks Kirsten is wearing too much makeup and is trying to hide something," I explained.

She snatched the towel out of his hands and started wiping off the layers of stuff caked on her face.

"What's the big deal, Keon? I'm wearing it too," I said.

He briefly cut his eyes at me and winked. "I've seen you without makeup on before. You're pretty without it, but I'm not so sure about your friend," he said. I could tell he was teasing her and deliberately trying to make her mad. This was like watching two high school kids go at each other.

"I'm going to slap you if you keep insulting me," she growled.

He gave a wide grin and shrugged his shoulders. "Won't be the first time a girl has slapped me."

Kirsten closed her eyes and nearly scrubbed her skin off. When she was finally satisfied everything was gone she threw the towel at Keon. "See? There's nothing wrong with my face. With or without makeup I look better than anybody you've ever been with," she snapped.

"If you say so," he replied, taking the towel into the laundry room.

She whirled around on her heels and stormed after him. I expected to hear a bunch of yelling, screaming, and the sound of things breaking, but silence was the only thing bouncing off the walls.

Jayce and I exchanged confused glances before the sudden loud slap drew our attention.

"Ow!" yelled Keon.

"Don't do it again," shouted Kirsten.

She came out first and he followed still clutching his face. "She slapped me!"

"Of course I slapped you. You kissed me without my permission," she said.

My eyes bounced back to Keon, waiting on an explanation. "You liked it or you wouldn't have kissed me twice before slapping me," he replied.

These two are definitely a match made in heaven. I have no clue as to what's going on.

"Let's play a game and squash all of this nonsense," suggested Jayce.

We followed him to the kitchen and I made sure to stay by Kirsten's side … just in case.

"What game?" I asked, taking a seat at the table. Jayce brought over the remaining tray of shots and placed them in the center. Keon and Kirsten exchanged glances with one another as they sat down to play.

"Truth or Dare," Jayce announced, sitting down next to me. "And Bri is on my team."

Chapter Twenty-One

I caught the mischievous glances being swapped between Keon and Jayce, and I wondered what they had up their sleeves.

"The rules are simple. You and your partner both have to agree on which side you choose. If you choose truth, you take a shot, and if you choose dare, you take a shot," Jayce explained.

"Those aren't rules. It sounds like we're drinking no matter what we choose," I said.

"Exactly," he replied, rubbing his hands together. "You guys can go first. Truth or Dare?"

"Truth," blurted Keon.

Kirsten promptly punched him in the leg. "You didn't ask me if I wanted truth," she said.

He turned to her with a playful spark in his eyes. "Are you going to hit me every time you don't get your way? Is our relationship built on violence?"

She looked shocked for a moment and blushed. "We don't have a relationship," she mumbled.

He leaned forward with his elbows on the table and tilted his head to the side. "Oh really? Give it some time, it'll all sink in," he murmured.

It was obvious she couldn't think of a witty response to him. Her mouth simply opened and closed a few times, before she cast a confused look in my direction.

Hell, don't look over here. I don't know what to tell you.

I shrugged my shoulders and locked eyes with Keon. "We're going with truth," he said with an understood finality to the question.

"Go on and take your shots," said Jayce.

They reached over, grabbed the tiny cups, and tossed them back. I felt Jayce's hand on my knee and my head jerked around toward him. "Let's think of a question," he whispered into my ear.

The warmth of his breath on my skin sent chills down my spine, causing me to involuntarily arch my back. "Okay," I muttered. "I think I've got one."

He nodded and leaned back over, but his hand stayed right on my knee. "Go on," he urged.

"Who's the last person you've undressed with your eyes," I asked with a seductive smile.

"Kirsten," said Keon with no hesitation.

Her eyes widened and the familiar sex kitten look blossomed across her face. "Keon," she replied. "And I'm not impressed."

"Oh really?" he laughed. "I need to change the picture in your mind."

"Your turn!" she yelled eagerly. "Truth or Dare?"

"Dare?" asked Jayce looking over at me.

My heart raced, there was no telling what Kirsten was going to come up with for a dare, but I didn't want to wimp out. "Yeah, dare," I said.

Keon and Kirsten leaned over and whispered to one another for a few seconds. The look on their faces told it all, and I knew something embarrassing was about to happen.

"I dare you to kiss each other, and I'm not talking about a peck on the cheek. I mean a real kiss," said Keon.

The second the dare crossed his lips, I felt my mouth get drier than a desert on the hottest day of the year. My hands trembled, and a thin layer of sweat instantly found its way onto my forehead. The hand on my knee glided up a bit and gave me a small squeeze. I reached out and grabbed my shot off the table. The liquid burned on the way down, and I chased it with another one for good measure. I exhaled slowly, forcing all of the air from my lungs until it hurt.

"Ready?" Jayce asked quietly.

I took several deep breaths and quickly licked my lips. He leaned in and paused just before our lips touched. After a few awkward seconds suspended in limbo, I closed the gap between us. His lips were soft, just like I imagined they would be. I felt his tongue tap my lips asking for permission to enter. My head attempted to jerk back, but Jayce moved his free hand up to cup my face and hold me in place. The wet tap against my lips was more urgent this time.

My lips parted slightly and that was all he needed to slide right in. I nervously allowed our tongues to meet as we took turns mingling in each other's mouths. I was thankful for the full coverage bra hiding my erect nipples this time. I squirmed uncomfortably in the growing wetness between my thighs as Jayce's hand snaked its way up my leg. The higher it got, the more urgent my need was for him to touch me. I panicked the moment his fingers finally grazed the warmth between my legs. I broke our connection and jumped up from the table.

"I need to use the bathroom!" I announced, running from the room. My name was called, but I didn't stop until I found the bathroom. Without turning on the light, I closed the door and leaned against it.

There's no way I can go back to the table with my panties soaking wet like this.

I flipped on the light and tried to regain my composure.

Damn, if I had my purse I could simply put my panties in there. What the hell just happened out there?

"Bri?" called Kirsten through the door. "Are you okay?"

I tried to steady my nerves by turning on the water so I could splash it on my face. If I kept the panties on, I'd have a rash in an hour. My eyes scanned the bathroom for something to put them in, but my search came up empty.

"Damn," I whispered.

A soft knock on the door interrupted my scavenger hunt.

Fine, I'll let Kirsten in and tell her to go get my purse.

I pulled the door open and Jayce was standing where my friend should be. He grabbed my face and brought our mouths together again as he barged into the bathroom. He kicked the door closed with his foot and pushed me against the counter. I moaned and wrapped my arms around him. Clearly I hadn't learned my lesson from the debacle I had with Connor. Alcohol and raging hormones didn't mix well with each other, but I couldn't stop myself.

Jayce reached down and cupped my ass with his hands before he picked me up and put me on the counter. I opened my legs to invite him into a more comfortable position. He maneuvered his way between my thighs pressing his rock hard erection into me. He broke our connection and yanked my shirt over my head. One of his hands unsnapped my bra and the other fumbled with the button and zipper on my pants.

"No ... wait," I whispered, slightly out of breath.

"You want to stop?" he asked, his chest rising and falling heavily.

"Yes ... no ... well, I just don't want to do it in the bathroom," I confessed.

He smiled and helped me completely take my bra off before dropping it to the floor. His arms wrapped around and picked me up again. My legs locked around his waist as he hoisted me into the air. He somehow managed to open the door and I was glad his back was to the living room, otherwise I would have flashed Keon and Kirsten. My breath came out in a slow hiss as his mouth latched onto my breast.

His mouth was warm and he gently rolled my nipple around with his tongue. The delicate nipping of his teeth sent a shockwave of pleasure and pain throughout my body. He made a left at the end of the hall and again kicked the door closed behind us. He put me down on the bed, and I watched his silhouette move against the darkness. His hands moved up my legs and pulled both my panties and pants off in one fell swoop. My legs instantly locked together, stopping him from going any further.

"Are you sure?" I asked nervously.

Leave it to me to be a buzzkill, but I have to be sure.

"I've wanted you since day one, but I had to be sure things were done with Vivianne," he said.

"Wow, really?" I croaked.

"Yes … really."

I inhaled deeply and allowed my legs to drop open on the exhale. Jayce was still dressed as he eased between my legs and hovered over my body. His mouth found its way to my neck and left a trail of wet kisses down my body. His hand moved down my thigh and circled around to massage my wet mound. I moaned and dropped my hips back away from his hand. One finger found its way inside as his thumb massaged my swollen bud. I don't know how he was able to keep up the two different rhythms at the same time and I didn't care. My hips moved with his hand in a hurried frenzy, and I could feel the orgasm building, but he removed his hand just as I was about to reach my peak. Despite the darkness in the room, I was able to clearly see his fingers disappear into his mouth as he moaned.

I hope I don't taste bad. I searched his face for some type of clue hinting to what I tasted like.

"I think I need some more," he whispered. His mouth moved down my body, each kiss ignited a new fire inside. His tongue danced on the inner crevice of one thigh, before he moved on to the other side.

It's a good thing I shaved everything before the party.

His tongue finally moved over to lap at my wetness. I bucked off the bed as his mouth closed in around my clit.

"Yessss," I hissed, biting my lip.

Jayce reached up, grabbed my hand, and placed it on his head. I took the hint and grabbed two fistfuls of his hair. My hips rolled with the rhythm of his mouth. He licked, sucked, and slurped me deeper into a heightened level of ecstasy. His arms wrapped around my legs and I felt myself reaching that point of no return. My breath hitched in my throat as the orgasm took control of my body. I jerked and tried to twist away from his mouth still working my overly sensitive clit, but he held on, rolling his tongue over it again and again. When my seizure-like pulses stopped, Jayce moved his mouth to nuzzle my inner thigh again.

I could call it a night and throw in the towel right now, but I know we were nowhere near through. He sat up, pulled off his shirt, and shimmied out of the lava-lava and shorts. I sat up too as my hands found their way to his chest and gently caressed the bulging muscles. I felt each one contract underneath the gentle glide of my hands. I reached down and attempted to wrap my palm around the length of him. Both hands ended up circled around him as I slowly moved them up and down. He moaned and I glanced up to see his head tossed back with his eyes closed. I stroked all the way up to the mushroomed head and back down again, smiling at the series of moans and groans coming from him.

It's now or never.

I licked my lips and brought my mouth down to return the favor.

"Bri," he moaned.

The sound of my name coming out as a muffled whisper excited me. My mouth slid down as far as my throat would allow, and even then I forced myself to take in more of him. I created a waving motion with my tongue and he really seemed to enjoy it based on the way he grabbed the back of my head. One of my hands tapped his thigh to get his attention. He dropped his head and looked down just as I lifted my eyes to meet his. I rolled my tongue again just so I could see the look on his face. He inhaled sharply and cursed under his breath.

"Lay down," I ordered, releasing him long enough for him to get comfortable.

As soon as he was flat on his back, I captured him with my mouth again. This time when I reached the end, I circled around the tip with my tongue and enlisted my hands to help. With both my mouth and hands at work, I knew it wouldn't be long before he finished. Just when I thought he was ready to explode, he quickly pushed me away. My jaw was tired, but I was not ready to stop yet.

"I'm not ready to finish," he whispered, pushing me down onto the bed. He reached over to the nightstand and grabbed a condom. Once he was ready, he positioned himself between my legs. He found my slippery opening with ease, but took his time pushing inside.

I inhaled just at the pressure of him bearing down on me. There was no way he was going to slide inside without it hurting. I dropped my knees down to open up my hips a little, but that didn't help. Jayce pushed forward and a pained sigh escaped my lips. I clearly underestimated his size, and I was having second thoughts about taking this any further.

"You're so wet," he murmured. "You're tight too, and I'm trying not to hurt you."

"Don't stop," I whispered.

What the fuck am I thinking? This is going to hurt like hell.

He slowly brought our hips together. I closed my eyes and concentrated on breathing through the pain. I refused to stop him … not now. We were too close, and I needed to have him every way I possibly could before shit hit the fan. Once he couldn't go in any further, he moved his hips in a slow motion in and out. The more he stroked the more I loosened up enough to accept the girth of him. The pain was over and quickly replaced with pleasure. He was able to touch and caress every part inside of my body. My hips arched off of the bed to match his rhythm.

"Yes … yes … yes. Don't stop," I moaned into the side of his neck.

Our breathing was synced and I could tell we were about to reach our breaking point together. A few more deep thrusts helped pitch me over the edge.

"Fuck," he barked as I bit down on his shoulder. He maintained our connection and rode the waves of the orgasm with me. I shuddered as the electric pulses mellowed out to subtle blips on the sex radar.

I'm not sure how much time passed, but we both eventually passed out from exhaustion.

Chapter Twenty-Two

I woke up a couple of hours later, trapped in the bed under the weight of Jayce's arm. My mind raced to put the last few hours of my life in order. What time was it anyway? I craned my head up to look around the room and spotted the alarm clock on the table.

Three o'clock? Shit, where's Kirsten?

I glanced over at Jayce and faked a few coughs as I eased out of bed. My feet barely touched the floor before I had to reach out and steady myself against the wall. Sore didn't quite describe the sensation I was feeling between my thighs. My legs were weak, and threatened to give out on me.

I'm going to have to soak in the tub for a week, and where the hell are my clothes?

The room was too dark to see much of anything, so I felt around the floor for my pants. A sense of dread covered me as I remembered where my bra and shirt were.

Maybe I can borrow his T-shirt to cover up with while I find the rest of my clothes?

I threw on his oversized shirt, which fit more like a dress, and tip toed to the door. Before my hand reached the knob, the lamp clicked on.

Busted.

"Going somewhere?"

"Umm ... yeah," I stammered. "It's late and I need to get some rest."

"Well get back into bed then," he said.

Damn ... strike one.

"No, I'm okay. Kirsten is probably pissed off, thinking I forgot about her," I explained nervously.

"I checked on her a couple of hours after you fell asleep, just to make sure Keon wasn't bothering her too bad. They are cuddling in each other's arms fast asleep," he said, folding his arms across his chest.

Strike two ... one more strike and I'll be out of excuses.

I sighed and dropped my hand away from the door. "Listen, I don't want to make things more awkward than they already are."

"Awkward?" he repeated. "Things weren't awkward for me until just now. Come have a seat and tell me what's on your mind."

Strike three ... time to come clean.

I inched over to the bed and gingerly sat down. Jayce reached over and pulled me into his lap.

"Thanks, Santa," I teased, attempting to cut the tension in the air.

Well, well, well … Santa has a hard on and it's stabbing me in the leg.

"What's going on, Bri? Your whole body is tense," he murmured into the side of my neck.

"Jayce, I don't want this to get weirder than it already is. We work together and you just broke up with Vivianne. I know I'm the rebound chick, and I'm not mad at you or anything. We were drinking and things got a little out of hand. It is what it is," I said in a rush.

He leaned back and loosened his hold around my waist. "What the hell do you mean rebound chick? Don't go there with me, Bri, we're adults and we had sex because we wanted to. I don't look at you like a rebound chick or a friend with benefits. This is only weird because you're making it that way," he said.

"I'm not asking you to define what this is, I'm just letting you know I'm aware of what it's not," I replied.

Did that come out right? I think I'm still a little drunk.

He sighed and pinched the bridge of his nose. "I've noticed you since the first time you walked into the shop, long before you started coming in without a bra," he grinned. "But I was in a relationship, and there wasn't a reason for me to cast a line and draw you into a messy situation. I'm not in a relationship anymore, and I don't want to waste any time getting with you. Please don't shut me out."

"It's too soon," I said. "Vivianne is still a new wound for you and I don't want to get pulled into any drama."

"We don't have to make any final decisions about anything right now," he said, wrapping his arms back around me. "I'm just asking you to stay open to the possibilities. What do you have to lose?"

Ugh ... everything. My heart could end up broken, and I could find myself without a job ... again. I've wanted this for so long, now I'm not sure what to do with it.

"Okay, I'll stay open," I muttered.

"Good," he said, planting soft kisses along my neck. "Now get back into bed."

He pulled me over to the other side of the bed and yanked his shirt over my head. "I need to feel your skin against mine."

The light clicked off and he settled in with his arms around me and not an inch of space between us.

Hours later a firm knock on the door jolted me awake. I yanked the sheet up to cover my body just in case someone came in.

Jayce slipped his shorts on and cracked the door just enough to see who it was, and I rolled over to check the time. It was well past nine and I was late for work. I waited until Jayce closed the door before I reached for my clothes.

"I'm late," I muttered, pulling my pants on. I clutched my still damp panties in my hand not sure what to do with them.

"Don't worry about it. There's somebody at the shop," he said. "You don't have to rush."

"Damn, I need my bra and shirt."

Jayce's eyes dipped low as he bit his bottom lip. "I don't know … I like the way you look without them. He sat down on the bed and kissed me on the mouth before venturing lower. He suckled at one breast and then the other.

"Stop," I whispered. "I can't walk out the room with a wet spot in the crotch of these pants."

"Take them off then," he growled, reaching for my buttons.

"I can't. I really need to go home so I can shower and get started on the account statements," I said.

He sat back pouting just a bit. "I'll get you later then. I already brought the rest of your stuff in here. It's on your side of the bed."

My side? We have sides now? When the hell did that happen?

We walked down the hall together and saw Keon and Kirsten sitting on the couch. Her hair was a tousled mess and she was wearing a too big T-shirt.

"Hey, Bri," she said with a big smile. "Good morning, Jayce."

"Morning. Are you ready to go?" I asked. I was a little embarrassed to do the walk of shame, but I was glad I was not alone.

I tried to make a beeline for the door, but Jayce pulled me back. The kiss he planted on me nearly made me forget Keon and Kirsten were still in the room. He let me go and I expected to hear a bunch of teasing, but I saw my friend in a similar position. Keon released her with a playful smile. My eyes automatically zeroed in on his protruding erection and I forced myself to quickly look around the room as if I didn't see it.

The men in this family give new meaning to the phrase "hung like a horse."

Kirsten smiled and wiggled her eyebrows at me as she stepped out the door. She linked our arms and leaned her head on my shoulder until we got to the car. Before I was able to successfully round the corner, she was already asking me a million questions.

"Did you have fun last night? I know you did ... the whole neighborhood heard you," she teased.

"Me?" I asked, feigning shock. "What about you? You're wearing Keon's shirt as a dress. I thought you didn't like him."

"I'm only wearing his shirt because it's more comfortable than what I had on. We didn't have sex last night, just cuddled, kissed, and talked. We'll get to me later, I want all the details on what went on after you bolted from the table," she ordered. "And don't say nothing happened, because like I said, the whole neighborhood heard you."

I cut my eyes over at her and tried to stop the smile from spreading. "Let's just say he's skilled, and did a very good job," I said.

Kirsten squealed and clapped her hands together. "This is just like high school all over again. Remember when we were dating the

Robinson brothers? Now we can go on double dates and everything," she gushed.

"I remember you dating the cute brother and I was left with the one covered in zits. And who said anything about dating?"

She rolled her eyes at me. "Really, Bri? You've done nothing but drool over Jayce since day one and now he's ripe for the picking. I know you don't expect me to believe you don't want to date him," she said.

My hands tightened on the steering wheel as I searched for the right words to say. "I guess you can say we're just going with the flow. He just broke up with Vivianne, and I don't want to put myself out there just for him to get right back with her," I explained.

"That's understandable," she said. "Well, Keon and I are doing the same. He was still being a jerk last night after you disappeared to Pleasure Island, but he opened up a little. We talked about his stint in the military, his family, and his plans for the future. I didn't expect to hit it off with him, but I did. We're planning to go out later."

She was giddy like a school girl and I couldn't help but laugh.

"Look at you! You're so excited about this huh?" I asked.

"Very excited," she beamed. "I'm going to grab my things from your house and head on home."

I was glad to see Mom's car parked in the driveway. We had so much catching up to do, but I needed to get ready to head to the shop.

"Hello, girls!" Mom yelled from the kitchen.

I closed the door behind us and followed Kirsten. "Wild night?" she asked with a suspicious gleam in her eye.

"Very wild," said Kirsten.

"So anyway," I said, trying to steer the conversation somewhere else, "how was your trip? Did you bring me something back?"

"It was wonderful. And no, I didn't bring you anything. You're lucky I even came back," she said.

"I hate to just grab my stuff and leave, but I need to head home and run some errands," said Kirsten, heading up the stairs.

"Mom, we'll catch up later. I have to get showered and get ready for work," I said.

"That's fine," she replied, taking a sip of her coffee. "I'm leaving soon to go visit Gram-Gram anyway."

I walked over for a quick hug before running up the stairs two at a time.

Chapter Twenty-Three

I headed straight for the office as soon as I got to the coffee shop. I hated taking care of the time sheets and other accounts at the last minute. My eyes strained to focus on the spreadsheets. The numbers were running together and my back was stiff. I tapped my head on the desk a few times, trying to pull myself together. My mind wandered over to last night's events and put them on instant replay. A chill raced over my skin, I shuddered and sighed loudly. My memory was so vivid and real, I could actually smell Jayce's cologne. I pictured myself leaning closer to him just to bury my face into his chest.

"You smell so good," I whispered.

"Thank you."

The sound of his voice made me jump out of the chair. I clutched my chest and waited for my heart to stop pounding.

"You scared the hell out of me," I gasped.

"I'm sorry, babe. I thought you knew I was behind you and that's why you said something," he said.

I shook my head and dropped down into the chair. "What are you doing here?"

Jayce pushed the door closed behind him and came toward me. He dropped down on his knees and cupped my face. Our lips touched with a subtle hint of familiarity. He had the softest lips ever and he knew what to do with them. I didn't want to let go yet, so I moved my mouth to suck gently on his bottom lip.

He moaned and pulled me in closer to him before jerking his head back. "If you keep it up I'm going to have you bent over this desk," he growled.

I smiled and sat back in the chair. "You still haven't told me what you're doing here."

"I'm supposed to be helping unload a truck. The delivery slipped my mind, but now you have me thinking of slipping inside of you," he murmured.

Who is this? This isn't the same Jayce at all. This version is making me feel things I shouldn't be feeling.

"Maybe later," I teased. My eyes caught the growing erection in his pants and if he didn't leave right now, I knew he would make good on his threat, and the time sheets would never get done.

"Go on and get the truck unloaded," I urged.

"Okay," he said, getting to his feet. "Keon will be gone later, and we'll have the house to ourselves."

"Does that mean you want me to come over?" I asked, wanting to be sure we were on the same page.

"Of course that's what it means," he laughed.

"All right, that's fine," I replied.

He walked out the door and gave me a sideways glance before he left. I tried to make myself finish my work, but the playful teasing had my blood pumping and my nerves standing on end.

My back started to hurt again from sitting in the same position for so long, so I decided to stretch my legs and grab a cup of coffee. It was not quite lunchtime, so we were nearly empty. I sipped the steaming hot liquid slowly and leaned against the counter.

I guess I can help restock and wipe down the tables before anybody comes in here.

I grabbed the cleaning supplies and got started. Leani was home from school and was manning the register. There was very little noise inside the shop, nothing other than the soft rustling of Mr. Jacobs' newspaper as he turned the pages. My brain teamed with questions and I found it hard to focus.

Am I better in bed than Vivianne? Does Jayce think I'm easy ... especially since it's not like he had to try very hard to get me to sleep with him. Should I ask?

Kirsten would probably tell me to keep my questions to myself, but I really wanted to know. The door opened and it took me a few seconds to register the chime in my head.

"Hello, welcome to Drip ... "

"Where the hell is Jayce?" growled Vivianne.

My stomach dropped down to my knees. The Queen Bitch of all things sparkly and evil stood before me with her hands planted on her hips and a scowl across her face.

The tight dress painted on her body was cut low enough to reveal her new prized possessions. Those things looked like two overly inflated basketballs.

I know her back is hurting from carrying those things around all day.

"Hello?" she snapped. "Is anybody going to answer my fucking question?"

"He's in the back, but you can't … "

The words barely escaped my lips before she stormed through the double doors.

"You can't come back here," I said, following her.

She stopped in her tracks and whirled around to face me. "I suggest you get your ass back up front and eat a bagel or something," she said. "This isn't any of your damn business."

It's my business now, bitch. And what does "eat a bagel" mean? Is that a dig at my weight? Calm down, Bri … don't whoop her ass just yet.

"Jayce!" I yelled.

I didn't get a response, and before I was able to call his name again, Vivianne had resumed her stampede into the walk-in fridge. Jayce's back was to us and his head bounced to the beat of whatever he was listening to. He turned around to grab another container of creamer and froze. His eyes locked with mine first and then Vivianne's. He snatched his earphones off and threw the creamer onto the shelf.

"What the fuck are you doing in here?" he said. The vein in his neck popped out, ready to explode.

"That's what I want to know. I told her to take her ass back up front," said Vivianne, glaring over at me.

"I'm talking to you!" he shouted, jabbing his finger in her face. "I told you to stay away from me and stay away from this shop. Did you think I was joking?"

"Can you get the fuck out of here!" she shrieked at me.

"Bri, don't you move one step," he ordered.

Okay ... this is hella awkward. Do I say something or just watch them yell at each other? I know one thing for sure, if Vivianne keeps yelling at me, she going to find those implants on the outside of her body.

"Let's get out of the fridge and go somewhere warmer," I suggested.

Jayce stormed out, but not before he turned around and grabbed my hand. Now, I'm sure he didn't mean to, but he nearly dislocated my arm.

"Wait a minute ... what the hell is this shit?" asked Vivianne, struggling to keep up with us.

Oh, shit. He's really poking the hornets' nest now.

We went into the office and closed the door.

"I asked you a question!" she screeched.

I reallyyy don't need to be in here.

"Listen, we're done. I'm done trying to make you happy and I'm done trying to fix things between us," he explained.

Even though Jayce was the one talking, Vivianne's eyes are burning holes into my head.

"Bri tried to help me figure out ways to keep you in my life, but you're not the woman I fell in love with. I don't know who you are," he said. "And I don't want you anymore."

"Did you sleep with him?" she asked calmly ... a little too calmly.

Okay, wasn't expecting that one.

"Vivianne," he hissed. "Are you even listening to me? It's over … what part of that don't you understand?"

"Did you?" she asked, taking a step closer to me.

She looked pissed off, but there was a smile on her face … a dark uncomfortable smile. Her eyes cut over to Jayce and then back to me again.

"Never mind, I know Jayce wouldn't stoop so low. You're a complete downgrade compared to me," she laughed.

Excuse me? Game on.

"As a matter of fact … yes," I replied smugly. "I had amazing sex with him, last night as a matter of fact. I'm actually still sore from it."

Checkmate, bitch.

It was a low blow, but Vivianne asked for it. Had she not insulted me, I would have kept my mouth closed.

She lunged for me, but Jayce got between us and faced the onslaught of her wrath instead.

I'm not sure what language she lapsed into, but I picked out a few choice words like … bitch, fat, and whore. Jayce picked her up and carried her out the back door.

"If you keep it up, I'm calling the police," he threatened.

She stood there with a red face and tear-stained cheeks. Her too tight dress was pulled up high on her thighs and she didn't bother to pull it down. "You're throwing away an opportunity to play football and the chance to build a life with me?" she asked between sniffles.

"Bye, Vivianne," he snapped.

The back door slammed shut, and we stood there with nothing but the sound of our ragged frustrated breaths. I don't know what he was thinking, but I was pissed off.

"Why did you do that?" I asked angrily.

"Are you serious? She came in here like a bull in a china shop," he said.

"I'm not talking about Vivianne. I want to know why you had to drag me into the middle of this mess," I snapped.

Jayce's mouth twisted sideways and his brow furrowed. "I intended to show both of you that I'm dead, damn serious. It let her know where I stood with her and it lets you know where I stand with you. I'm not trying to hide anything from anybody," he grumbled. "I didn't plan on putting you on the spot like that. It just sort of happened that way."

"It's okay," I muttered, opening my arms to him for a hug because we needed it.

The aggravation was plastered all over his face, and I didn't like seeing him this way. He still had feelings for Vivianne, but it was obvious he was trying to force himself to move on. I wanted him, but I didn't plan to have him like this. It was hard, but I kept my concerns to myself … for now.

Chapter Twenty-Four

I called Kirsten as soon as I got off work, but the call ended up going straight to voicemail. My nerves were fried and I needed somebody to talk to. Relief washed over me when Jayce left the shop to take care of some other errands, because I used his absence to think.

He'd never given me a reason to doubt his word in the past. His love and devotion to Vivianne was out there for the world to see and I appreciated the fact that he didn't hide his feelings. My heart was screaming for me to stop thinking so hard about everything. But I couldn't stop my brain from questioning every hug, every smile, and every word exchanged between us, even the ones during our friendship.

There was a soft knock on my door just before it cracked opened. "Bri, we're having dinner with Gram-Gram at six," said Mom.

I rolled over and tossed the pillow covering my head to the side. "I can't tonight!" I yelled.

Mom opened the door wider and poked her head inside. "Why not? We have some catching up to do."

"I have a date," I muttered.

She finally pushed the door completely open and invited herself inside. "A date? Is it with the guy that came over and met Gram-Gram?" she asked, her eyes lighting up.

"Yes," I grumbled. I should have known Gram-Gram told her about him. "We're going to grab some food and maybe watch a movie at his house."

"He can come eat dinner with us," she suggested. "That way I can meet him too. From what I've heard, he has the potential to be my son-in-law."

"What?" I croaked.

"Invite him to dinner, Bri, or I'll do it myself," she threatened playfully as she backed out of the room.

Crap.

Despite the smile on her face, she meant business and wouldn't hesitate to embarrass me if I didn't do what she asked. I grabbed the phone and scrolled down to Jayce's number.

"Hey, babe," he answered.

"Hey, do you mind coming over to have dinner with my mom and grandmother?"

"You know I don't mind. I would love to meet your mom and see Gram-Gram again," he said. "What time?"

"Six," I muttered.

"Awesome, I'll be there."

"All right, bye."

My stomach flipped, flopped, and twisted in knots. There was no telling how this was going to turn out. I headed downstairs and started cleaning up a bit. Mom preferred cooking alone and I didn't want to get in her way. Typically I just stood around watching and sneaking tastes when her back was turned.

"What are we having?" I asked, unable to resist the tempting scent wafting from the kitchen.

"Homemade lasagna, garlic bread, and a salad. Do you think your boyfriend will like it?" she asked, opening the oven.

"He's not my boyfriend," I muttered. "He's my … well I don't know what he is."

"What do you mean you don't know?" she asked, waving the oven mitt over the pan. "You haven't established the guidelines for your relationship yet?"

"Mom, we haven't gotten that far," I said.

"Well, Bri, don't give him your cookies until you know where you stand," she said.

Too late. He's had my cookies and dipped them in milk too.

"We're not discussing this right now," I grumbled. "Everything is fine for now."

She shook her head and grabbed the garlic bread off the counter. "I'm giving you great advice, and I suggest you listen. Make him work for it."

Shut up, shut up, shut up!

"I'm going back into the living room," I said.

I plopped down on the couch and snatched a magazine off of the coffee table. Keys rattled outside the door and I groaned to myself. The door opened and in walked Gram-Gram.

"You're not dressed for dinner?" she snapped.

"Not yet," I sighed.

"Bri, go on upstairs and come back presentable. You can't have a gentleman caller seeing you like this," she said.

Gentleman caller? Have I somehow time traveled into the past? Am I the black Scarlet O'Hara?

"Jayce has seen me in pajamas with uncombed hair and no makeup before. I would go to the coffee shop like that all the time before I started working there," I huffed.

She put her hands on her bony hips and glared at me over her glasses. The message for me to get my ass up and moving was written all over her face. I pursed my lips and stormed up the steps.

I need to get my own apartment sooner rather than later.

My phone was ringing from somewhere on the bed and I nosedived into the tangle of sheets to retrieve it.

"Hello?" I said, breathing heavily into the phone

"Ummm, did I interrupt something?" asked Kirsten.

"No, I couldn't find my phone," I said. "What happened to your antennas earlier? You completely went ghost on me."

"Bri, I've had the most wonderful day ever. I've been with Keon all day. Once you get past his assholishness, is that a word? Whatever … you know what I mean. He's a big cuddly bear. I've never been hugged so much in my life. I actually don't want to go back to work," she sighed.

"You better take your ass to work," I teased. "I'm glad you're really hitting it off with him. For a minute I thought you hated each other. Where is he now?"

"He's in the bathroom," she said. "So when he comes out don't get mad when I hang up on you."

"I guess I can go ahead and fill you in on what happened earlier, because I need some advice," I grumbled.

I gave her the short version of today's events. She gasped, moaned, and groaned all throughout the conversation.

"Wow, that's a big mess. Personally, I think you need to kick Vivianne's ass and tell her to kick rocks. But you really shouldn't worry about that crazy bitch. I told you I have a good feeling about Jayce and I don't want you to mess up your own happiness by getting caught up in a brawl with Vivianne. The time for love is now, and I plan to ride this rollercoaster until the wheels fall off. Based on the bits and pieces of conversation I've overheard, Jayce sounds serious about his feelings. Uh oh … gotta go."

She ended the call before I had a chance to quiz her on what she heard.

Oh well ... I guess I'll get dressed before Gram-Gram comes up here to do it for me.

I looked down at my clothes and then over toward the closet. I actually didn't plan on changing, but I wanted to keep the peace in the house. Since I planned on getting undressed anyway, I decided to hop in the shower.

I came out, and sat on the edge of the bed with my towel wrapped around me. My phone flashed with a text message notification.

Jayce: Are we still on for tonight after dinner?

My thumbs started typing my response and just before hitting send I erased the entire message. An idea popped into my head to take a few pictures instead. I dropped the towel to my waist and smiled for the camera. I hit send and waited. His response was instant.

Jayce: Really, Bri? I'm in public with a hard on

Hmmm I wonder what kind of response he'll have if I send a few more.

I dropped the towel completely and posed so my pudgy stomach wouldn't show. My mind was so focused on teasing Jayce that I didn't hear the door open.

"Oh my goodness, Brianna Marie! What in the world are you doing?" shrieked Gram-Gram.

Holy ... fuck.

I fell over and grabbed the towel to cover up.

"Are you in here making sex videos? Evelyn, get in here!" she yelled.

"Gram-Gram get out and shut the door!"

Mom stumbled up the stairs, still wearing her oven mitts. "What? What happened?" she asked, panting, as she tried to catch her breath.

Gram-Gram pointed her finger at me. "She's in here making porn."

"Bri," Mom hissed.

"I'm not making porn. Mom can you please leave and take Gram-Gram with you," I begged.

"Evelyn, I saw her with my own two eyes. She had her legs wide open and was ... "

"Come on, let's give Bri some privacy. She'll explain herself once she gets dressed," said Mom, taking Gram-Gram by the elbow.

She closed the door behind her giving me one last wide-eyed glance.

I can't believe I didn't lock the door.

It took a few minutes for my heart to beat normally again. I couldn't even think of a logical lie I could tell in order to explain my "delicate situation."

`Brianna: You won't believe what just happened.`

I texted to Jayce.

`Jayce: What?`

I quickly typed out the horrifying experience that just transpired, and his response made me fall off of the bed holding my sides laughing.

`Jayce: Do I still get the pictures?`

After telling him I may have scarred my grandmother for life, the first thing he asked was whether or not he could still see the pictures. It was so funny because I would have asked the same exact thing.

I sent three more pictures and slipped a navy blue maxi dress over my head. If I could stay in my room all night, I would, because I didn't want to explain what I was doing.

"Bri!" yelled Mom. "Your company is here."

My feet couldn't get me down the stairs fast enough. Jayce stood there with a bouquet of flowers. Mom and Gram-Gram were holding bouquets of roses and their smiles were almost ten miles wide.

I was surprised he remembered to get me lilies and calla lilies. I tilted my head up to thank him and he kissed me instead. The moment was sweet and awkward because we had a giggling audience in the background.

"All right, young man," said Gram-Gram. "Let's not put the cart before the horse. Come have a seat while we get the table set."

Jayce stepped back, but my head was still tilted, eyes closed, and lips puckered. I didn't want the kiss to end just yet. He leaned down and gave me a quick peck on the lips and a light swat on the ass once Gram-Gram and Mom were out of sight.

"Brianna, come give us a hand!" yelled Mom.

I took my flowers into the kitchen and found an empty vase in the cabinet.

"How sweet for him to bring us all something," whispered Mom.

"Brianna, you need to fix his plate when we sit down at the table," Gram-Gram ordered. "It'll show him you don't mind being submissive. Men like that kind of stuff."

Here we go with that again. I have to slip into the 50's and be the good housewife in order to make her happy.

I grabbed the plates and food and made my way to the table. "Jayce, we're ready to eat!" I yelled.

"Stop yelling, Brianna, it's not lady like," said Gram-Gram.

"The food smells wonderful," said Jayce. He walked around the table and pulled out each one of our chairs. I had to admit, it was a rather smooth move and definitely scored a few points with me.

"Brianna," muttered Gram-Gram through clenched teeth. Her eyes landed on Jayce's plate and then back to me, so I leaned over and took his plate.

"Thanks, babe," he said rubbing my lower back.

Once everybody had food in front of them, Gram-Gram gave a long winded prayer. Mom cleared her throat loudly a couple of times.

The food is going to get cold. Good grief, is she praying or preaching?

"Amen," said Mom quickly. Gram-Gram had paused for a moment to catch her breath and thankfully Mom capitalized on the opportunity.

It didn't take long for us to dig in and suddenly all that could be heard was the sound of forks hitting the plates. Jayce used one hand to shovel food into his mouth and the other one caressed my thigh. I was glad we were the only ones on that side of the table because I moved his hand and slowly pulled up my dress. He paused for a moment and cut his eyes at me when I placed his hand against my bare skin. He stroked my inner thigh gently and pretended like nothing happened.

"So, Jayce, what are your plans with my daughter?" asked Mom.

"Mommm," I whined, dropping my fork onto my plate. "It's too soon for that kind of question."

He squeezed my leg and put his fork down. "I don't mind answering," he said. "Bri and I are still in the beginning stage of our relationship. I'm not sure where it will go, but I can honestly say, I don't jump into relationships without planning for a possible future with the person."

What? What plans? What future? With who ... me?

"I think Bri is a wonderful person and I'm lucky she came into my life as a friend first," he said.

Mom nodded her approval, Gram-Gram smiled, and I tried to remember to breathe.

I was so happy when the conversation steered away from the topic of our relationship and possible wedding bells.

I'm not going to get my hopes up at all, not even if we get to the long-term point.

I knew in my heart I'd go on a murderous rampage if things turned out the same way my last engagement did. Stephan left me high and dry before marrying another woman a couple of months after he abandoned me. I guess none of that mattered because it was too soon to start worrying about all of that anyway.

My plate was cleared but Jayce was only halfway finished because he wouldn't stop talking long enough to eat. I grabbed his hand

and slid it high enough for him to notice I wasn't wearing panties. He stopped mid-sentence and looked directly at me.

"You're food is getting cold. Do you want me to wrap it up so you can eat the rest at home?" I asked sweetly.

"Oh, I'm sorry," said Mom. "I'm sitting here running my mouth and you should be eating your food."

"Don't worry," he replied. "I'll definitely eat later." He wiggled his fingers and I smiled at the double meaning.

"We'll go into the living room and let the two of you have some privacy," she said.

He waited until they were gone before turning toward me. "You're a big tease," he whispered, bringing his lips to meet mine.

"Let's go," I urged. "I can wrap your food up and we can leave."

"You know we don't have to have sex," he said, cutting his eyes to the living room.

"What will we be having then?" I asked.

"We can cuddle on the couch and watch TV," he said. "I don't want you to think we need to have sex every time we're alone."

I smiled and pressed myself against his hand, which was still planted between my legs. "I'm a Scorpio, sex is a part of my being. We're also very passionate and deeply rooted in our emotions," I explained.

He arched his eyebrow up and looked at me suspiciously. "Quoting your daily horoscope now? You're horny … just say you're horny."

"Okay, I'm a horny Scorpio, and you're getting your food to go."

Chapter Twenty-Five

We made it to Jayce's house in six minutes instead of the usual fifteen. Keon was still out canoodling with Kirsten so the house was nice and quiet.

"I'm just going to put my plate in the fridge," said Jayce, going past me into the kitchen. "Go on and find us a good movie to watch."

I carefully walked into the darkened living room. My toes didn't need any more run-ins with any gym equipment laying around. I turned on the lamp next to the couch and flipped on the TV. After channel surfing for a bit, I tossed the remote to the side. An idea crossed my mind and I searched around the living room for a good starting point. The coat closet was a perfect hiding place. I tiptoed inside and quietly closed the door the behind me. The light from my cell phone illuminated the small space and I prayed Jayce couldn't see the glow from under the door.

Brianna: You can have me … if you find me.

Seconds later I heard him come into the living room. "Bri?" he called.

He moved a few things around and mumbled under his breath. My hands flew up to my mouth to stifle my laughter.

"You have no idea what's going to happen when I find you!" he yelled.

I held my breath and waited, but the sound of him rummaging around was a lot more distant.

Maybe he's checking the bedroom?

I cracked the door to peek out, but ended up toppling over as Jayce snatched the door completely open. His arm shot out to catch me before I hit the floor, and he hoisted me over his shoulder like a sack of potatoes. I kicked my feet and squealed as he playfully grabbed my ass.

"You should have never opened the door," he grumbled.

He tossed me onto the couch and got on top to pin me down. "Give up?"

"The people of the republic will never surrender," I said.

He's either going to get it or he's going to think I'm crazy.

"Oh really? You'll surrender or face the consequences," he muttered.

Yes! Yes! Yes! He gets it!

I pursed my lips and closed my eyes defiantly.

"I can last a lot longer than you can," he said. "I'll come out victorious in the end."

He was supporting his own weight before, but he suddenly collapsed down and forced all of the air out of my lungs.

"Jayce ... I can't breathe and you're hurting my legs," I wheezed.

"Open them so I can readjust myself."

I tried to move around but my stupid dress was wrapped around my legs. "My dress is in the way," I whined.

As soon as he reached down to help me, I tried to wiggle out from under him. He grabbed my wrists and pinned them above my head.

"I tried to give you an opportunity to do the right thing," he growled, reaching down to pull my dress up with his other hand. He pushed my legs apart with his knees and buried his hand between my thighs. His fingers found me wet, swollen, and ready. First one finger slipped inside and then another. My hips jacked up off the couch and the sensation took my breath away.

This man has magic fingers dipped in gold.

My inner thoughts were quieted by the outer moan I could no longer contain. I twisted and squirmed, trying to get away from the pleasure overload, but I was still pinned down.

"Open your eyes, Bri," he ordered.

I opened my eyes just as he changed his rhythm and dove deeper inside. The change took me by surprise, I bit my lip and turned my head to the side.

"Keep your eyes open and look at me. I want to see your face," he growled.

My eyes locked with his again. He released my hands and pulled down the front of my dress to free my breasts. I buried my hands in his hair as he flicked his tongue over my nipple. His fingers built momentum and stroked places I didn't know existed. Every nerve ending was on fire and just as I was about to finish, Jayce's head snapped up. The instant he met my glazed over eyes, I was pushed over the edge. My breath froze in my chest, and the orgasm washed over me like rolling waves. Each stroke brought the intensity level higher. I exhaled one last time and slowed my breathing until my chest barely moved at all.

Dear God, I hope I wasn't making ugly faces when I finished.

"Do the people of the republic surrender now?" he whispered.

"Is what just happened punishment for not giving in to your demands?"

The playful exchange was funny and a huge turn on for me. I was just happy he didn't think I was a nut job.

"Yes, but it will be worse next time," he muttered.

"Well in that case, we'll never, ever surrender," I laughed.

"How about we negotiate?"

"Okay, shoot," I said.

He somehow managed to shimmy his jeans and boxers down. He thrust his hips forward and released a hiss of air into my ear. "Oh my God, you feel so good," he murmured. "So warm and wet."

"What happened to negotiating?" I moaned.

He reached down and slipped his hand under my thigh, opening my legs wider.

"I prefer a hostile takeover," he grunted.

Despite the punishing thrusts of his hips, his mouth was gentle and warm against the crook of my neck. I tilted my pelvis upward to allow him more room because my goal was to get him deeper inside of me. He succeeded and slammed into my walls seemingly unable to push any further. Pleasure and pain mingled together as I bit down on my bottom lip. He growled into the side of my neck and pushed himself deeper and deeper. I heard the jingling of keys at the door but I couldn't stop him, we were too close to just stop.

The door flung open and I heard Keon curse loudly as he quickly slammed the door. Jayce didn't slow his rhythm at all, in fact his movements became more hurried. His breath came in short ragged bursts as his hands dug deeper into my thigh.

"Fuck," he moaned with one final thrust.

His body relaxed and I braced myself to accept his deadweight. He loomed over me, supporting himself as he tried to catch his breath.

"We need to get out of the living room," I mumbled. "Keon is waiting outside."

"Yeah," he muttered. "Give me a second."

I ran my tongue up the center of his throat right over his Adam's apple. The guttural response he gave made me smile.

"If you keep it up Keon will end up spending the night out there," he whispered. "Go on into the bathroom and get cleaned up."

Jayce shifted his weight and made himself decent enough to answer the door just as I power walked down the hall.

"Damn, cousin, not on the couch," teased Keon. "Now my lady and I have to sit in a wet spot."

"Shut up, there's no wet spot," replied Jayce.

"Sorry, Keon!" I shouted.

There was a knock on the door and I cracked it just a bit to peek out. Kirsten stood there with a devious smirk.

"You horny little toad," she whispered.

I pulled the door open further and yanked her inside. "You're supposed to be gone," I hissed.

She rolled her eyes and jumped up to sit on the counter. "I have plenty of time to get to my appointment in the morning. That's enough about me, let's talk about you getting it on in the living room."

"It just sort of happened," I muttered.

"Bri got caught doing the nasty with her man. From what I could see, it looked like he was really working," she laughed. "He really had his back into it."

"Oh my goodness, Kirsten, shut up!" I yelled, covering my face.

"You know I love you, Ms. McNasty. I'm happy one of us is getting more than kissing and heavy petting. Keon refuses to take our relationship there just yet. Which is understandable considering we haven't known each other long. I'm horny and frustrated, but I actually like the fact he wants to wait," she said. "But the next time I come home, I'm expecting my ankles to be pushed up behind my head ... kind of like how yours were."

I shook my head while she covered her mouth to stifle another stomach-shaking chuckle.

"Did the party move in here?" asked Keon through the door.

I opened the door and he stood there with a knowing grin on his face.

"Hey, Bri, now I can greet you properly. I'd like to say hello to your face and not your legs," he said with a wink over to Kirsten.

"Ha ha, shut up," I mumbled. Today had turned out to be a rather embarrassing one. First I scarred Gram-Gram for life and now this.

I brushed past them and found Jayce leaning against the door of his bedroom with the smug look of satisfaction on his face.

"Let's go in the room so we can have some privacy," he said.

"Yeah … so you can finish where you left off," joked Keon.

"We did finish," I shot back.

Jayce closed the door on the hooting and hollering behind us and stripped down to his boxers.

Damn, at this rate I'm going to end up walking funny.

"Do you want a T-shirt to sleep in?" he asked.

Sleep? I'm staying the night?

"Um … yeah that's fine," I said.

He handed me one of his shirts and helped pull my dress over my head. I slipped it on and followed him to the bed. He pulled the sheets back and motioned for me to get in. We got comfortable and Jayce turned the TV on.

"I'm glad we're spending this time together," he mumbled into my hair. "I didn't think I would feel this way again with another person. Everything feels so comfortable."

"It feels a little surreal to be in this situation right now. I'm just waiting to see where it all leads. But even if things don't work out, I'm okay with it," I lied.

Actually, I would not be okay at all ... I'll probably have a mental meltdown and shave all the hair off of my head.

"Everything will work out just fine," he said. "Like I said, I feel like I know you. I even know when you're about to climax just based on how your body responds to me."

"Yeah right," I scoffed. "How do you know I'm not faking it?"

"Oh I know," he said. "You stop breathing just before it happens and I can feel your body tighten. So I know for a fact you're not just moaning for no reason."

"I hope I'm not making weird faces or anything."

"You do have one face you make that reminds me of a zombie. Your mouth opens and you looked zoned out for a while," he chuckled.

"Shut up," I said, hitting his chest. "All of my faces are cute."

"It's cute if you like zombies," he teased.

Somewhere between the laughing and cuddling, I fell asleep in his arms.

Chapter Twenty-Six

I'd been walking on cloud nine for the past month. I rarely spent any time away from Jayce at all. If we were not at the coffee shop together, we were at his house or having dinner with Mom and Gram-Gram. The day I "met" his parents, who were vacationing in Samoa, was one to remember. The video call lasted well over two hours and I had a blast.

I hardly ever saw my bestie anymore because she was just as busy with Keon as I was with Jayce. Everything was perfect, I finally found my knight in shining armor and I certainly didn't want to let him go.

My eyes followed his body as he maneuvered around the cash register. He turned around and caught me staring.

"See something you like?" he teased, wiggling his hips a little.

"Absolutely," I murmured.

He walked over and leaned down. The front door chimed and he stopped before our lips had time to meet.

"Welcome to Drip Drop," he said turning around to face the customer.

I sidestepped him so I could help complete the customer's order. Vivianne's eyes zeroed in on me the instant I came into view.

"What the hell are you doing here?" Jayce barked.

This chick has horrible timing.

While he was questioning her, I took the time to really take in her appearance. The normally overly-groomed Vivianne looked like something the cat coughed up. Her hair was in a lopsided bun on top of her head and she had dark smudges around her eyes.

Either that's mascara or this bitch has gotten into a fight and lost.

"Can I talk to you?" she sniffled. "Privately? It won't take long … I swear."

Jayce shifted his attention around to me. "Do you mind?" he asked.

"Why are you asking her?" she huffed.

His head whipped around like it wasn't attached to his spine. "Because she's my girlfriend and if she's says no, you're going to get your ass out of here," he snarled.

Her eyes darted over to mine in surprise.

Hell, I'm just as shocked as you are. Girlfriend? When did that happen? We haven't discussed labels yet.

I wanted to break into a little dance. There was something exciting about having that label because it made me feel … wanted, but most importantly, it made me feel superior to Vivianne.

My chin jutted up a little, empowered with a sense of authority. "It's okay, I don't mind."

Jayce jerked his head toward the office and fell in step behind Vivianne. She glared at me with a hatred that chilled my blood.

I'm doing you a favor you hateful cow.

The lunch rush started and ended with no sign of Jayce or Vivianne. Keon came into the shop with his eyes narrowed and searching.

"Hey, Keon, I thought you were off today?" I said.

"So did I," he muttered. "What the hell is going on? Jayce called me and said to get down here immediately. I thought the building was on fire or something."

My lips pulled into a tight line and my brow furrowed. "Vivianne showed up and they went into the back to talk. I haven't seen either one of them for quite some time."

"Oh God," he groaned. "I should have known. Every emergency he's ever had has her name written all over it."

After another twenty minutes of waiting, the door to the office finally opened. I didn't bother to scramble away from the hallway and look busy as Vivianne sashayed her way past me. Obviously she's in a better mood. She batted her lashes and flashed her teeth as she headed out the door without uttering a single word.

What the hell just happened?

Keon and I glanced at each other and then back down the hall. Jayce stepped out of the office and looked positively sick. He was pale and fidgeting all over the place.

"What's wrong, hun?" I asked, stepping in front of him. My hands cupped his face to get his attention. It was easy to tell his mind was somewhere else. It took a few moments for him to finally acknowledge me.

My heart thudded loudly and my body tingled with nervous anticipation. "Jayce?"

His eyes lowered and he offered a weak smile. He brought his hands up to rest on top of mine. "I need to leave for a little while. Keon is here to help out until closing time," he muttered.

"What's wrong, Jayce? You're scaring me," I said, unable to keep the shaking out of my voice.

He leaned down to kiss my forehead. "I'll explain everything a little later. I just need to clear my head first," he replied.

He gave a slight nod toward Keon and walked out the door.

"What the hell was that about?" I asked.

Keon shook his head and looked equally as worried. "I've never seen him look like that before. But I know one thing … it can't be good."

The rest of the day was slow and uneventful. I was on imaginary pins and needles to get away from the shop and over to Jayce's house. We pulled up into the driveway and exchanged baffled glances.

"I thought he would be here," Keon muttered. "If you hear from him first, give me a call and I'll do the same."

I nodded and waited for him to get out of the car. My eyes roamed the streets as I headed home with more questions in my head than answers.

What the hell went on in that office? Queen crazy bitch looked quite satisfied with herself when she came out. Or did he give her a reason to be satisfied? No ... don't go there, Bri. Jayce is a better man than that.

After several deep breaths, I wiped my damp hands on my pants. I made it home, parked, and pulled out my cell phone. There was no missed call or text message. The inner stalker in me wanted to throw the car in reverse and cruise past Vivianne's mom's house. An internal tug-o-war began in my head.

What if he's there with her while I sit here like an idiot? What if he's not there ... then what? Am I supposed to contact him first?

Something told me it was too soon to be in a relationship with Jayce. My greatest fear was coming to life. I forced myself out of the car and into the house. After I peeled away my clothes and took a shower, I snuggled under the blanket on my bed. I kept my eyes glued on the phone waiting on him to call, but eventually my eyes dimmed, pitching me into a fitful sleep.

I woke up every hour to check my phone, and all I saw was the brightened screen displaying the time. My fingers nervously scrolled for Keon's phone number.

Brianna: Any word?

My feet bounced to the beat of nervousness. I waited and waited and waited some more. I was still tempted to hop in my car and patrol the streets.

Keon: Nothing yet. I've called the rest of the family and even Vivianne. No sign of him.

My pulse raced as my blood boiled in my veins. What the hell is going on? I bet my left tit that cow is pregnant or something. God help her if she is.

There was no point in closing my eyes again. Panic set in and I broke out into a cold sweat.

I have to do something ... but what?

I grabbed my phone again and immediately started checking with local police departments and hospitals. Nobody had any information for a Jayce Kanoi. My only option at this point was to simply wait.

The oranges and pinks of morning blanketed the sky and I was still fucking waiting. I got dressed for work and drove by Jayce's house, but there was no sign of him.

What do I do now?

I arrived at the shop and unlocked the door. Keon was there already, frowning at his phone.

"What is it?" I asked, edging closer to him.

His eyes darted up from the phone, zeroed in on my face, and then back down at the phone again. "Jayce's mom heard from him early this morning. He didn't say much, just that he'll be back soon with an explanation."

"Huh? Wait … what? That's all he said?" I asked.

He nodded slowly and slipped the phone into his back pocket. "Sorry, Bri, I wish I had more info for you, but that's all I know."

With that little nugget of information not really answering any of my questions, I was completely in zombie mode the rest of the day. I occasionally checked my phone for some form of communication from Jayce.

Who the hell does something like this? He called me his girlfriend and then disappeared like a thief in the night. This is driving me absolutely insane.

As soon as I finished my shift, I made a beeline for my house. After my shower, I lounged around the house and tried to continue on with my night. I fanned my face with my hands as small beads of sweat formed on my forehead and upper lip.

Great ... now I'm sweating all over creation.

When my nerves were extremely rattled I got hot and started sweating. Once it started, it's hard for me to stop. If I didn't hear something soon, I'd be changing clothes four times a day.

My eyes were itchy and dry, and I was pretty sure I wasn't blinking regularly. An infomercial promising me rock hard abs in thirty days played in the background, but I wasn't really paying attention. My phone buzzed around on the table, I grabbed it, and subsequently dropped it.

Damn sweaty palms.

I finally picked it up and glanced at the screen. My hands shook, but I willed them to be still long enough for me to read the message.

Jayce: Can you come over?

I didn't bother texting a response. The message from Jayce was one I'd been waiting for, so I didn't even slip on my shoes. I stubbed my toe on the table as I dashed out of the house, and half ran, half hopped to my car. My tires sounded off loudly as I screeched to halt in front of his house. It took me two attempts to get out of the car, because the first time resulted in me jumping out of the car with the engine still running. My feet carried me across the wet grass toward the front door. I had my fist poised to knock, but the door flew open on its own.

Jayce pulled me inside and wrapped his arms around me, but not before I glimpsed the grim look on his face. I allowed him to swaddle me in his arms anyway. The feeling of him was both comforting and unsettling. This wasn't the time for hugs, this was the time for some damn answers.

"Jayce … what the hell?" I asked, pushing back against his chest.

His arms dropped down to his sides and he reached out to take my hand. I followed him into his bedroom so we could speak privately.

He closed the door and paused for a few moments. His back was to me and I watched anxiously as he took several deep breaths.

Damn, did he murder somebody? This is too much for my train-wrecked nerves to handle.

"Jayce … " I muttered.

"Have a seat, Bri," he said, motioning toward the bed.

To hell with that.

"I'll stand," I said, folding my arms across my chest.

He turned around with his head down, allowing his hair to cover his face. The dark strands I fell in love with were blocking my view, making me wish I had a pair of scissors handy. I needed to see his face, I needed to see the truth in his eyes.

"Bri … listen," he said.

"Is this about Vivianne?" I blurted out, unable to hold in my aggravation any longer.

He nodded, sending his hair in a wave back and forth. "I really think you should sit down," he murmured.

"No," I whispered. "I can't wait any longer, please just tell me what's going on. Did you sleep with her or something?"

Please say no ... please say no.

"No."

Whew! Thank you, Lord.

"Well?" I pressed. My first instinct wanted me to walk over and shake him until he coughed up the information I was looking for. "Is she …"

"Pregnant," he muttered. "She's fucking pregnant."

"What?" The word rolled off my lips in a whisper.

Pregnant? I knew it ... I freaking knew it.

I figured out she was knocked up before he confirmed it, but my brain refused to do the word association game.

"Oh … um … o-okay," I stammered.

Jayce used one hand to sweep his hair out of his face and I noticed the other one was clinched into a tight fist.

"She came to the shop to deliver the news and give me an ultimatum," he said.

My mind scrambled for the right words to use in order to reassure him. "Don't worry, whatever it is, I'm sure we can figure things out," I said, reaching out for him.

"I can't see you anymore," he whispered.

My hand slowly dropped down to my side, and my heart stopped.

"You … can't see me anymore?" I repeated.

It was like an alarm had gone off and all I could hear was a very annoying whistle. The temperature in my body dropped to an arctic level.

"I don't understand," I said, twisting my head to the side.

He closed his eyes and exhaled. "That's part of the ultimatum she delivered. If I want a relationship with my child then I have to at least try to work on the relationship with her, and I can't do that if I'm with you."

The cold was quickly replaced by an inferno of absolute rage. "That's bullshit," I spat.

"Bri … "

"No!" I shouted. "Don't you 'Bri' me. You expect me to believe that load of crap? That's why people get lawyers. You don't have to be with her in order to see your child. If you want to be with that selfish bitch then just say so."

He brought his hands up to either side of his head and paced the floor. "You think I haven't thought of taking the legal route? Bri, by the time everything gets sorted out in court I'll have missed some pretty major events in my child's life. I don't want to bring a person into a broken family … not if there's a chance to salvage it. Believe me when I say I don't want Vivianne, but this isn't about her at this point."

All of my emotions took turns going haywire inside my head. First I was sad, then mad, then relieved, and then sad all over again. Each emotion was coupled with rage.

"I should have never trusted you. You lied to my face and said you wanted to be with me. My mom was practically planning our wedding based on the things you've led us all to believe. I gave myself over to you!" I shouted.

The anger had infiltrated every fiber of my being. Now I was the one pacing the floor, fists clenched. I didn't notice the hot tears rolling down my face. Jayce grabbed me and pulled me in for an embrace. I fought him like a trapped wild cat fighting for its life. He tightened his hold on me and said my name over and over, but none of it truly registered with me. The river of tears turned into sobs, and finally the sobs turned into silence.

"This isn't what I wanted for you … for us," he whispered into my hair. "I meant every word I said to you and your mother. Our relationship wouldn't have existed if I didn't think I could possibly take things to the next level with you."

My breath came out in short ragged bursts. A quiet storm brewed just beneath the surface of my skin.

Happiness has no home here, because something about me is broken. Every time I get a sliver of happiness, something always happens.

"I loved you," I whispered.

"Loved? As in past tense? No, Bri, don't say that. I love you. I love you now and I'll love you no matter what happens."

Wow … this is our first time mentioning the "L" word and it's under horrible circumstances.

He dropped down to his knees and wrapped his arms around my waist. "I'm sorry," he muttered into my stomach over and over.

My arms were raised above him because I couldn't bring myself to touch any part of him. I was on sensory overload and there was only one thing on my mind and that was leaving. I took him by surprise and slipped free from his grasp. I yanked open the door and sprinted out of the house. He was right on my heels, but I think I shocked us both at my level of speed. The tires on my car churned recklessly out of control before they lurched me forward into the darkness of the night.

Chapter Twenty-Seven

This was a bad dream come to life. I was yet again driving blindly with tears in my eyes. My lids fluttered as I tried to blink them away, but as soon as one set was gone, another took their place. This situation was the icing on a shit-flavored cake. I would probably have a different reaction if this was something new to me, but it wasn't. The feeling of being humiliated was a dish I'd sampled on more than one occasion.

I clearly had a streak of bad luck when it came to men. Even my ex-fiancé turned out to be a total disaster. Not only did he leave me without a parting word, but all of the venues we booked came in handy when he got married later on to some other woman. What a way to end an engagement. I had dress fittings, a bridal shower, and Save the Date invitations in the mail.

I should have known better, but I never noticed the red flags until it was too late. The only flag I saw with Jayce was that we got together too soon.

This whole situation could have been avoided if I would have avoided the relationship bullshit, and just had sex with him.

The streets were becoming less and less familiar as I made another left turn. I couldn't go to my usual spots because Jayce could be there waiting for me. My phone was going crazy with calls and text messages. I briefly contemplated tossing it out the window just so I could have a moment of silence. The perfect hideout came to mind.

I'll go to Kirsten's house and pull myself together. She's out of town and no one will think to look for me there.

I jerked the steering wheel with enough force to tip the car onto two wheels. Once I got to the apartment, I let myself in and collapsed onto the bed with my face buried in the pillow.

With any luck I'll suffocate to death.

Instead of suffocating, I cried until my eyes were swollen shut. I woke up hours later with a pounding headache. My eyes were puffy and I couldn't breathe through my nose. I shuffled to the bathroom and nearly peed on myself when I saw my face. My eyes were bloodshot red and I had dark circles around them.

What do I do now?

I couldn't go back to the coffee shop. Not only would I be forced to see Jayce, but I was sure Vivianne would use any and every excuse to come flaunt her baby bump in my face. There were a lot of things I could handle, but that was not one of them. Basically I was back where I started, jobless and single. I was still living at home, so I didn't have to add that one back to the list of tragedies. I checked my phone just to see who all the calls and texts came from. Half were from Jayce and the rest were a nice blend of Keon, Kirsten, and Mom.

I can't believe he dragged my mom into this.

Great. Now I got to see the unwelcomed pity in her eyes as soon as I went home. Everything in my life was upended during one conversation. I kept putting my heart on the line and it always got stepped on. Maybe I should become a heartless bitch like Vivianne. It seemed to work just fine for her. I rolled my eyes and released a deep sigh of frustration.

I guess I'll be the weird lady with a bunch of pets since I can't get my relationships to work out.

Mom would call for a search party if I kept ignoring her, so I sent a short message letting her know I was okay. With that bit of business out of the way, I was finally able to be alone inside my own head. Every time my mind wandered over to Jayce, I felt a tightening in my chest. I wanted to be numb and not feel anything. My socked feet shuffled me to the bathroom, to the couch, and back to the bathroom again. I couldn't cry anymore even if I wanted to. A loud rumble bounced off the walls, drawing my attention to my empty stomach.

When's the last time I ate something?

I had zero concept of time at this point. One … maybe two days had passed. I answered myself with a shrug. I was too drained to drag myself off the couch and find food. My stomach protested loudly with another loud rumble. I closed my eyes and searched my mind for at least one coherent thought. This whole situation had left me feeling so empty. The first few stages of a breakup are always difficult to get through. I knew what I was feeling wouldn't last forever, but my heart was having a hard time understanding that concept. My plan was to close my eyes, go to sleep, and wake up from this nightmare. But every time I closed my eyes the only thing that happened was time continued to pass me by.

My phone was completely dead now and I had no idea who was trying to reach me, and I really didn't care. I grasped the remote control in my hand, turned the volume down, and browsed the stations. A jingling of keys at the door quickly silenced my breathing altogether.

"All right, give me just a second to get dressed," said Kirsten. Her voice was muffled, but I could clearly make her out even through the door.

Light illuminated the room and I was too weak to move, so I did the only thing I could do … I closed my eyes.

"Oh my God, Bri! We've been looking all over town for you. Are you okay? Say something!" she urged.

My lips moved, but I was pretty sure there was no sound coming out.

"We found her … I don't know … She looks spaced out or something … " said Keon. "Okay, I'll text you the address."

I'm not spaced out … I'm … I'm … well I don't know what I am.

"Bri, honey … I'm going to help you get cleaned up," said Kirsten, her hand stroking the side of my face. "Keon can you help me get her into the bedroom?"

His arms found their way underneath me and I was suddenly hoisted into the air.

"Just put her on the bed. I can take it from here."

A brief conversation was exchanged, but I couldn't hear them because they were deliberately speaking in hushed tones. The bedroom door closed and Kirsten made her way into the bathroom. The shower turned on and she reappeared in the doorway.

"What's it gonna be? Are you showering solo or will this be a group effort?" she asked.

"I can do it," I muttered. It took a few tries, but I finally got undressed. I shuffled to the bathroom and allowed Kirsten to help me step into the shower.

The scalding hot water felt good on my skin and I ignored the fact that I was probably getting third degree burns.

"You shouldn't be in here right now," said Kirsten.

"Move ... I just want to see her," growled Jayce.

He pulled back the shower curtain and I froze like a deer caught in headlights.

"Bri," he whispered.

"Get out," I replied coldly.

His eyes dimmed a bit as he searched my face for answers. "W-what?" he stammered.

"Get out!" I yelled.

He swallowed a few times, sending his Adam's apple up and down. His eyes stayed glued to mine as he backed out of the bathroom.

I took my time in the shower, using it as an opportunity to rid my head from the fog of depression. The water eventually turned ice cold and I stepped out into the frigid air.

I thought Kirsten left a towel out for me?

I gave the bathroom a quick once over before I ventured out into her room. The fluffy white bath towel was clutched in Jayce's hands. I stood there dripping wet and cold, waiting on him to give me the towel, but neither of us made an attempt to move toward the other.

Finally my hand opened, palm up, motioning for the towel. Instead of giving it to me, he opened his arms and wrapped it around me.

"You shouldn't be here," I muttered against his chest. The scent of his cologne, the cologne I helped him pick out, was all I could smell. It was a struggle, but I kept the tears at bay. I would never smell Tom Ford again without it dredging up memories of Jayce.

"You scared me," he muttered. "I didn't know what happened to you."

I pushed against his chest, but he had me locked in a bear hug. "I'm fine, now let me go."

His arms slacked and I stumbled backwards away from him. He sat on the edge of the bed and rested his elbows on his legs.

"What happens to me is no longer your problem anyway. You need to focus on pampers," I snapped.

"Bri … tell me what to do. Just tell me how to make things right," he said. His voice was strained and he sounded tired.

"There's nothing you can do," I said. "You've made your decision and I've no choice but to respect it. However, I do choose to keep myself from witnessing any part of it, so I quit. I guess you can bring Vivianne back to handle the accounts."

"No," he said. "You don't have to do that." He reached for me, but I couldn't let him touch me. If I did, I knew the stone wall around me would crumble into a million pieces.

"Yes I do," I said defiantly. "I can't come to that coffee shop and see you each day. I don't want to get too close and accidentally bump into you or say the wrong thing. I'm holding on by a thread right now and it's quickly unraveling. I don't need to put myself in the position to have my will tested. You chose Vivianne, and I refuse to be your woman on the side."

"No one asked you to be my woman on the side. I would never put you in that type of situation. I'm telling you not to quit because I've decided to accept the football offer," he said.

"W-what?" I stuttered. "You're taking it?"

He pressed his lips together into a tight line until they nearly disappeared. "It's the only way to handle the situation. Plus it's part of the ultimatum Vivianne gave."

"When did you become her puppet?"

Jayce recoiled and his face grew dark. "What did you just say to me?"

I placed my hands on my hips and cocked my head to the left. "You heard me. She's calling all the shots and dictating your life and you're allowing it to happen."

He jumped to his feet and stomped toward the door. "You're right. She has my balls in a vice grip right now. I'm trying to do things as painlessly as possible and you're not making this easy. I know this is a fucked up situation for you, but it's no picnic for me either. No matter what happens, Vivianne doesn't control my heart."

He didn't offer a goodbye as he stormed out of the bedroom. The front door slammed closed just as I collapsed to the floor. Kirsten ran into the room and put her arms around my shoulders.

"It's okay, Bri," she whispered.

Keon was right on her heels. "Listen, I love you like a sister and if I could make the situation better I would. But you should give Jayce some slack. This isn't easy for anybody involved. Just let things run its course and the chips will fall where they may. Based on Vivianne's track record, she won't hold up her end of the bargain anyway … trust me," he said.

"I feel like I lost a part of me I didn't know existed until now," I mumbled.

He dropped down to his knees and put his hand on my shoulder. "He feels the same way. We spent the last few days looking for you and trying to find a way out of this shit storm. He's trying … he really is."

I was a melting pot of emotions and I didn't know which one to listen to. One thing was crystal clear … my heart was broken, and I knew it wouldn't be repaired any time soon.

Chapter Twenty-Eight

I decided to go home a few days later, but it was a mistake. Mom and I tiptoed around the issue because neither of us wanted to address my derailed life. I'd been walking on eggshells ever since I stepped foot in the house. My eyes were puffy and I was wearing some of Kirsten's pajamas which were two sizes too small.

My bedroom served as both a sanctuary and a prison. Jayce did text and call, but I avoided him like he had the plague. I simply didn't have anything to say to him right now. I wanted to invite him over so we could have our last goodbye before he headed to training camp, but I couldn't bring myself to call him. What would I say anyway?

I was down to my last few dollars so a trip to the bank was in order. This was my first trip outside the house in days and I decided I wouldn't dress for the occasion. The flyaways milling about my head would stay that way until someone other than me forcibly slicked them down. Today I was wearing a once forgotten sports bra, which was a major step up from my standard no bra policy. I did however opt for toe socks instead of shoes because I wasn't getting out the car.

I'd mentally prepared myself for the anorexic check waiting in my account. This was my last check and I hadn't worked much these last couple of weeks so I already knew what to expect. I jumped in my little dune buggy and turned the key.

Click. Click. Click.

What the hell? This can't be happening.

I sent up a small fervent prayer to Jesus, Allah, Buddha, and whoever else was listening.

"C'mon baby, let's go for a ride. Please crank this time," I whispered. I closed my eyes and turned the key again. This time the faint sound of clicking was gone and complete silence had taken its place.

"Shit!" I screamed, shaking the steering wheel back and forth. I wanted to rip the car apart and yell, "Hulk smash!" but my poor attempt at comedy to lighten the mood would be wasted since nobody was around to witness it.

I could ask to borrow Mom's car, but that would require an actual conversation.

The idea of going inside made my stomach clench in knots. In order for me to ask we'll have to exchange words which would most definitely lead to awkward silences and nervous chuckles.

Mom wasn't exactly the best person to talk to when I was in a funk. She could always find the positive side to any situation and sometimes I just wanted to stew in my feelings for a while, and not turn my frown upside down. She already knew it grated over my nerves, so our conversations end up strained and uncomfortable. I banged my head on the wheel hard enough to make me flinch.

I can add this to the pile of never-ending shit gone wrong in my life.

I dragged myself from the car and back into the house. Mom was sitting in her office hunched over her laptop.

"Mom?"

She was in the zone and had already tuned the world out. She was clearly editing manuscripts for her clients, it was the only time I had to throw something to get her attention. I grabbed one of the stress balls off the small table next to the door and tossed it in her direction.

"H-huh … what? What is it, honey? What's wrong?" she asked.

"Hard at work?" I asked, motioning to the laptop.

She blinked at me several times and then glanced down at the screen. "Yeah, just a little. I'm frustrated over how many times this author uses the word pleasure button. This is an adult novel, just say clit for crying out loud," she mumbled.

Okay ... too much info.

"How are you doing, honey? Do you want to have a seat? I can take a short break if I need to."

"No, you don't have to do that. I just want to borrow your car. Mine is making a weird noise and I need to run to the bank. I shouldn't be gone long," I said.

She gave me a warm motherly smile. A smile that told me she understood my life sucked right now and she'd fix it if she could.

"Sure, honey, you know you don't have to ask, especially while I'm cooped up in here. Be careful and I'll see you in a little while."

"Thanks," I mumbled, shuffling my way toward the door.

"Gram-Gram is coming over for dinner ... if you're up to it," she said gently.

I nodded and nervously cracked my knuckles. "I'm up to it. I'll hurry back so I can help you in the kitchen."

She gazed at me with an unspoken understanding before allowing her eyes to drift over to the laptop.

I snatched the keys off the hook and shot out the door. The bank was right around the corner, I could actually walk there, but I had plans to stop and get a couple of donuts … and maybe a sandwich. I pulled up at the ATM, removed my seatbelt, rolled down the window, and still had to open the door just to reach the card slot. God gave me T-rex arms for some strange reason. Nobody else in my family was cursed with these short arms. In my case, I had short everything, and it made simple tasks like going through the drive-thru difficult. I punched in my pin number and waited for the balance to display.

No point in sending the account into overdraft … at least not yet.

The machine issued the receipt and I had to look at it twice.

What the hell?

I clutched my chest and tried to breathe through the tightening in my lungs. Either the bank or the coffee shop had made a major mistake. With this amount I could simply buy a new car and several other things.

Shit ... I need to go inside, but I can't.

My decision to go shoeless proved problematic. I circled around the building and pulled up to the window.

"Ma'am, I need you to review something for me. I believe my deposit amount is incorrect and I want to make sure the glitch isn't on your end," I said into the loudspeaker.

I provided all of my account information and waited for her to explain the error. Staring at the account printout made my stomach hurt.

"Ms. Davis, I've reviewed your account and the deposit posted at midnight and it is indeed correct on our end. Do you have any more questions?"

"N-no ... um ... I'll take care of it," I stammered.

I put the pedal to the metal and floored it to the coffee shop.

"If my check is this messed up ... there's no telling what's going on with the other accounts," I mumbled under my breath.

The shop was a couple of miles away and I made it there driving on two wheels. I glanced down at my feet and gave a frustrated sigh.

This is too important to worry about dress code.

I hopped out of the car and headed inside with the printout still in my hand. Luckily the shop wasn't that busy. Keon smiled and tossed the towel down onto the counter.

"Hey, Bri!" he said, opening his arms for a hug. He didn't give me a chance to close the space between us before he wrapped his arms around me and nearly cracked one of my ribs. "I'm glad you came out of the house for a change."

"I ... can't ... breathe," I gasped.

His grip loosened and I sucked in a deep gulp of much needed air.

"Where are your shoes?" he asked.

"I didn't wear any because I didn't plan on getting out of my car," I said. "Hey listen, there's something wrong with my check."

Keon folded his arms across his massive chest, leaned against the counter, and crossed his legs at the ankles. "Wrong in what way?"

"Wrong as in a few thousands kind of way," I whispered, thrusting the receipt in his face.

He took the slip of paper and examined. "Nope," he said handing it back to me. "It's right. I took care of your account myself."

"Since when have I ever been paid five grand? Plus I barely worked any this last pay period."

He shrugged his shoulders and picked up his towel. "I guess you need to ask Jayce, I just did what he told me to do."

My head snapped back as he delivered the shocking news. "What?" I hissed.

"Jayce said to put the money in your account whether you came to work or not," he whispered.

"No ... no," I murmured. "I'll have the bank reverse the deposit."

Keon flicked the towel at me. "Chill out with the hysterics, Bri. If you reverse the deposit, I'm just going to bring it to your house. If you refuse to take it ... I'll give it to your mom. Trust me, I've thought about the possible outcomes to this situation."

"He can't do this," I snapped.

"Well he did," he said with a shrug. "Hey, if you don't like it then fine, come back to work and consider it your paycheck plus a small bonus."

I pinched the bridge of my nose and tried to think clearly. "This is wrong," I mumbled.

"Depends on your point of view. I would do the same thing if I were him. Just because he's in this messed up situation doesn't mean his feelings have changed. I wish you would understand that," he huffed.

My mouth flapped open, closed, and then opened again. I had things to say, but the right words weren't forming. "Are the rest of the accounts right?" I asked.

A grin trickled across his face. "Yeah, I had to hire a lady to help out with those. I'd prefer you to come back and give me a hand. It's boring as hell without you."

"Fine," I muttered, turning on my heels toward the door. "I'll be back tomorrow."

"Atta girl, just make sure you wear shoes!" he yelled.

Chapter Twenty-Nine

I caught a whiff of whatever Mom was cooking before I entered the house. Gram-Gram's car was parked haphazardly in the driveway already, so I parked on the street. I struggled to steady my hand long enough to open the front door.

It's just dinner ... just dinner.

I quickly manufactured a smile and stepped inside. "Hey, I'm back."

"Hi, honey, I know you wanted to help, but Gram-Gram showed up a little early so I went ahead and got started," said Mom.

Gram-Gram peered over her glasses and followed my every move. "Hello, Brianna. Where have you been with no shoes on?"

"I had to run an errand and I didn't need to get out of the car. Your hair is pretty today," I said, hoping the compliment would help change the direction of the conversation.

"Mmmhmm, I did something a little different this time. I just hope the curls last until Sunday," she said, smoothing down a nonexistent flyaway.

I found a spot on the couch and tried to appear really interested in something on my phone. Gram-Gram didn't need to know I was just scrolling through my apps over and over.

"So, Brianna, are you excited for football season to get started?" she asked, her tone steady and cool.

Well damn, she held out a lot longer than I thought she would.

"Not really, you know I'm not into sports like that," I replied. My foot started to bob up and down. I know from experience my hands would be the next thing to start doing something weird.

"Oh," she said slowly. "I just figured you would want to watch now since your boyfriend is a ball player."

Thanks, Gram-Gram, for twisting the knife that's already lodged in my heart.

"No, ma'am," I grumbled. "We broke up not too long ago. His ex-girlfriend found out she's pregnant and he wanted to give things with her a fighting chance. So he's now officially hers again."

There! Satisfied now? Maybe I should run off crying just to make her feel bad for bringing it up.

"Humph … he'll be back. I saw it in his eyes. You can't deny love like that for too long. You just make sure you don't shut him out when the time comes. You do that sometimes, you know. When your feelings get hurt, you shut down and shut people out. Now give me the remote control, I think Wheel of Fortune is on," she said.

I picked up the remote, dropped it, and tried again. My mouth was wide open and I tried to find the right words to say.

How many times will I be at a total loss for words today? I wasn't expecting that kind of response, especially from Gram-Gram.

"I … I don't know if I can," I muttered.

"You can, and you will," she said, seeming very sure of herself. "I already prayed about it. Just make sure you're ready for it."

Chapter Thirty

It had taken several weeks for me to undo the damage done by the other account manager. I was dreading today's payroll fiasco, but I sulked my way to the coffee shop anyway and tried to get a jumpstart on fixing it.

My head dropped against the desk for the third time in the past half hour.

It's a good a thing I came back when I did.

"Bri?"

"Yes?" I mumbled against the stack of papers.

"I'm glad you came back. It wasn't the same without you," said Keon, stepping further into the office.

"Thanks," I said, grabbing the sides of my head. I felt a migraine starting to form.

"Don't take what I'm about to say the wrong way … okay?" he said.

My ears burned and I perked up a little as I waited for him to continue.

I'm probably going to take this the wrong way.

"Your clothes don't fit anymore, are you eating?" he asked gently.

I hadn't really paid attention to my clothes lately, but I did recall needing to readjust my clothes more often.

"Oh … um, not really. I mean I eat, but I guess I'm not as focused on it as before," I mumbled.

"Oh, okay," he replied skeptically. His mouth twisted to the side as he gave a slow nod in my direction.

"Do I look bad or something?"

"Well, to be honest, I don't know. Your clothes are too big for me to really see what you look like. I'm only saying something because you filled out your clothes a couple of weeks ago and I haven't seen you eat anything while you're at work," he said.

Damn, why are you watching me like that?

"I'm fine, I promise. I need to finish payroll, so if you want to get paid, I suggest you scoot on up front," I said, flashing a wide phony grin.

He narrowed his eyes and nodded again, but at least he retreated from the office. As soon as he rounded the corner, I dropped the act and banged my head on the desk again. My phone vibrated against my thigh, I retrieved it, pushed the button, and answered.

"Hey, Kirsten," I muttered.

"Bri!" she shrieked. "I need to go out tonight."

"Aren't you supposed to be with Keon later?" I asked.

She practically growled at me through the phone causing me to sit up a little. "We're together all of the time and I just need a break. I go to work, come home, and I'm with Keon. When I'm out of town, I get off work, go to my hotel, and I talk to Keon. My entire life at this point revolves around Keon and I need to have a day for myself before I snap."

"Oh ... wow. Well you know I'm not doing anything later. What do you want to do?"

"I wanna dance with somebody!" she sang.

I snorted a laugh. "All right, sounds good."

"Great! I'll be at your house when you get home," she said before hanging up.

It usually took more time to convince me to go anywhere, but I had the dancing bug tonight too. I was determined to have fun even if it killed me.

Kirsten proved just how serious she was about needing a break by showing up at my house two hours before I actually made it there.

I walked inside and paused right outside Mom's office.

"You're right, pleasure pole does sound out of place," said Kirsten.

"Exactly, people don't say stuff like that in real life," Mom replied.

"I'm home!" I announced before bursting into the office.

"Hi, honey," said Mom.

Kirsten looked me up and down and then glanced over at my Mom.

"What?" I asked.

"Nothing," she said quickly. "We need to add shopping to our list of things to do this weekend."

I frowned and looked down at myself.

What's the big deal? I've dropped a little weight, but we all know if I eat a donut it'll come right back again.

"Keon isn't going to let you get away for two days straight," I teased. "I'm sure you have some canoodling to do with him."

"Let's go upstairs and I'll update you," she said. "Talk to you later, Mama Ev."

"All right," said Mom before focusing back on her computer screen.

Kirsten beat me to the stairs and I noticed she was not dressed in her usual super glam style. In fact, the last few times I'd seen her she was dressed in a very reserved fashion.

She entered my room and fell face first onto the bed. "We're alone now, go ahead and spill it," I said, closing the door behind me.

She rolled over and made a face. "He doesn't know I'm home," she muttered.

"Um … what?" I asked, not believing what I just heard. "The two of you have been peas in a pod since day one. What happened?"

"He basically hates everything about me. Don't get me wrong, he's an amazing boyfriend, and excellent in bed, but he is sucking the life out of me. He didn't like the sexy clothes or makeup so I toned it down … toned it down a lot. I'm used to going out and partying, but he prefers for it to be the two of us at all times. He's smothering me to death," she huffed. "And on top of all that, he has some serious mental issues."

"Mental issues? Keon?" I asked in disbelief. "What kind of issues?"

"Please don't say anything. He's very private about that part of his life," she said, sitting straight up on the bed. "He has nightmares, really bad nightmares. He goes to counseling for post-traumatic stress disorder. This is something I'm not used to dealing with and it's hard for both of us," she whispered.

"Aww," I murmured. "That's so sad."

"I just … I just need a break from it all," she said. "We'll get through it eventually. Speaking of getting through things, how's the Jayce situation?

I shrugged my shoulders to give the illusion of a carefree attitude. "There's really no situation to speak of. I haven't talked to him since the night we broke up. He calls and texts regularly, but I don't respond. I need more time. He's still depositing money into my account though," I said.

Kirsten nodded slowly and cut her eyes at me. "Explains why you look like a hobo."

"What? No I don't," I said defensively.

"Yes … you do," she said, jumping to her feet. She grabbed a fistful of my clothes and pulled them snugly against my body. "Your clothes are huge and your body is a lot smaller. I'm positive you'll be able to fit some of my stuff now."

"I seriously doubt that," I scoffed.

She reached for her overnight bag and started flinging clothes on the bed. "Well there's only one way to find out."

We took turns in the shower and then the real magic started. Kirsten glammed up her own face first and then mine.

"Honey, our faces are beat!" she said, snapping her fingers.

"What the hell does that mean?" I laughed.

"It's a slang term. It basically means our makeup is fierce. Don't question the logic, just roll with it, girl," she said. "Now let's take a look at this body."

I stood there and allowed her to poke and pull me into her clothes. They were extremely fitted, but I managed to get in them. I turned around slowly in the mirror and I was floored by what I saw. The kangaroo pouch was nearly gone and my hips weren't as wide as before.

"Wow," I mumbled.

"Wow is right," said Kirsten, joining me in front of the mirror. "Now let's go have some fun."

She quickly put on the shortest dress in existence and posed for several pictures. "I feel like myself again" she sighed.

We grabbed our purses and headed out the door. After thirty minutes of driving, I started to get concerned. "Where are we going?" I asked.

"Sorry, Bri, I don't want to risk running into Keon so we're going to party in the next town over," she explained.

The moment was oddly reminiscent of our high school days when we would sneak out of the house. Kirsten tried to convince me we wouldn't get caught if we went to the next town then too. Oddly enough, we did get caught, we wrecked the car on the way back, and that was the end of our little outings.

"What are you going to do if he finds out?" I asked.

I for one don't intend to be in the middle of your bullshit.

"Nothing," she said with a shrug. "The only thing I can do it fess up and hope he'll be understanding."

She swerved the car into a crowded parking lot and stopped in front of the valet booth. "Are you ready to have some fun?" she asked with a familiar spark in her eyes.

"Ready when you are."

We stepped out of the car together and made our way to join the hoard of other people waiting to get in. Fortunately for us, it was not long before one of the bouncers tapped Kirsten on the shoulder and escorted us to the front of the line. The huge mammoth of a man moved the velvet rope and ushered us inside. Kirsten leaned over and smiled at him while I surveyed the club. Without the multicolored strobe lights it would be pitch black inside the large open space. I could see three different levels hosting half-drunk, sweaty people grinding on one another. And there were several platforms with nearly naked go-go dancers putting on an amazing show.

One part of me wanted to get drunk and join them, and the other part wanted to find somewhere to sit so I could people watch and guard the purses. As I struggled to decide which voice to listen to, Kirsten suddenly appeared by my side.

She mouthed something to me, but the steady bump of the music drowned her out. I leaned in closer in an attempt to hear her better, but she grabbed my arm and dragged me to the dance floor. The crowd closed in on us and I was pitched into a wave of movement. Kirsten released my hand and started to get lost in the music. I nodded my head to the beat and searched for a way off the dance floor. I needed a little liquid courage in my system if I was going to break my wallflower habit. A man the size of a redwood blocked my escape. My eyes traveled the length of his body all the way up to his smile. His skin was dark, several shades darker than mine, and it looked great against the bright yellow polo shirt he was wearing.

I gave a tight, polite smile and ducked to the left to get around him. He blocked me again and his smile doubled in size. I narrowed my eyes and tried to move to the right, and he did the whole block and smile thing again. He playfully slapped my thigh and started to dance. The wild gyrating of his hips was funny and sad at the same time, and I couldn't contain the laughter any longer. My laughing encouraged him to continue his rendition of so-called dancing. I wasn't sure which one of us looked the silliest, him for the flamingo-on-fire dance he was doing, or me for standing there allowing this travesty to continue. He slowed down a little and reached for my hand. I thought he wanted to dance, but he led me over to the bar instead.

He pulled out the barstool and motioned for me to sit down. All the other seats were taken so he stood next to me.

"Did you like my dancing?" he asked.

"Yes," I said, clapping my hands. "That was unreal. You're clearly a professional."

He gave a small bow and laughed. "Thank you so much, I trained with the best of them. My name is Darren and you are?"

"I'm Bri," I replied. I waved the bartender over, placed my order, and waited on Darren to do the same.

"So, Bri, are you having a good time?" he asked, leaning in close.

I nodded and took a welcomed sip from my drink.

"I know you are, and it got even better when you met me, right?" he asked, nudging me in my side with his elbow.

I had to admit, his smile and playful demeanor was contagious. "Right, the little show you put on for me was the icing on the cake."

"I had to showcase my moves. Ladies go wild when I dance," he said, spinning around. "I think you should give me your number. The fun doesn't have to end here."

"Oh really?"

"Yes, ma'am," he said. "I would love to see more of you. Will you give me that chance? Please? I'm not above begging."

My lips turned up at the corners as I considered his request.

"Wait," he said, drawing his face into a frown. "Are you married, pregnant, or really a man?"

"I look like a man?" I asked defensively.

"No … no, I'm not saying that. I'm only asking because I've encountered some interesting people here."

"No to all of those questions," I replied.

"Good," he said with a sigh. "So how about that number?"

"I just got out of a relationship," I said, trying to let him down easy.

"What's your point? I'm new in town and I'm just looking to get to know some people that's all. C'mon … live a little. Plus, any man stupid enough to let you go doesn't deserve you anyway."

"It's complicated," I said.

"Doesn't matter in the least little bit," he said smugly. He retrieved his cell phone and thrust it over to me.

Giving him my number won't hurt anything. Besides, I need to move on … right?

I punched in my info and hit save. The satisfied smirk on his face told it all.

"See, don't you feel good about that? You made the right decision, kid," he said.

I rolled my eyes and focused my attention back on the dance floor.

Where's Kirsten? She has completely disappeared into the crowd.

"Are you ready to get out there? If it'll make you feel better, I can bring my skills down a little so I don't show you up," he joked, reaching for my hand.

I happily grasped his open palm and followed him out into the crowd. This moment wouldn't last forever, but I was determined to enjoy it for what it is. As sweat poured down into my eyes, I kept right on dancing even though my feet begged me to stop. This was the most fun I'd had in a very long time and I didn't want the night to end.

Chapter Thirty-One

I spent the next couple of days trying to recover from my night out on the town. The blisters on my feet were a testament to the good time I had, and my pronounced limp didn't go unnoticed.

"Do you need to go to the hospital or something?" asked Keon.

"No, I'm fine," I muttered. My shoes were kicked off under the desk and I was slowly massaging the aches and pains.

Damn, Jayce is way better at doing this than I am.

"I probably shouldn't bring this up because I don't want to put you in the middle, but I'm having some issues with Kirsten," said Keon. He rubbed his hand over his cropped hair and leaned against the side of my desk.

Shit. Confess nothing, and deny everything.

"Issues? Are these good issues or bad issues?" I asked nervously.

"I'm not really sure," he said with a shrug. "She's not answering my phone calls as often as before and it takes her forever to text back. She used to come home all of the time and now I barely get the chance to see her."

"All couples need time apart," I said.

His head whipped around toward me and his eyes flashed with the same hint of anger I'd witnessed with Jayce. "Time apart? She doesn't want to be with me anymore? Did she say something to you?"

"Whoa there, cowboy, calm down," I said, putting my hands up. "No, she didn't say anything about breaking up with you. I'm speaking in general, that's all. You know Kirsten is a free spirit."

"Free spirit?" The vein in his neck throbbed angrily as his face turned several shades of red.

Crap, I'm saying all of the wrong things.

"I know what that sounded like and that's not what I meant," I said. My tongue got heavy and my palms slicked with sweat.

"Don't get upset … er … um … well don't get even more upset. All I'm saying is, in general, some people feel smothered when they're together all the time. This is something new for Kirsten. She's used to being alone, doing her own thing," I said.

Keon breathed heavily and his nostrils flared.

He looks ready to punch something.

"Did you feel that way about Jayce?"

"W-what?" I stammered.

"Did. You. Feel. That. Way. About. Jayce?" he asked. The stilted rhythm in his voice grinded against my nerves. I tried to inconspicuously scoot over a little, just in case he decided to go postal.

"No, but Kirsten and I are two different people. You can't compare us like that. Don't blow this out of proportion. Maybe you need to sit down with her and just talk," I suggested. I placed my hand on his forearm in a show of support.

His eyes travelled down from my face to my hand. The look in his eyes forewarned me that I'd lose it if I didn't get it off him. I snatched it away and clasped my hands together in my lap.

Message received loud and clear. Roger that.

"Sorry," I mumbled.

He blinked a few times and dropped his head. "No, I'm the one that needs to apologize. It's just … my head is a mess right now. Don't hold this against me, please," he said. He wrapped his arms around me and I couldn't stop my body from tensing up at his touch. In fact, I stopped breathing all together, and simply waited to see what he'd do next.

"You're right, I need to sit down and talk to her," he mumbled.

This hug is getting increasingly awkward.

A few painstaking minutes later, he finally dropped his arms. "I'm planning a party for Jayce's first game. I'd really like for you to come."

"I guess I can come … if I'm not busy," I said.

My stomach cramped and I felt a sense of restlessness.

"Great," he said cheerfully. "I'm going to get everything planned out."

He moved toward the door and smiled. "Thanks, Bri … for listening."

My lips thinned into a tight line and I nodded. "Anytime."

I waited until he disappeared around the corner before I released the air in my lungs. Keon was scary as hell when he's mad and that's not a side of him I wanted to see ever again. I watched the door for a few minutes just to see if he would come back.

I'm going to tell Kirsten to talk to him and get her shit straight.

My phone vibrated against the desk and I rushed to answer it.

"Hello?"

"Hey, pretty lady, how's your day going so far?" asked Darren.

I smiled at the sound of his voice and leaned back in my chair. "It's great. How about you?"

"I'm better now because I'm talking to you. So I'm ready to pop the big question, are you ready to answer yes?" he asked.

"I don't think I want to say yes," I laughed.

"Of course you do," he said. "No other response will work. Bri, I enjoyed the hours we spent together, and the sporadic text messages and phone calls we've shared, and in my heart I'm ready for you to be my … lunch date."

My sides ached as I leaned over the desk laughing. His quirky, carefree demeanor was what I liked about him the most.

"Really?" I asked between chuckles. "That's the big question you needed to ask me? I hope you're down on one knee."

"Of course I am. That's the proper way to propose a lunch date, right? So go on and make my day by saying yes."

"You're so dramatic," I teased.

"Is that a yes? My knee is hurting," he said.

"Yes, Darren, we can have lunch."

"You've made me the happiest man alive. I can't wait to take you out. I'm letting you know upfront you can only order off the kids menu, I'm on a budget," he said.

"You're so silly. Bye, Darren, I have work to do," I replied.

"All right, all right, get back to your work. I'll text you later and we can hash out the details of our date. Bye, beautiful."

"Bye."

I placed the phone back on the desk and grinned. My phone vibrated again and I answered it without looking.

"Darren, I told you I have work to do," I laughed.

"Darren? Who's Darren?"

My heart sank to the bottom of my stomach and it rumbled anxiously to bring it back up again.

Fuck me sideways to Sunday.

"Jayce," I croaked.

"Bri, who the hell is Darren?" he demanded.

"You do not get to take that tone with me," I snapped. "Darren is just my friend so don't go there. It's not like I had unprotected sex with him and got pregnant … like some people."

My heart beat loudly enough to drive me insane. I counted to ten in an attempt to bring it down to a normal rate.

The silence was unnerving too. I could hear subtle breathing on the other end of the phone.

"How are you?" asked Jayce, his voice strained and rugged.

"I'm good … everything is just … good," I replied.

I filled the awkward silence that followed with a steady tapping of my fingers against the desk.

"How are things with you?" I asked, forcing myself to return some semblance of polite banter.

"They're okay. My first game is coming up, so I'm a little nervous about it," he mumbled.

You could cut the tension in the air with knife and it was starting to get to me.

"He's not my boyfriend," I whispered. "I don't owe you an explanation or anything, but … I thought you should know."

"Thank you, Bri, and you're right, you don't owe me anything. I appreciate your honesty though. We don't have to talk about that anymore, okay?"

I flexed my feet and tried to think of something else to say in order to keep the conversation going. Even though I accidently answered the phone, I found it increasingly difficult to end the call.

"How's the baby? Do you know what it is yet?" I asked.

He sighed, but it sounded more like a growl. "No. Vivianne's being really weird about the whole thing. She doesn't even tell me about doctor's appointments until after the fact. Actually, she refuses to discuss baby names or anything. In fact, I call bullshit on this whole thing. Too many things aren't adding up."

"Wow, so you think she's faking it? I wouldn't put it past her but until you know for sure just give her the benefit of the doubt. Maybe she just needs time to adjust," I suggested.

"Oh, she's adjusting just fine. She's adjusted to spending every dime I make on designer clothes and shoes. And she's managed to alienate herself from all of the wives and girlfriends of my teammates by being an absolute nightmare. I'm locked in a prison and she has the key. You don't know how happy I am to actually hear your voice," he said.

"Thanks … I actually feel the same way," I said in a rush. "Keon is planning a party for your first game."

I hoped he would take the hint and change the subject. The last thing I wanted to do was get ensnared in a conversation about our feelings.

"Yeah, he told me about it. I hope you're able to make it," he said. "My break is over, I need to get back to practice. I hope I'm able to talk to you again sooner rather than later."

"Okay, I'm sure that won't be problem," I lied.

"Bri?"

"Hmmm?"

"I still love you."

I wanted to respond, but he ended the call before I had the chance.

Way to twist the knife in my chest. I don't need you to love me ... I need you to let me go so I can do the same.

Chapter Thirty-Two

I finally had lunch with Darren and it turned out to be an everyday event. Being with him helped take away some of the loneliness. The one thing I admired about him the most was his sense of humor. I found it impossible to be around him and not smile.

"So, Bri, tell me about this guy that's keeping me from getting to know you better?"

He propped his head up on hands and waited. I wasn't prepared to really answer that question and nearly choked on the food in my mouth

"W-what? We are getting to know each other," I coughed.

"No," he said slowly. "I'm in the friend zone. Don't get me wrong, you're an excellent friend to have, I'm just curious to know if I have a real shot or not."

"I'm sorry," I muttered.

He waved his hand and dismissed my apology. "Don't be sorry, and don't feel pressured to go to the next level with me. We're just making conversation. So go on, tell me all about him."

I took a deep breath and started at the beginning with my weight and unemployment issues all the way to the present day. Darren even made me whip out my phone to show him proof of my waist size.

"Humph," he said. "That is some serious drama right there. Don't take this the wrong way … but I don't think you should be mad at the guy."

"What?" I asked in disbelief.

Everybody's on Jayce's side, even the guy who doesn't even know him.

Darren smiled and shrugged his shoulders. "If I were in his shoes, I'd do the same thing. I'd rather work on things with my child's mother if possible rather than go through a nasty custody battle. Based on what you've described I don't think his child's mother is the cooperating type of woman. He's just trying to keep the peace."

"But where does that leave me? Out in the cold, tossed to the side," I snapped.

"Give him some time, you never know how things will turn out. I still want to hang out with you though. Things will happen when they're supposed to."

I reached for my phone to check the time and noticed several missed calls from both Keon and Kirsten.

"Excuse me just a second, my friends have been calling me back-to-back and I need to see if anything is wrong."

"Do you need some privacy?" he asked.

"No, this shouldn't take long."

I dialed Kirsten's number and waited. "Hey, Kirsten, what's going on? You and Keon are blowing my phone up like something's wrong."

"Something is wrong! Where are you, did you forget about the party today?" she snapped.

"Crappp," I moaned. "It totally slipped my mind."

"Bri, get here now! Keon is about to blow a fuse and Jayce keeps texting too, and he's not even supposed to have his phone right now."

"Kirsten, I can't come right now, I'm with Darren," I hissed.

"What's wrong?" he whispered.

I tapped the mute icon on the phone while Kirsten started ranting about my absence. "I'm supposed to be at my friend's house. My ex, the guy I was just telling you about, is playing his first game and we're supposed to be watching."

Darren's eye lit up. "Seriously? Aww man, do you think they'll mind if I tag along? I was just sitting here trying to think of a way to convince you to watch the game with me. I love football."

"Really, Darren? You wanted to blow me off to watch football?" I laughed.

"Blow you off? No, my plan was to invite you to watch, and then ignore you while I shout at the TV."

I rolled my eyes and hit the unmute button. Kirsten was fire-red mad and shouting into the phone.

"Hello!" she shrieked.

"I'm here. Calm down, I'm on my way. Ask Keon if he minds Darren coming over to watch the game too."

"Sure, fine … whatever. Hurry up please!"

She ended the call and I rolled my eyes at the phone. "I don't know if I mentioned this before, but my best friend is dating my ex's cousin. He's the one throwing the party," I said.

"That's cool. I hope there's some chicken wings and beer, I can't watch football without those," he said. "Well let's go, it's almost game time."

He seriously just goes with the flow.

Darren parked in front of the house and I struggled to get out of the car. This was the first time I'd been inside since Jayce left. I felt jittery and nauseated all at the same time.

Why am I so nervous? He's not even in there. Calm down, Bri ... just calm down.

"You okay?" asked Darren.

"I'm fine," I said, trying to swallow the lump in my throat.

I eased out of the car and knocked on the front door. A shirtless Keon, with a towel around his shoulders, snatched it open and wrapped his arms around me tightly. I was positive I'd end up with bruised ribs from his hugs.

"Why the hell are you knocking on the door? You know you can come right in," he said.

I could tell the instant he noticed Darren because his whole body tensed as he put me back down on the ground.

"Hi, I'm Darren, Bri's friend," he said, extending his hand out.

The moment was tense and awkward as we all stared at Darren's hand. I wanted to shake his hand my damn self just so he could put it down.

"A man is extending his hand to you," he said, his voice rumbled through my body making me feel even less at ease.

A look of surprise glossed over Keon's face and I prepared myself to duck so I didn't end up in the middle of their brawl.

Instead of exchanging punches, Keon gave a lazy grin and actually shook Darren's hand.

"What the hell?" I whispered.

"It's a military thing. Come in and get settled," said Keon.

It's a military thing? Did I miss something?

I stepped past him and looked back with my brow furrowed. Kirsten looked equally confused as she placed the platter of chicken wings on the table.

"You brought him here?" she whispered.

"Kirsten, I told you to make sure it was cool with Keon, remember?"

Her lips twisted as she crinkled her nose. "Hell no I don't remember, because I've been dodging hot grease all day. I had to fry this chicken all by myself."

"Aww, friend," I said, leaning on her shoulder. "I'm sorry, but seriously I forgot all about the game today."

"Mmmhmm. I'm just happy Keon didn't punch the guy in the face or something. They seem to be hitting it off somehow," she said, nodding in their direction.

It was odd seeing them engaged in deep friendly conversation. I felt like I was observing new animals at the zoo. One second Keon was ready to spit on the man's hand and the next second they were hamming it up like new best friends.

I poured myself a drink and got comfortable on the couch. Darren walked over with a beer and a plate of food perched on top of it.

"We just ate," I said, shocked at the amount of food he's scarfing down.

He devoured two wings, licked his fingers, and smiled. "I told you I need chicken wings and a cold beer before I'm able to effectively watch the game."

Keon plopped down with a similar setup in his hands. Both guys elected to sit in the recliners in the living room and not the couch. Kirsten and I exchanged frowns as they smacked their food and slurped their beers.

"What number is Jayce?" I asked.

"Number ninety-six, defensive tackle," said Keon.

"Oh," I said.

Kirsten cut her eyes over to me and shrugged.

Yeah, I don't know what any of it means either. I guess we'll cheer when the guys cheer. All of the players look the same to me.

I couldn't even begin to put the pieces of football together. One dude had the ball, another one threw it, and then everybody tried to knock the other person down. By the time Jayce took the field, I was a little tipsy and ready for a nap. But the cheers and yelling from the guys snapped me out of my downward spiral into sleepy land.

"W-what happened?" I asked.

"It's Jayce, he's about to do whatever it is that he does," whispered Kirsten.

We quickly learned early on in the game to whisper any questions or comments, or wait until a commercial break. Apparently, men can't focus on sports and answer questions at the same time.

I perked up a little and tried to focus on the TV. It was weird seeing Jayce again and not being able to touch him. It sucked I couldn't be there to hug him after the game and help him unwind. My eyes stay glued to his jersey as they ran play after play. For somebody who didn't want to play professional football he was really good at what he did. Seeing him run and block was actually turning me on. I should have been paying closer attention to the game overall but I'd only managed to zero in on his lower body. The tight material of his pants made his ass look great, and the thought of what I knew he was sporting in the front was enough to make me squirm in my seat.

He was running again and those strong powerful legs moved lightning fast. Suddenly those same legs were knocked out from under him, and a pile of men the size of commercial buses were on top of him. The play was over and the men slowly got up one by one. Jayce was on the bottom of the pile, and we all waited for him to get up. We waited … and then we waited some more.

My chest tightened and I jumped up off the couch. "He's not moving, why isn't he moving!" I shouted, looking around the living room.

I searched the faces in the room for answers, but no one answered. Kirsten's hand covered her mouth as she blinked away tears, and people from the sidelines rushed onto the field.

No ... no ... no, this can't be happening. People get hit in football all the time. That's the whole basis for the fucking game. Jayce is going to get up.

They cut to a commercial just as the medics made it to him.

"Oh my God," I muttered over and over.

"Bri," said Keon slowly. "Calm down, injuries happen in football. This isn't unusual, okay?"

"He wasn't moving, Keon!" I shouted.

"We have to wait, Bri. If there was somebody to call right now I would. We have to let the medical personnel do their jobs. Jayce is in good hands, just be patient," he replied.

My legs refused to support my weight any longer and I collapsed onto the couch.

What if he's paralyzed or has some type of brain injury? What if he has internal bleeding and the doctors don't find it in time?

My foot tapped against the floor and my stomach cramped in knots. Just sitting there doing nothing was killing me.

My breath froze in my lungs mid-exhale as the screen cut back to the game. The players were back in formation minus Jayce. The announcers quickly glossed over his injury and went back to detailing the game plays.

I needed to know how he was doing. I was desperate and the only solution I saw in sight was to call Vivianne. "Keon, do you mind calling Vivianne? She probably won't tell me anything if I called."

"I can try," he muttered. "She'll likely ignore me too."

He dialed her number and waited. After a few tries back-to-back with no answer, he decided to send a text message.

"We'll have to wait for her to respond," he said. His voice was low and teemed with doubt just like my inner thoughts.

Please don't let that spiteful bitch be heartless enough to ignore Jayce's family calling to check on him.

The game continued and we stared at the TV quietly. I wasn't sure about everybody else in the room, but I was hoping and praying they gave some kind of update on his condition. But everything ended without them giving us a kernel of information.

"Maybe we should call the hospital?" suggested Kirsten.

Darren leaned over with his elbows planted on his thighs. "They won't give you any info on how he's doing. Bri, I need to leave so I can get ready for work, but I don't want to leave you like this."

"I'm o-okay," I stammered. "You need to go to work."

"It's cool, man, we'll take care of her. Grab a plate to take with you and give me your number too," said Keon.

Darren reached over and gave my knee a gentle squeeze before following Keon to the kitchen.

"He's going to be fine," whispered Kirsten.

I wanted to believe her, but I wasn't so sure of anything anymore.

Chapter Thirty-Three

I ended up falling asleep on the couch with Keon and Kirsten around me. We still didn't have an update and Vivianne hadn't offered any type of response either.

"Can one of you take me to the airport?" I asked.

Kirsten raised up a little from her spot on the couch. "The airport? For what?"

"I have to go check on him. Waiting is no longer an option for me," I said, putting on my shoes. "I'm going to find out what I need to know."

"Let's wait a couple of hours. I've been talking to my aunt and she should have an update on Jayce real soon. If we don't hear anything by then I'll take you to the airport myself," said Keon.

I wiped away the stray tears that started to fall. Unlike before, these weren't sad tears, but angry ones. I was pissed off to the highest level possible.

"That miserable bitch could send a text and tell us something. Pregnant or not, I want to punch her in the face," I fumed.

"I know exactly how you feel," muttered Keon.

Over the next two hours we struggled to remain busy until I simply couldn't take it anymore.

"All right," I said, shouldering my purse. "I'm leaving one way or the other."

Keon jumped up, slipped on his shoes, and grabbed his keys. "I'm a man of my word, so let's go."

"Wait," said Kirsten, scrambling toward the door. "Are you seriously going to the airport? Bri, you can't just show up where the man is and expect to get answers. His psycho baby mama is there and I refuse to let you go to jail for hitting a pregnant woman."

"So does that mean you're coming too?" I asked.

"Damn straight I'm coming too. I can't let you go to jail by yourself," she laughed.

"You two are absolutely crazy," said Keon. "But I guess it's only right if we make this duo a trio. Nobody plans to pack any bags?"

"Nope," we answered in unison.

We arrived at the airport and it suddenly dawned on me, we didn't exactly know which hospital to go to.

"Guys, I know we probably should have hashed out the details before we bought our tickets, but how are we going to actually find Jayce?"

"We'll cross that bridge when we get to it," said Keon. "Hopefully my aunt responds to me before we land."

I settled back into my seat and waited for the plane to get into the sky. Just as the seatbelt light popped on, Keon grabbed his phone.

"Hey!" he yelled. "Jayce just text me."

I snatched the phone out of his hand and read the message.

Jayce: I'm all good. A little banged up.

My fingers started moving faster than my mind could process what to type.

"Ma'am, I need you to put your cell phone away," said the flight attendant.

Naturally, I ignored her until my own phone started buzzing. I answered and brought my trembling hand up to my ear.

"Jayce," I sighed.

"Hey, babe," he said. His voice was strained and he sounded like he was in pain.

"Ma'am, we can't take off until you turn off your phone," snapped the flight attendant. We proceeded to have a staring contest as I continued my conversation.

"Take off?" he asked. "Take off where?"

"I'm on a plane with Keon and Kirsten. We're coming to see you so I need to get off the phone. I'll call you just as soon as I can," I said.

"Okay, babe," he croaked. "Hey, Bri?"

"Hmm?" I said, glaring at the attendant. Her arms were folded tightly across her chest and I could almost see flames shooting out of her nose.

"I love you," he whispered.

"I love you too, Jayce, bye."

I ended the call and tucked my phone away into my purse. "Sorry," I muttered.

The flight attendant narrowed her eyes and shook her head as she stalked up the aisle to the front of the plane.

"At least we know he's okay," said Keon.

"Yeah," whispered Kirsten. "I'm glad you talked to him."

"Me too," I said. Even though I was relieved to hear his voice and know he was okay, this situation was like ripping a Band-Aid off a fresh wound. But this time … I'd rather bleed than take a chance on not having Jayce in my life.

I ran off the plane as soon as the door opened. I was focused on one thing and one thing only and that was getting to Jayce. I whipped out my phone and hit his number just as soon as I had enough bars to complete the call.

"Hey, babe," he moaned.

"Hi, hun, where are you? We're about to hop in a cab and come to wherever you are."

"I'm back in my hotel room right now. Room 208 at the Intercontinental Towers on Lincoln Avenue."

"Got it, we're on our way," I said.

"Okay, I'll call down and let the front desk know to let you in. I don't think I'll be able to make it to the door," he said.

"Do you need us to bring you anything?" I asked.

"Nope, you're the only thing I want right now."

"All right," I said. "I'm on my way."

I ended the call and walked with my friends to the lower level of the airport to flag down a cab. We jumped in the first one we saw and gave the driver the address. The cab smelled like cigarettes and my hand touched something sticky on the seat.

Please let that be candy or something not related to a body fluid of some kind.

The driver maneuvered the streets like a madman and we had several close calls with the back end of other cars. He slammed on the brakes in front of the hotel, and I wanted to kiss the pavement when I got out of the cab.

I headed for the front desk and plopped my purse down on the counter. "I'm Brianna Davis and—"

"Yes, ma'am," said the attendant. "Mr. Kanoi said we were to expect you and two other guests. Here's the room key and I trust you'll let us know if you need anything during your stay."

I nodded and clutched the key card to my chest. *Jayce is here, and I'm about to see him.*

"This might be a bad time to bring this up, but did you at least ask Jayce where Vivianne is?" asked Kirsten.

"No," I said as I reached out to press the button for the elevator. "I guess we're about to find out firsthand where she is."

I shifted my weight from one foot to the other as we waited for the elevator. *Damn, maybe we should have taken the stairs.*

I pressed myself inside the elevator before the doors fully opened. Beads of sweat formed on my upper lip as it shot up one floor. They opened and I made a beeline for room 208. My knuckles were poised to give a few taps on the door and I realized I didn't need to. I slid the key into the slot and waited for the little red light to turn green. The automatic click of the door unlocking made my heart skip two beats.

"Jayce," I called out nervously.

"Hey, beautiful, I'm in here," he said.

I braced myself and pushed the door open. My mind scrambled to mentally prepare itself to see him. I cleared the foyer area and rounded the corner to face a king-sized bed. Jayce was perched on the edge of the bed, bandaged and bruised. His smile widened and he opened his arms.

Part of me wanted to tackle him and never let go, and the other half stood frozen in place. A firm nudge from behind me helped move things along. I stepped forward and eased down next to him. Our hug was brief, but to simply feel his skin against mine made this trip out here totally worth it.

"Hey, guys, c'mon in and have a seat. Where are your bags?" he asked.

"Well, somebody was in such a hurry to get to you, we didn't pack any bags," said Keon. He wiggled his eyebrows at me and plopped down in a chair by the window. Kirsten followed him over to the seat and made herself comfortable in his lap.

"Wow," he murmured. "I feel so loved right now." He wrapped his arm around my hips and I leaned in against his shoulder.

God, he still smells the same.

"All right," said Keon. "I guess I'll be the first to bring up Queen of the Crazy People. Where is she and how long do we have before she comes back?"

My skin pimpled at the reminder of her existence.

"Where is she? Hell, I don't know. And if I had to guess, she'll never come back," replied Jayce.

"Say what?" said Kirsten. "You get hurt and she skipped out on you when you needed her the most?"

"No," he said. "It's a lot more complicated than that. Let me get comfortable first, and then I'll explain."

He slid off the bed and clutched his side as he hobbled toward the headboard. I jumped up to beat him there and pulled the sheets back.

"Thanks, babe," he said. He winced as he settled down into the bed and I pulled the comforter up high on his chest. He reached out and patted the spot next to him. I eagerly obliged and nestled myself next to him, trying to keep from leaning against him too much.

"Well," he groaned. I could tell just moving around from one end of the bed to the other took a lot out of him. He needed to take a pain pill or something and simply relax.

"I really tried to be there for her, but in the end it just didn't work out. The whole baby drama really weighed on my mind. I talked to some of the guys on the team just to get a clear picture of the pros and cons of what it means to be a ball player. They have this love, dedication, and passion for the sport that I simply don't have. But no matter how much love they have for football the one thing they all agreed on is they wished they had more time with their families. It made me think about all the things I've missed so far and the baby isn't even here yet. Of course Vivianne didn't see things that way."

Of course not, as long as she has a credit card in her hand and diamonds everywhere, she's perfectly happy.

"I gave her an ultimatum of my own. I told her we could open a business together instead of me playing ball and being away from her and the baby. She wigged out and said that's not what we agreed on. In the end, I told her I planned to have my contract reviewed again to see what steps I needed to take in order to get out of it. I let her know we could work together and move forward or I would take her to court for my rights to the child. In her own special kind of way, she told me I don't have any rights because there's no baby."

"Wait a minute, Jayce," said Keon. "What do you mean no baby?"

He gave a dry laugh and tried to shrug his shoulders. "You heard me. There's no baby. I figured she was lying, but I wanted to be understanding. I noticed her belly wasn't getting any bigger and she always had excuses for why she never told me about any doctor's appointments. She finally confessed and told the truth. I mean there was no reason for her to keep up the charade any longer."

"That … bitch," I murmured.

"She knew I would do anything she asked just so I could be with my child, so she lied to get what she wanted. All of this happened right before the game and my mind was still trying to wrap itself around everything. I wasn't all that upset about the nonexistent baby because I had a hunch she was making it all up. What pissed me off is I initially believed her and ultimately turned my life upside down for nothing. In the end I wasn't focused on what was going on around me. Luckily, the hit I took wasn't as bad as it looked."

"Really?" I asked in disbelief. "Because it looked like you were dead."

"No," he chuckled. "Knocked unconscious? Yes. But not dead. Few bruised ribs and a lot of soreness. But I'm better now that you're here."

I smiled and leaned in to kiss him. His lips were smooth, soft, and familiar. After a few exaggerated coughs from Keon, we finally broke up our lip-lock.

"What would you rate that, babe?" asked Keon.

Kirsten laughed and crossed her legs. "I'll give them a seven on a scale of one to ten."

"A seven?" I repeated, pretending to be offended.

"Hey," she said, tossing her hands up in the air. "I'm being generous considering your boyfriend is dealing with an injury."

"Whatever," I said, throwing a pillow at them both.

"I'm going to call down to the front desk and get a room for you guys," said Jayce.

"Thanks, cousin," said Keon. "We need to find a store or something so we can get some clothes."

Jayce dialed the front desk and got everything arranged. We agreed to meet in a couple of hours and order room service. The door had barely closed behind them before Jayce had his lips pressed against mine again.

"Wait … wait," I moaned, leaning away from him.

"What?" he asked, cupping my face. "I don't appreciate our kiss being rated a seven, I want all tens."

He tilted my chin up and I leaned out of the way again. "Let's talk first … please."

"All right, babe, let's talk," he sighed.

"How are you really feeling?" I asked. "Honestly?"

The façade started to slowly peel away and I could clearly see the hurt and anger in his eyes.

"Honestly? I'm pissed the fuck off, Bri. This is actually the second room they had to give me, because I broke several things in the other one. Vivianne robbed me of time I could have been spending with you. I allowed her to manipulate me into playing ball again. Even though I didn't want her, I wanted the baby, a baby that never existed," he said.

He clamped his eyes closed and pinched the bridge of his nose. "I thought the love I used to have for Vivianne was enough, but after being with you, nothing compares."

"Why?" I murmured.

"What?"

"Why doesn't it compare? I mean … Vivianne and I are nothing alike," I said.

Jayce twisted his face into a pained expression as he wrapped his arm around my waist. "Of course you're nothing alike. You're so much better than her. With Vivianne, loving her came with a set of rules and I tried to play the game for a little while. Buying stuff for her is a requirement of the relationship. But you value time and people above everything else. I've watched you grow and change so much. I know what I want, and what I want is you."

Hot tears rolled down my cheeks and I quickly brushed them away. "Jayce, I don't think I need to tell you how much this killed me. If you really want me and want to move forward then let's do it. But I need to let the guy I've been seeing know what's going on. He's a really great guy and I honestly don't want to hurt his feelings," I said.

"Of course," he said, resting his chin on top of my head. "Let him down easy and tell him he doesn't have a snowballs' chance in hell with you."

"Oh really? Are you jealous, sir?" I teased.

"Absolutely. And from what I hear, I have a good reason to be jealous. I know if Keon liked the guy then I need to be worried. There's something I want you to know."

"What's that?" I asked.

"I didn't touch her," he said. "Not once. In fact, we never even slept in the same bed. She definitely wanted to, but I couldn't bring myself to go that far."

"Jayce?"

"Hmmm?"

"After today, I don't ever want you to mention Vivianne or even say her name again. Let's leave her in the past."

"You know the best way to do that?" he asked, his fingers slowly stroking up my arm toward my breasts.

"How?" I sighed.

"You. Me. Naked in this bed right now," he hissed.

"And run the risk of hurting you even more? No, sir. Plus, I need a shower."

"You go shower, and I'll do some light stretching. Come back in nothing but a towel," he whispered. "If it makes you feel better, I'll let you get on top and do most of the work."

I scurried out of the bed, got tangled in the sheets … and nearly fell. Nothing, not even falling out of the bed was going to stop me from getting back to my man.

Chapter Thirty-Four

As soon as I got back in town, I called Darren to let him know how everything turned out. Luckily, he took everything in stride just like I thought he would. I was definitely floating on cloud nine. Jayce managed to get out of his contract, but things weren't able to get back to normal just yet. He still had weeks of physical therapy to endure and I stayed right by his side during each appointment. I felt guilty considering he hurt his back and leg that night in the hotel room with me.

"Don't go in to work today," begged Jayce.

"I have to, hun, and you better be still before you hurt your back again," I laughed, darting out of the bed. "You know I have to take care of the bills today."

"Do it from home then," he suggested.

"I'll still need to leave to get the documents for the accounts. You'll see me later for dinner remember?"

"Yes," he replied. "Make sure you're dressed and ready to go. Our reservation is at eight."

Jayce insisted on planning a "fancy fun night" for us. I was excited to see what he arranged.

"We could stay home and just relax," I suggested.

"No, I worked really hard to make tonight special," he said. "Hurry up and leave so you can hurry up and come back."

I jumped in the shower, got dressed, and headed for the coffee shop. "Good morning, Leani," I said, waltzing past her and into the office. I'd had an extra bit of pep in my step since Jayce came home.

With my shoulders hunched over the desk, I slipped into accounting mode. Drip Drop had been doing so much better financially in these last few weeks.

Maybe we need to have a customer appreciation day or something?

A knock on the door drew my attention away from the ledgers. "Hey, Bri, is Jayce here?" asked Keon.

"Oh, no, he's not here. Where did you come from? Aren't you supposed to be off today," I asked, dropping my pen on the desk.

Keon's eyes flickered from my face and then down to his phone. "Yeah," he said slowly.

"Is something wrong?" I asked. It was rare for Keon to fidget, but he was definitely doing a lot of it right now.

"Yes … no … well, I thought Jayce told you?" he stammered.

"What?" I asked, jumping out of my chair. "What's going on?"

"Nothing," he replied, making me seriously doubt the truthfulness of his response.

"Okay, Keon," I snapped. "Check the house, he's not here, and he hasn't been here."

"All right," he muttered, glancing back down to his phone.

I narrowed my eyes and watched him leave the office.

Follow him.

I had no clue where the voice came from, but I grabbed my keys and darted out the door behind him.

Here I am sleuthing again. Something I haven't done since I interrupted my ex-fiancé's wedding.

I rounded the corner going toward Jayce's house and slammed on the brakes. Luckily, no one was behind me because my little car would have been completely wrecked. I rubbed my eyes and opened the door to get a better look at what was in the driveway. A black drop-top

Jaguar with a personalized plate on it was parked in front of the garage. The car by itself was disturbing enough because I knew it was not something Jayce would drive, but it was the damn license plate that sent a steady stream of rage through my body. VIVI was scrawled across the back of the car and I set my mind to "seek and destroy."

I turned around yanked open the back door to my own little dingy car. Jayce and I attempted to learn how to play tennis a couple of weeks ago, and right now the racquet was about to become my new best friend.

Just as I raised it over my head the front door opened and Keon ran out. "Bri, no!" he shouted.

I swung and missed the car by inches, because he swooped in and tossed me over his shoulder.

"Calm down," he yelled. "It's not what it looks like I swear!"

Jayce appeared in the doorway and jogged over to help. "Bri!"

I could hear them both calling my name, but I felt like I was having an out of body experience.

This explains it all. There's nothing he can say to explain why Vivianne's car is here. Look at me! Out here embarrassing myself for this man.

I managed to slip free from the tree-trunk-like arms trying to restrain me and ran for my car. My foot pressed down on the gas pedal long before I ever shifted the car into drive. Black smoke billowed out and I threw the car into the right gear. Jayce and Keon ran to keep up but it was too late, I was already halfway down the block.

My phone rang, I pressed ignore and considered tossing it out the window.

I'm done trying to make things work. Fuck this. Vivianne can have him.

Kirsten's ringtone started and I snatched the phone off the seat next to me. "I don't want to fucking talking about it!" I yelled.

"Whoa, whoa … wait a minute, calm down. Talk about what? I called to see what time I needed to come over and do your hair and makeup for tonight," she said.

"To hell with tonight," I growled. "I'm not going anywhere, especially with Jayce."

"Take a deep breath and tell me what happened," she said.

"Keon came in the shop acting weird, I followed him home, and Vivianne's car is parked in the driveway."

"How do you know it's her car?" she asked.

"What other psycho bitch around here has personalized plates on their car that say 'Vivi'?" I snapped.

"Wow," she murmured. "Listen, just go home and I'll be there in just a few minutes."

I tossed the phone back onto the seat and wiped my nose on my sleeve. It was not the most lady like of gestures but I didn't care at that point. I tried to hurry up and get home before Jayce showed up there trying to talk. The last thing I needed was him in my driveway.

I pulled up at home and grabbed the spare key from under the mat before I went inside. Mom was out of the house, so I was relieved I didn't have to explain my red eyes or why I was slamming the doors. I stomped up the steps to my room and sat on the edge of the bed. The front door opened and closed and Kirsten's heavy feet brought her up the steps.

"Bri?"

"Yeah," I muttered.

"Hey, chick," she said, dropping her bag on the floor.

"Cute top," I mumbled. She glanced down at the oversized sequined sweater and frowned.

"Um, thanks?" she said. "Have you talked to Jayce?"

"Nope," I replied. "And I don't plan to."

"Bri, you should hear the man out," she said.

"No, Kirsten … just no."

She looked at her phone, and then back at me with a pleading look in her eyes.

"No," I said firmly.

"Fine," she huffed, plopping down next to me. "Well what do you want to do?"

"I'm already doing it. I want to sit here on my bed."

"I drove a long way and I haven't had any sleep just so I could make it here to help you get ready for your date night and you're going on a damn date with somebody even if it's with me," she snapped. "I'm going to take a shower and get ready. I expect you to start doing the same."

She stalked off mumbling to herself as I sulked on the bed. The water turned on and subsequently shut off twenty minutes later. Kirsten came out wrapped in a towel and gently kicked my shin with her damp foot.

"Your turn," she said.

"I don't want to go," I whined. "Let's just order food and stay in so I can cry."

"No," she snapped.

I rolled off the bed, trudged into the muggy bathroom, and leaned against the counter.

"I don't hear the shower!" yelled Kirsten.

I know she came a long way to be here, but damn, she's acting like Gram-Gram.

The water was scorching hot, but I ignored the stinging against my skin. I closed my eyes as the water washed away my pain.

Love isn't supposed to hurt. Be a little complicated? Maybe. But it definitely isn't supposed to hurt.

I opened my eyes and allowed my tears to mix with the spray of water splashing against my face.

"Bri, it's been an hour already. I'm sure you're clean by now!" yelled Kirsten.

An hour? I only closed my eyes for a second.

I turned the water off and stepped out into the cold air. The oversized terry cloth towel wasn't enough to stop my teeth from chattering or my body from shivering.

"C'mon, let's get started," said Kirsten.

Her hair was in rollers and she had her makeup apron on over her dress.

"I don't want to go to a bar," I mumbled.

"We're not," she said, grabbing a handful of my hair. "I'm hungry and I'm sure you are too. Where was Jayce supposed to take you?"

"I don't want to go there," I said.

Kirsten rolled her eyes and reached for the hairpins. "Fine, we can go to the Crab Shack," she suggested.

"We're going to be overdressed don't you think?"

She shrugged her shoulders and pinned my hair up one side. "There's no such thing as being overdressed."

Once my hair was out of the way, she moved on to my face. "Bri," she mumbled.

"Yeah?"

"I can't put your makeup on if you're going to keep crying," she said.

"Sorry," I whispered.

I didn't realize the tears were still flowing and I wasn't sure I knew how to make them stop.

"It's going to be okay," she said, wrapping her arms around me. "You just need to calm down. It will all fall into place once you let him explain."

"Go on and get finished," I said, drying my eyes on the towel.

My eyes were still a little red but other than that my face was flawless after Kirsten finished. The hair left out cascaded down the side in beautiful ringlets and framed my face perfectly.

"Once you slip on your dress and heels, we'll be ready to go," she said.

The dress she selected hugged every curve. She paired it with a smoking hot pair of heels that were sure to have my feet hurting by the time I made it downstairs.

Luckily, Kirsten volunteered to drive because I was in no mood to get behind the wheel. We rode in silence to the restaurant, but my mind was loudly asking me a million hypothetical questions.

Maybe I should kill Vivianne and Jayce? Maybe even throw in Keon for helping add to this entire mess of a situation. But if I kill them, I'll have to see Mom's sad face staring at me through plexiglass and endure handwritten letters from Gram-Gram expressing how disappointed she is in me.

"Come on, Bri," said Kirsten.

I didn't even realize we made it to the restaurant. Jayce was all I could think about as I grabbed my clutch. We walked inside and Kirsten made a beeline for the hostess. After a few minutes of whispered conversation, we were finally escorted to a semi-private room.

"Can't we get a booth?" I asked.

"No," said Kirsten. "We need some privacy."

She stepped to the side and shoved me into the room … right into Jayce. I whipped around and practically hissed at her.

"You're SO not my friend anymore," I growled.

"Shut up and listen," she said.

I faced Jayce again, and searched for the right words to tell him how I never wanted to see him again. A hiccupped sob escaped my lips instead of words. I turned on my heels and tried to go out the door, but Keon blocked my exit.

"Bri," said Jayce. "I want you to listen to me, please."

"Move," I muttered.

"Sorry, Bri, I can't do it, not yet," said Keon.

"Brianna Marie Davis, hush up and let the man say his peace!"

"Gram-Gram?" I asked in disbelief. I ducked down to look around Keon's legs.

"Why is my grandmother here?" I asked, turning back to face Jayce.

The sight of him changed my blood from boiling hot to an icy Antarctic temperature. Seeing him down on one knee reaching for my hand made me forget about everybody else in the room. I heard the shuffling of feet behind me, but I couldn't move my head to turn around.

"W-what's going on?" I stammered.

He smiled up at me and shoved a satin black box into my face. Someone behind me nudged me closer to him and I accepted his open hand.

"Bri, let me clear the air before I give my little speech. The car you saw in the driveway did belong to Vivianne, but she wasn't there. I paid for that car and it's registered to me so I wanted it back. Things got a little hectic when I went to get it from her which is why Keon was a little off his rocker when he came looking for me. Okay, are we good now?"

My breathing was labored and I couldn't think, let alone form words at this point. I nodded slowly with my eyes fixated on Jayce. My eyes clouded with tears and I tried to blink them away.

"Good," he said. He licked his lips and offered a sly smile. "Now let's move on to the good stuff. We've had some shaky situations to deal with, one very recent one involving a tennis racket."

A wave a heat rushed to the surface of my skin as someone behind us laughed.

Not my proudest moment, but hey, my emotions were running high.

"But even through all of that, my love for you has never wavered. You accept me for who I am and I love that about you. You're everything I hoped for in finding my other half. You get lost inside your own head sometimes, but that's one of the quirks I love about you. I want nothing more than to come home to you every day, grow as a couple, and one day have children of our own … but first there's one question I need an answer to," he said, flipping open the box. "Will you marry me?"

My heart stopped and everything started going black. I did the only logical thing I knew to do … I dropped down onto both of my knees to avoid passing out completely. My eyes bounced back and forth between Jayce's eyes and the gigantic ring shining brightly from the box. I wasn't sure how much time passed, but someone coughed nervously in the background and Jayce's forehead had a light sheen of sweat forming across it.

"Bri, if you go ahead and give me an answer, we'll both be able to get off of the floor," he whispered.

"I … I," I stammered. "I wish … well I … um … are you sure?"

"More than anything in this world, so what do you say?"

"Yes," I said so low, I barely heard my own response.

"What? What did she say? Brianna, open up your mouth and talk so we can hear you girl!" shouted Gram-Gram.

I turned toward the growing crowd behind me and smiled. "Yes!" I shouted. The cheering and clapping was loud enough to shatter glass, but I tuned it all out and focused on Jayce. Suddenly, I was off the floor and cradled in his arms. My hand found his face and helped guide our lips together. We broke our lip-lock as he put me down to officially put the ring on my finger.

"I'm glad this is finally out of the way," said Kirsten, circling her arms around me. "You almost ruined the night by refusing to leave the damn house."

"Yeah," said Keon, "We rushed to get over here and get everything in place, but it turned out perfect."

Mom and Gram-Gram tackled me with tears, hugs, and kisses. Once they were done with me, they moved on to Jayce.

I hope they understand he's only marrying one of us.

"Well it looks like we're getting a new daughter," boomed a loud voice. Jayce's dad and mom came toward me with their arms outstretched. This was the first time we'd met in person and I suddenly became a babbling idiot again.

"Mr. and Mrs. Kanoi!" I said, excitedly returning their tight embraces.

"No, none of that, we're family now," said Mrs. Kanoi.

After all of the hugs and congratulations from the crowd, Jayce moved to be by my side.

"I planned a more formal setting for all of this," said Jayce. "But my bride-to-be had other plans. Nevertheless here we all are, and she said yes, so that's all that matters. Grab a seat and a menu, and let's get the party started!"

I sat in awe watching our friends and family socialize and laugh their way through dinner. My stomach was in too many knots and I could barely swallow a sip of water.

Jayce nudged my leg and leaned over to whisper in my ear. "That ring looks good on you."

"This ring looks huge on me," I said, holding my hand out to admire the rock for the hundredth time. "I feel like I'm going to wake up and this would have all been a dream."

"It's real," he said, rubbing his hand against my thigh. "That ring is never supposed to be taken off, okay?"

"Okay," I whispered. "I feel like I should give something to you though."

Jayce brought our faces together until our noses touched. "You did give me something. You gave me the answer I was looking for. Of course, you took your time giving it to me, but I would have given you the moon if I needed to just to hear you say it again."

Our lips lightly touched and the knots in my stomach loosened just a bit. "As long as I have my coffee cup and a kiss from you every day, I think you can leave the moon where it is."

Grab BOOK 2
LATTES OF LOVE
By clicking link

https://www.amazon.com/dp/B07FVT84SG/

Keep scrolling for a sneak peek!!

Lattes of Love Sneak Peek

Chapter One

Keon collapsed on top of me in a sweaty heap and panted.

"Wanna go again?" he heaved.

I squirmed underneath him, trying to take a full breath. My writhing was pointless, not only am I trapped under him, I'm somehow wrapped up in the sheets too.

"Keon, move … I can't freaking breathe," I whined, pushing on his shoulders.

He laughed at my distress, but ultimately rolled off to the side.

"I'm not that heavy, Kirsten."

He flashed a toothy grin at me and flipped his damp black hair back. I make it a point to tell him as often as possible how much I love the longer look as opposed to his previous Marine regulation cut. Despite being honorably discharged and open to live life on his own terms he stubbornly holds on to a lot of his military ways. His "once a

Marine always a Marine" mantra was wearing my nerves thin, so the compromise with his hair was a welcome relief.

"Like hell you aren't," I said. With the pressure gone, I can now take a full breath. "Between you, my breasts, and my asthma, you know my breathing is limited. I need all the air I can get."

I think I may need my damn inhaler, but being forced to use it in front of him is so unattractive. In all fairness, passing out isn't attractive either so if it comes down to it, the inhaler wins.

Before I knew what was happening, Keon reached over and snaked his hand between my thighs.

"Still wet," he murmured. "I think you can go another round."

I moaned as he slipped his fingers inside me. "Keon," I hissed. "We can't … we both have work to do."

"I'll make you a deal … if I stop, do you promise to go two rounds later?"

"Mmmhmm. Hell, if you do this same thing later on, you may get three rounds, a massage, and a puppy."

Keon laughed as his hand drifted away from my body. "I'll hold you to the puppy deal later, but for now I'll take the three rounds and a massage."

I blinked a few times to clear my head and watched with anticipation as he slid out of bed and headed for the bathroom. I stared at the hard lines of his body as they relaxed and contracted with every slight movement. His naturally tan skin, beautiful hair, and massive size was evidence of his strong Samoan genes, but the muscle definition came from his dedication to the gym.

Ah, the gym ... a not so friendly foe of mine. It's not like I have time for it anyway.

I've never been too big or too small, and I've definitely been nothing less than confident about my size, but these last few months with Keon have packed at least thirty pounds on me. He calls it happy weight, but I call it what it is, plain-old-buttered-biscuit-eating fat.

"You're looking at me like you want those extra rounds now," he teased.

"Don't worry," I said, pulling the sheets back. "It'll be worth the wait later."

I walked over to our closet and thumbed through the hangers. Picking out Keon's clothes had become my new favorite past-time.

"Let's play hooky ... just for today," he suggested. "We can have a day for us with no real plans, no phones, and no obligations to do anything."

I shook my head and rolled my eyes. "You have to get down to the café and I have to get down to the filming studio. I have at least four faces to complete before the cameras start rolling. Besides, what will the people do if they can't tackle their sleepiness with a refreshing cup of hot joe from Drip Drop Café, owned and operated by former NFL star, Jayce Kanoi," I recited from memory.

Keon laughed and popped my bare ass. "You know he didn't write that himself. Don't make my cousin's commercial sound so corny."

I joined in on the laughter and grabbed a shirt that hugged the curves of his muscles perfectly. "It sounds corny because it is corny," I teased.

"I know," he said, slipping into the bathroom. "I wouldn't exactly coin him as a star considering he only played one game. But hey, it sounded good, and it helps keep the place packed."

I grabbed my robe off the end of the bed and slipped it on. My feet dragged my aching body towards the living room.

I don't know if Keon will get those extra rounds later on. He really put his back into it this time so an Epsom salt soak will be in order.

I aimlessly picked up my to-do list and skimmed over everything.

"There's still so much to get done," I muttered, flipping through the pages.

"And it'll all get done," said Keon coming up behind me, fresh from the shower.

His arms circled around my waist and helped pull me in closer.

"You will run yourself crazy looking at that list."

I sighed and turned the page in my little notebook. "I know, but helping Bri plan this wedding has taken over my life. You promised to help or did you forget? I'm sure Jayce gave you some best man duties to accomplish."

"Mmmhmm," he murmured into my neck. "He gave me a few things to do. I sent out a handful of invitations. Most went to our side of the family, and I sent one to Bri's dad."

I twisted away hard enough for it to hurt and turned to face him.

"Are you fucking kidding me?" I shrieked. "I thought you understood why that was a bad idea. I flat out told you it was a terrible idea, hell even Bri said don't send that man a damn thing."

Keon ran his hand through his pitch-black hair and scowled at me.

"Kirsten, don't you think you're overacting? He wasn't invited to the engagement party and Jayce honestly felt bad about it, you know how he is. The least we can do is have him at the wedding. It's not like he asked him to walk Bri down the aisle or anything."

He leaned against the counter and folded his arms as I continued my rage filled rant.

I scratched at a spot on the side of my face and fought the urge to hit my boyfriend.

It would probably hurt me more than it would hurt him.

I shook my head, closed my eyes, and pinched the bridge of my nose.

"If I would have known you would throw a tantrum, I wouldn't have sent the damn thing."

"You did know!" I yelled, arms flailing. "I explicitly said 'don't send Bri's dad an invitation or anything else.'"

Keon shifted his weight and stared at me. "What did he do to make the two of you hate him so much?"

"Everything," I muttered.

My own daddy issues flood to the forefront of my mind and I scrambled to wipe away the angry tears.

I shook my head again as Keon wrapped his arms back around me.

"Fuck," he whispered. "C'mon, let's have a seat and talk this shit out. I hate seeing you cry."

I allowed him to lead me toward the couch still wrapped in his arms. He sat down first and pulled me into his lap.

His hulking six-foot frame dwarfed my little five-foot-three even sitting down. I always felt comforted by his touch ... relaxed.

"He cheated on her Mom. I got that part. But Ms. Evelyn has moved on and as far as I can tell ... she's happy."

"It's more than the fact he cheated. It's 'who' he cheated with," I said, still brushing tears away. I inhaled sharply, wishing the conversation was over before it even started.

"Back when Bri and I lived right next to each other, our other neighbor had a daughter named Makenzie. We all grew up together, in fact most people called us the Three Musketeers. We were literally always together. Hell, for a year we went to school in matching outfits."

"So, her dad cheated on her mom with your best friend?" he asked twisting his lips into a frown.

"No," I snapped. "Stop interrupting, I only want to tell this story once."

I shifted around nervously in his lap before continuing, ignoring his below the waist response to my wiggling.

"Back to what I was saying ... our best friend at the time had a little sister, and that's who he cheated with. Well, Miranda, that's the little sister, is barely twenty, and she takes every opportunity to rub it in Bri's face that she's knocking boots with her dad. He left Bri and her mom for this little bitch so we can't stand to be around either of them. It broke Evelyn, and she stayed that way for a long time. It hurt me to see her like that and it pissed me off knowing he treated her that way. You know how messed up my family tree is so Bri's family became my family."

"Look, I'm sorry, babe. I didn't know things were that crazy. The last thing I want is to have Bri's big day ruined. I'll call Jayce and tell him he can meet Bri's dad some other time because I still think he deserves to get to know the man marrying his daughter."

Keon gave my thigh a light squeeze before gently pressing his lips to mine.

"No," I muttered, pulling back. "It's high time Bri faces this thing head on so we can all stop walking on eggshells about it. I'll handle it."

"Are you sure? I feel like shit for putting you in this position."

You should feel like shit. The shittiest of shit since I told you point blank not to send the damn invitation.

"I'm sure," I snapped. "I've got it covered … just like everything else."

I tried and failed to break free from his vice grip like hold.

"Whoa … whoa. What the hell does that mean?" he asked squeezing me tighter.

I sighed and didn't erase the scowl from my face.

"Did you pick up the backdrops I asked you to get? Did you get the guys together to get measured for the tuxes?" I asked, marking items off my mental checklist.

Keon dropped his head and tried to nuzzle my neck.

"I'm not in the mood," I snapped.

"Alright, fine," he muttered. "No, I have none of that stuff done. But in my defense … you're upset over nothing. I always deliver. Stop micromanaging everything … just relax."

His hold on me momentarily loosened, and I seized my opportunity to scramble out of his arms.

"*Micromanaging?*" I hissed. "You consider me trying to ensure my best friend's wedding isn't a complete shit show, *micromanaging?* Excuse the hell out of me for caring whether stuff gets done and gets done right. Jayce is your cousin, and you should care about how this all works out too. Your nonchalant attitude is charming sometimes, but right now it's annoying as hell and I'm already stressed out."

"I don't want to argue," said Keon getting up from the couch. "I'll pick up the backdrops today and I'll work on getting the guys together."

"Fine," I growled. I snatched my phone off of the counter and stalked off towards our bedroom.

"Kirsten?"

"Have a great day at work. I won't be there to micromanage you."

I slammed the door behind me, muffling any response from Keon. My fingers scrolled down my list of contacts and found Bri's number. I needed to break the bad news to her and help figure out this disaster.

Chapter Two

My ears are still ringing from the phone call with Bri. She took the situation just like I thought she would by pitching a complete fit. I don't think I've ever heard her scream so much at one time. Luckily, only part of her anger was directed at me with the other part being directed at her fiancé and my meddling boyfriend. Although, I don't get why the hell she's mad at me in the first damn place. I tossed my phone into my purse and popped the trunk to get my makeup kit out.

Today would be a long day but I'm looking forward to the surgery I'm about to perform. I don't consider what I do as just slathering on some makeup. Hell no, I'm an artist and I can literally transform how someone looks with the wave of a brush. I fluff my hair one final time before walking into the already overly active dressing room.

"Well, well, well, look what the lion coughed up," said Finley. His perfectly sculpted brow shooting upwards.

Finley, the resident diva and best hair slayer in the city, waved his comb at me. The bright lights cast a blinding glare on his bald head and I can't help but notice he took the time to cut a different design in his beard for tonight's special occasion.

I shook my head and rolled my eyes as I hoisted my heavy ass kit up on the table. "Now I know you know the saying is 'look what the cat coughed up' not the lion," I said.

"Oh no honey," he said sauntering over to join me. "I said exactly what I meant to say. You look like a damn lion with that hair all over your head."

I reached up and gingerly pat my wild coils. It's true, my afro hair is far from the sleek bun I'm used to wearing.

"My boyfriend likes my hair like this," I said defensively.

Finley shook his head and folded his arms across his chest. "Well, bitch is he here? Don't worry, I'll answer that with a big fat hell no. The dick must be good to have you switching up your entire vibe on me."

I stopped organizing my brushes and mirror Finley's stance. "How am I switching up my vibe by changing my hair?"

A smirk replaced the shit-eating grin on Finley's face as he waved his hand to get Damon's attention. Damon, the resident stylist for the crew, sauntered over and gave me the once over.

"Oh sweetie, what is this?" asked Damon, gesturing to my outfit.

Finley laughed and playfully hit my arm as I glanced down at my clothes. I still don't get what the big damn deal is. My dress was a simple black maxi, and my shoes are flats.

"See," said Finley. "I didn't even have to say anything and Damon immediately caught on. You're practically dressed like a nun. What happened to the stilettos? Where's the Kirsten the sex kitten with the severe cut crease on her eyelids? Bitch, where is the glitter! You used to give us looks, now you're giving us whatever this is."

Damon shook his head as he circled around me. "New dick will do that to you. At least you're glowing, so this man is obviously laying it down."

I rolled my eyes and finish up unpacking my trunk. "First of all, Damon, you get new dick every other month and I don't jump all over you about it."

"I am a dick specialist, Kirsten, having a bit of variety is necessary to perfect my craft."

My gaze turned to Finley who's helping to organize the makeup brushes I spent hours cleaning last night. "And I thought you had my back? You're the one that told me to stop running from this relationship and that I should jump in full force."

Finley wrapped his arms around me and gave me a squeeze. "Oh, honey I said that because you needed dick in your life. I don't think you realize how uptight you used to be sometimes. We just didn't expect you to turn into Miss. Muffet."

"And don't get me started on these hips," said Damon. "He is obviously feeding you quite well too."

"Well, damn," I snapped. "Is today shit on Kirsten day?"

Both men exchanged glances and laughed.

"You're being so sensitive, Kirsten. Look, I'm sorry if we struck a nerve or something. We love you and want you to change because you want to, not because some man with good wood comes swinging into your life," said Finley.

"Mmmhmm," echoed Damon in the background. "Don't lose yourself just because you found a man."

I stomped back over to my station and rearranged everything repeatedly as I replayed the attack on me.

They have no fucking idea. Sure, I've changed a little, but Keon has changed for me too ... kinda, sorta, but not really. Shit, maybe those assholes are right? To be fair, the less complicated version of me gets ready faster since I don't have to do my makeup or dress on trend.

"Miranda is ready to get started," said one of the backstage assistants poking her head through the curtains.

I pulled the corners of my mouth into a smile and forced my brain to switch over to the artistic side so I can do my job.

It's not long before I transform Miranda from her straight-off-the-plane bare face to an evening look that would last under the scorching hot set lights.

"You are amazing," said Miranda leaning forward to get a closer look in the mirror. "I need to take you on the tour with me, because no one can cut a crease better than you."

She reclined back in the chair and folded her arms across her chest. Miranda, the host of tonight's drama filled filming session taking place, was a well-known jetsetter and fashion icon. Being on her payroll would not only add zeros to my account, but it would boost my reputation up a few notches.

"Take her," said Finley. He reached up to take out the clips holding Miranda's curls in place and tossed them on the counter next to me.

"Kirsten is due for a little adventure anyway. Can you imagine the three of us traveling around the world with you slaying every city we step in?"

I wanted to punch him right in the face, but that would look bad to a potential client. I would let his ass have it as soon as Miranda was out of earshot.

She narrowed her eyes and nodded. "You know what, I like that idea. I like that idea a lot. What do you say, Kirsten? Is your schedule open?"

"Yes," I replied faster than probably necessary. "My schedule is whatever you need it to be. I have a few days I need to block out for my best friend's wedding, but other than that, I'm all yours."

Miranda flashed me a grin, practically blinding me with the white from her teeth.

"Awesome," she drawled. "I'll have my assistant link up with you and take care of the other details."

After closing the deal, I was on cloud nine the rest of the night. I had another thing to add to my resume, more exposure for my work, and I get to see some new places. The downside to the new adventure is Keon. He loves our quality time together so breaking the news to him would be a little tricky. Despite the asshole-ish way Damon and Finley broke things down, they're right, and I know for a fact Keon will probably throw a fit. I'll just have to make him understand that this is my job, and I was doing this way before him. If I put it that way, what could possibly go wrong?

Chapter Three

I've been dodging landmines for a couple of days and I'm not sure how much longer I can keep this up. Between Bri and Keon, I might step on one on purpose. My brain hurts from thinking of different ways to break the news to Keon about my new contract. I literally couldn't think of the right words to say and it's never the right time.

"No," I muttered. "We've seen that movie four times already."

"It's a good movie," said Keon flipping through the extensive movie list. "But for you, babe, we'll find something else to watch, even though I really want to watch that one again."

I snuggled down into his side just as my phone chimed. My eyes cut over to him briefly.

"Don't you dare. We're having our time right now. You know the rules, we agreed on the no phones policy during our quality time."

I exhaled and tried to resolve myself to this temporary yet voluntary hostage situation.

What if it's someone scheduling an appointment? My clients are my freaking livelihood. It could be a bride needing a last-minute makeup artist. Oh shit, what if it's Miranda calling me? I could use the money to buy that cute purse I saw last week.

"Cut it out, Kirsten. It's not work, and no one is having an emergency. Relax. Whoever is calling can leave a message and whatever is going on will still be there in two hours," said Keon.

"How do you do that? Better yet … why do you do that? It makes me feel like you can read my mind," I murmured, looking up at him.

Keon laughed, the rise and fall of his chest coupled with his hearty chuckles, jostled me around.

"The military trained me to be the best at what I do," he said. "Plus, your face is a dead giveaway for what's going on in that head of yours. And don't even think about sneaking off to the bathroom to check your phone either."

"Got me all figured out, huh?" I asked, playfully elbowing him in the side. He looked down and smiled. His smile was enough to make me lose touch with reality. I reached up and stroked the side of his face.

"If you keep up this lovey-dovey touching and carrying on, we're not gonna watch the movie," he whispered.

He leaned down and gently pressed his lips to mine. I rubbed the top of his hair and turned up the heat on our lip-lock. His hand snaked inside my shirt and cupped my breast. My nipple hardened as his thumb grazed over it.

Keon leaned back and continued to look down at me. "You mean the world to me."

"Aww, babe. Now who's being lovey-dovey? You know it's okay for us to fool around and just fuck. We don't have to stroke and caress every single time. Sometimes I just want to get to it."

"I kno-"

The front door and my phone simultaneously interrupted everything. Keon rolled his eyes as I sat up and dug around in my pocket.

"This is your one and only pass to check your phone while I get the door," he said.

I mouthed what he said and rolled my eyes in response. Keon was my sweetie bear but I still couldn't get him to understand I needed to interact with other people.

"Do you know how many times I've called you?" shrieked Bri. I moved my cell away from my ear and glanced at the screen. Her yelling was loud enough to make Keon glance over his shoulder.

"I'll just take this in the other room," I whispered. "Bri, what's going on?"

I made my way down the hall and looked back towards the door. Jamison waved at me as he stepped inside, but he didn't smile. He always made me feel uneasy and Keon was never in a good mood after he left

"Hold on for two seconds, Bri, and stop screaming," I said.

I pushed the door closed with my foot and plopped down on the bed. "Okay, now calmly tell me what's going on."

"Jayce doesn't want to marry me," she wailed.

Here we go again.

"Your paranoia is really starting to chap my ass," I snapped. "I can't believe you called me screaming bloody murder with another conspiracy theory."

"It's the truth this time and I have proof," she said. "We've been arguing about my dad nonstop."

I shook my head at the phone and waited for whatever proof her mind had cooked up.

"He still thinks we should invite him."

"What is it with these Kanoi men? How many times do we need to explain this situation to them," I snapped.

"My point exactly," sighed Bri. "He said it was the right thing to do."

"Bullshit," I hissed. "No fucking way. Don't even worry about it. I'll make sure security keeps him out."

"No … I don't need any type of scene going on at the wedding. If there even is a wedding. At this rate I'm not so sure."

I cut my eyes to the closet and glimpsed the floor length white bag protecting my maid of honor dress.

Wedding or no wedding. I'm wearing that damn dress.

"Don't be ridiculous. There will be a wedding. There has to be … I've already bought this dress."

"Girl, forget the dress. My life is falling to pieces over here. Jayce is so nonchalant about everything and it's pissing me off. And now I need to handle this bullshit with my dad once and for all. Maybe I really do need to just go talk to him."

I scowled and trudged over to my makeup vanity. I grabbed my brush cleaner and my brushes. Cleaning my makeup brushes always helped me clear my head.

"I thought that was the plan anyway? Anything I can do?" I asked.

"Yes, have Keon stay on Jayce about the rest of the wedding stuff. He's the one person he actually listens to."

"I'll try," I replied. "It's hard as hell to get Keon to stay on track too."

"There's one more thing, I need you to come with me to see my dad," said Bri in a rush.

I dropped the brush in my hand and frowned. "Say what?"

"Please, Kirsten," she pleaded. "I can't ask anyone else. My friendship circle is small."

I laughed and picked up the brush again. "Sweetie, your circle is nonexistent. It's more like a straight line that leads directly to me."

"Blah blah. Look, I want to get this over and done with as soon as possible. Can I come over right now to pick you up?"

I paused and thought for a moment. "I guess so, but if Keon gets pissed at me for bailing on cuddle time, just know I'm blaming you."

"I'm good with that. See you in a bit."

I ended the call and headed for the door. My hand was about to turn the knob but something told me to wait. Silence now replaced the steady rhythm of voices that was coming from the living room.

Hopefully Jamison is still here and Keon won't be too upset about me leaving.

I cracked the door and listened. After a few more seconds of silence I stepped out and headed towards the living room, which was now empty.

"Keon?"

My ears strained to hear some sort of clue as to whether he was still in the house and I noticed the door to the patio was slightly open.

I poked my head out the door and saw Keon. Moments dragged by and I watched him take a long drink from the cup in his hand before going back to his blank stare.

"Babe?" I whispered.

It was best to avoid startling him when he had that look on his face. I paused and waited for some type of acknowledgment. This exact reason is why I hate Jamison coming over. Keon was always a mess afterwards, completely despondent like a freaking zombie.

If he wakes up again in the middle of the night screaming, I'm kicking Jamison's ass.

Keon was skittish on occasion but visits from his Marine buddies always made things ten times worse. I can't handle him being so out of whack, not right now.

"Keon," I said a little louder, trying not to startle him.

His eyes flickered over to me briefly before going back to that vacant stare.

"Going somewhere?" he asked quietly, his voice barely above a whisper.

"Uh, yeah," I said glancing down at my keys and purse. "Are you okay? What's going on? What happened?"

"McKinley killed himself," he said flatly. "Blew his fucking brains out."

Oh shit.

I dropped my things and kneeled down in front of Keon. If I knew nothing else, I knew McKinley and Keon were closer than anybody else from their squad. I also knew that like Keon, McKinley was dealing with PTSD too.

I never thought I would date someone with post-traumatic stress disorder, but here I am, struggling to figure all of this out day by day. Judging by Keon's behavior, I'm not doing very well with the figuring it all out part. I never know what kind of mood he'll be in or what small thing will trigger him. His condition would probably be ten times better if he would go to the meetings and take his medication properly though.

"I'll call Bri and let her know I can't make it," I said quickly.

He drained the cup and looked down at me. "No. Go ahead and meet Bri. I actually want to be alone. Besides, I wouldn't be great company right now. I just need to process all of this and I can't do that with you here."

"I'll be back as soon as possible," I said patting his massive thigh gently.

He nodded and reached down to grab the bottle of whatever he was drinking and quickly refilled his cup.

I hated seeing him like this, even worse … I hated leaving him like this. But one thing I learned the hard way was to give him his space when he asked for it.

Chapter Four

"That's so sad," murmured Bri. "Are you sure you don't need to go back home?"

I gave her the cliff notes version of what was unfolding at my house, and she's right, it is sad. Unfortunately, there's not a damn thing I can do about it.

"I'm sure. He doesn't really like me hovering when he's inside his head," I said.

I glanced over at Bri and catch her looking back at me with a lopsided grin plastered on her face.

"What?"

Her grin widened tenfold and her huge afro reflected the sunlight brightly. "I like this look on you," she drawled.

I gave myself a once over and frowned. I'm completely dressed down in a plain white tank top and distressed jeans.

"This outfit is basic as hell, Bri."

"I know," said Bri. "But this is a major shift from what you usually look like. This may seem basic to you but you still look runway ready in my opinion. This version of you is a lot more toned down. I mean I love your party girl escort look too, but this is nice."

I'm tired of this ongoing theme. What the hell was wrong with the way I was before?

"Everybody has a lot to say about how I look lately," I grumbled.

Bri furrowed her brow and tilted her head. "What do you mean?"

"You like this look, but if I go to work dressed like this, the fellas hate it. I can't win for losing," I snapped throwing my hands up.

Bri nodded and flashed another smile at me. "It doesn't matter what we like. Dress however you want. You look amazing either way."

I folded my arms across my chest and glanced around the car. "Where did these wrappers come from?" I asked, changing the subject.

"I had a light snack," explained Bri. I noticed her hands tighten on the steering wheel.

Light snack my ass.

I fished around and picked up the fast food bag on the floor.

"A light snack is two burgers and fries?" I asked.

"Actually, that included an apple pie too," she replied calmly.

"Seriously, Bri? We've already had to let your dress out once," I snapped. "You have got to stop all of this eating."

"I know, but I eat when I'm stressed," she muttered. "Don't worry, I'm on a new diet starting next week. You guys have no idea what a basket case this whole wedding planning thing is making me. So, cut me some damn slack."

I leaned over to give Bri a reassuring pat on the knee. "You're right. I've been pitching a fit about everybody critiquing me and here I am doing the same thing to you. Hell, I've gained some weight too. My dress still fits, but I'm in the same boat. Let's change the subject and figure out our plan once we get to your dad's house."

I think we should burst into the house with torches, kill the witch, Miranda, and burn the house to the ground.

"I don't really have a plan ... I just hope Miranda isn't there. In fact, if luck is on our side we can catch the mailman right after he puts the mail in the mailbox and just take the invitation out. No harm no foul if they never know it even existed," said Bri.

"I thought you wanted to sit down and talk to him, but now you're proposing we steal your dad's mail?" I asked, arching my brow.

A little breaking and entering is right up my alley. It's been a while since we've gotten into a little trouble.

She rolled her eyes and tightened her grip on the steering wheel again. "Well, it sounds crazy when you say it like that."

"That's because it is crazy," I said with a smile. "Don't worry, everything is going to be fine."

She nodded and exhaled deeply as we turned into the neighborhood.

"I kinda want to throw up those burgers right now," mumbled Bri.

"Bri?"

"Hmm?"

"Relax," I said, gently putting my hand on her shaking thigh.

"I am relaxed," she said glancing over at me with that manufactured smile plastered on her face.

"Oh, really?" I asked, raising both brows up to accompany my skepticism. "In that case, why are we practically stopped in the middle of the road?"

Bri looked around and exhaled. The car was inching along at a snail's pace and I know she's trying to delay the inevitable.

"Listen, I've got your back. And if all else fails, we'll burn the house down," I suggested playfully.

A smile tugged at the corners of Bri's lips. "Great minds think alike."

"That's my little arsonist," I teased.

We relaxed even more as Bri brought the car to a complete stop two houses down from our destination.

"Well, he's not home," she said, observing the empty driveway. She beamed from ear to ear and started to leave.

"Whew, confrontation averted," she muttered.

"Wait," I said. "You said we should check the mailbox, remember?"

"I was joking," she replied.

"Yeah," I said glancing around. "I don't see anybody outside though. He *is* your dad. There's nothing wrong with you checking the mailbox for him. And if we happen to beat him to getting the invitation …"

"You know that's a crime, right? We established that a while ago. In fact, I think it's a felony," said Bri.

I put my hands up and closed my eyes. "Just hear me out, you're the one that suggested it in the first place, I'm just running through the options. It's not technically stealing because it's your invitation."

"Fine," she said in defeat. "You be the lookout."

Bri pulled into the driveway and eased out of the car. Unfortunately, her dad had one of those mailboxes that was attached to the house just outside the front door. Which meant she had a short trek up the walkway.

She slowly approached the box and looked back over her shoulder. I waved my hand to usher her forward.

Just as she reached her hand into the box, someone suddenly snatched the front door open. I let the window down so I could hear better just in case Bri needed backup.

"What do you think you're doing?" asked the most annoying voice ever.

Bri turned towards Miranda with her hand still poised to grab the invitation.

"Girl grab the damn thing and let's go," I whispered.

"Miranda, who in the hell answers the door with lingerie and a bathrobe on?" snapped Bri.

Miranda glanced down at her ridiculous outfit and smiled.

"It makes it easier for my fiancé if I'm already partially undressed," she purred.

Did that little twat say what I think she just said?

"Did you say ... fiancé?" asked Bri, her voice cracking.

Miranda smiled and wiggled her fingers at Bri showing off the glistening rock.

"Don't worry, you won't have to call me mom. That would be weird since you're like ten years older than me or something."

Alright enough of this bullshit, this bitch is really asking for it.

"Get the damn invitation!" I yelled.

Bri snatched the envelope out of the box and turned on her heels.

"Wait, get back here. What is that you're taking?" snapped Miranda.

The muscles in my jaw flexed as I struggled to keep myself from exploding. Bri's gaze locked on me and I knew shit was about to hit the fan.

"Bitch, I know you heard me," Miranda growled.

Bri's foot didn't have a chance to touch the ground before she whipped around.

"What did you say to me?" she hissed.

I had zero time to think and process the disaster unfolding in front of me. I quickly scrambled out of the car but Miranda hauled off and sucker punched Bri right in the face before I could close the gap between us.

"You crazy bitch!" Bri screamed, clutching her eye.

She launched herself at Miranda and gave her a few good whacks, but I tackled her to the ground to try and separate them.

"No, Bri!" I shouted.

Deep down, I wanted Bri to beat Miranda's wig off, but I don't want her doing it out in the open in front of the entire neighborhood.

She wrestled to break the bear hug I had on her, and just as we were fumbling to get to our feet, a stream of what felt like acid greeted us both.

Miranda screamed bloody murder as Bri and I collapsed and writhed on the ground in complete agony.

So, this is how it all ends? I came to support my friend in rescinding her invitation and end up blind. Miranda's screaming, but we're the ones with our pupils scorched out of the sockets.

After a few moments a brief sense of relief washed over me that felt better than sex.

Sirens.

The approaching sirens got louder as they wailed in the background.

Thank you, baby Jesus, help is on the way.

***

"You assholes are supposed to protect and serve," snapped Bri, rubbing her wrists just as the door slammed shut.

I looked at Bri's swollen red eyes and assumed mine mirrored hers. I smirked and dropped my head into my palms.

"What?" she asked.

"I pictured us beating up Miranda one day and gladly going to jail for it, but this wasn't what I had in mind."

Bri shook her head and joined me on the bench.

"The worse part about all of this, aside from being maced …. I didn't even hit her like I really wanted to."

"Right, the scene was too public," I muttered. "So, what's the plan?"

"I don't have a plan," mumbled Bri. "Do you think they'll go ahead and give us something to eat, or do we wait for a certain time?"

I dropped my hands away from my face and scowled over at her.

"You've got to be joking? We're locked up, car towed, maced for no reason, and you're asking about food?"

She shrugged her shoulders and leaned her head against the dingy wall.

"Well, what do you suggest?"

I stood up and wandered over to our little sliver of window. "We have to call someone to bail us out."

"Fine," she muttered. "Call Keon down here and I'll pay him back as soon as we get out."

I shook my head and paced the floor. "Hell no," I hissed. "He's in a bad head space, Bri. I can't dump this shit in his lap."

"Well then, our options are limited," she replied.

"Why can't we call, Jayce?" I asked. "I'm sure he'll come right down."

She rolled her neck and touched the tender spot on her cheek where that string bean hooker clocked her.

"Keon is a lot more understanding. I told you, Jayce and I are already rubbing each other the wrong way today."

I finally joined her on the bench and leaned against the wall.

"We're screwed," I muttered.

Now I'm hungry too.

She cracked open her eye and nodded. "Basically."

Somehow, I drifted off into a fitful sleep, but a loud banging on the door startled me awake. I glanced around, slightly shaken, and struggled to get up. Bri was draped over my lap and squeezing out from under her was easier said than done.

"You ladies are free to go, someone posted your bail," said a voice.

"What? How?" I asked, finally breaking free from the dead weight of my friend.

The officer looked at me and frowned. "Are you saying you rather stay here?"

"No," I sighed, shaking Bri slightly. "It's just strange considering we didn't call anyone."

"Lady, I get the names … I come down here … and I read them off this clipboard."

I shook my head and sighed again as I continued to attempt to wake sleep beauty.

"Bri, get up. We got bailed out."

She yawned and took her time stretching.

"Get a move on ladies. I have other things to do," said the now irritated officer.

I hooked my arm around Bri's waist and steadied her on her feet. You would think she took something based on out of it she was.

"This is like trying to get a corpse to walk," I mumbled.

She yawned again as we followed the officer down the hall. As soon as we rounded the corner our saving grace came into view and he was standing next to Bri's furious fiancé.

"Honey, are you alright?" asked her father. He almost came toward her with his arms outstretched, but I supposed the look on her face canceled that idea.

Well, that's awkward as hell, but he deserves it.

Ignoring him completely, Bri turned toward Jayce.

He grabbed her chin and turned her head to inspect the bruise on her cheek. She placed her hand over his and tried to smile. Jayce smelled like freshly roasted coffee and vanilla. The scent was familiar and comforting ... *Keon smells like that when he comes home from work.*

"This morning when you said you'd handle things with your dad, I didn't expect to have to pick up the two of you from the police station," he said.

"I know and I'm sorry. This wasn't exactly how I imagined things would turn out either," she mumbled.

I cleared my throat loudly behind them. "You didn't call Keon, did you?"

Please don't say you poked the hornet's nest right now.

Jayce gazed over Bri's head at me. "Of course, I did, but he didn't answer."

Good. The last thing I need is for him to come down here too.

"Bri-bear?"

My blood boiled at the mere sound of Bri's dad's voice, so I can only imagine what it's doing to her. She cut her eyes to the left to stare at him and scowl. I turned to look at him too and it's easy to see why Miranda had her talons hooked in so deep.

His tailored suit blanketed his hulking six-five frame. He looked more like a retired football player than an executive. Muscles, dazzling smile, impressive bank account, hell if I was a backstabbing bitch like Miranda, I'd probably give him a second glance too.

"I'm sorry about all of this. I came down as soon as I heard what happened. Mr. Thompson next door saw the whole incident and called me immediately. Miranda sort of stretched the truth when she gave me her version of events."

My eyes bucked as Bri waved her arms around. "Stretched the truth? She attacked us, sucker punched me, maced us, and now we're being bailed out because of her!" she yelled. "That's a hell of a truth to stretch."

"Ma'am, you will have to keep it down," said a different officer sitting behind the desk.

Jayce grabbed Bri's hand and I helped usher her out the door.

"I wish I could undo it, honey," said her dad.

"I don't need your apology … I need hers," she hissed. "You're always apologizing and making excuses for her. And don't get me started about the ring on her finger."

"I can explain if you'll just hear me out, I promise I'll make things right," he said.

You just don't get it, Bri wants blood.

Bri walked over to the car and placed her hand on the handle.

"The only way you could do that is if you had a time machine," she muttered. She pulled the door and seethed as we both waited for Jayce to push the unlock button.

Way to blow her grand exit.

Jayce finally unlocked the door and Bri scrambled inside without mumbling another word. I climbed into the backseat and sighed loudly.

"I really need to go check on Keon," I mumbled.

I crossed my arms and shot daggers at both Bri's dad and Jayce. They spoke a few moments longer, shook hands, and parted ways.

Jayce slid into the driver's seat and looked at her face again. "Let's get you some ice," he said.

We rode in silence as Jayce gently rubbed her thigh.

Hell, I need a good thigh rub and a stiff drink. I could use something a lot stiffer, but I'm sure Keon isn't in the mood.

"I'll go pick up your car later," he said. "Kirsten, are you okay? Do you need anything?"

"Nope, I'm good. This is what best friends are for. We ride together and get mugshots together. Just drop me off so I can check on my man."

Jayce looked over at Bri before glancing in the rearview mirror. "What's up? Is he okay?"

I gave him the condensed version of what was going on and I watched his whole mood change.

His jaw tensed, and he shook his head as he raked his fingers through his hair.

"Is he off his meds again?" he asked.

"Everything is fine, I promise," I said in a rush.

He gave me a hard stare similar to the one I've become accustomed to receiving from Keon. It meant he didn't believe a word being said but wouldn't press the issue.

Thank you again baby Jesus. You are really coming through for me today. The last thing I need is a barrage of questions I'll have to lie my way through.

We pulled up in front of my apartment and I hurried to get out of the car.

"Call me if you need anything," said Jayce.

I nodded and closed the door. "Don't worry guys, everything is fine," I said trying to reassure myself just as much as them.

End of sneak peek!

But you can click the link to purchase

and finish reading!

books2read.com/u/b5rMd1

Don't forget to add that butter to my bread by leaving a review!!!!! Also, don't forget about the newsletter, it's the only way you'll be able to receive ARC's. I'm also looking to add to my Beta Reader Group, but you have to be on the newsletter to get the alert.

Newsletter Signup

https://mailchi.mp/cd4d69a732cf/mlspannsignup

ACKNOWLEDGEMENTS

I'm so excited to write these acknowledgments! This has been a long but worthwhile endeavor and I'm happy to see the end result. Special thanks to my friends and families for allowing me to shoot ideas by them, and not rolling their eyes when my ideas made absolutely no sense. Double thanks to the beta readers that offered their thoughts on the story, without you I would have never gotten this far. Hugs and chocolate to everyone who has offered input!

M. L. Spann

Megan Spann also known as M. L. Spann is an eclectic blend of sex, sarcasm, and a dash of darkness. Her love of books blossomed at an early age and it has developed into a passion for writing as well. She also writes darker fiction under the pen name M. T. Harrte. She's definitely one of those people that carries around books in their bag. She adds a touch of sass to her novels by using her southern roots to set the tone.

She spent a great deal of her life moving from state to state with her military family, until finally settling down in Mississippi. Despite graduating from Ole Miss with a business degree and going on to gain a

Master's degree, she has decided to truly follow her heart by pursing a writing career.

Instagram: @mtharrte

Twitter: @mtharrte